ALSO BY TATE JAMES

MADISON KATE
Hate
Liar
Fake
Kate

HADES
7th Circle
Anarchy
Club 22
Timber

7TH CIRCLE

TATE JAMES

Bloom books

Published by Bloom Books, an imprint of Sourcebooks
P.O. Box 4410, Naperville, Illinois 60567-4410
(630) 961-3900
sourcebooks.com

Originally self-published in 2020 by Tate James.

Cataloging-in-Publication data is on file with the Library of Congress

Printed and bound in the United States of America.
LSC 10 9 8 7 6 5 4 3 2 1

For Petey, who inspired so many good parts of this story.

CHAPTER 1

Ice clinked in my glass as I swirled the amber liquid. It was my fourth straight whiskey, and it'd barely dented my shitty mood.

It was my own fucking fault. I knew better. I knew he didn't feel the same way about me, but...ugh. I was such an idiot!

I'd all but thrown myself at him—at a man I still needed to deal with in a professional capacity on a far-too-frequent basis. Well, as professional as anyone was in our line of work.

Keeping the upper hand with him was going to be all too uncomfortable now that I'd gone and made a pass at him. And been rejected.

His harsh words still echoed in my mind. *"I don't fuck children."* Like I was a fucking teenager or something. I wasn't. I was a twenty-three-year-old successful businesswoman—among other things—and I was far from the immature, blushing virgin he must think I was. Maybe he was getting me confused with my eighteen-year-old, naive-as-fuck sister, Persephone. That's how he'd just treated me, anyway. Like a little kid with a crush.

"Rough night?" a smooth voice asked, and I glanced over as a gorgeous man slid onto the barstool beside me. The bar was busy, no question, but not so busy that there weren't other seats available.

I cocked a brow at the ballsy stranger and sipped my drink. "Nope," I lied, baring my teeth in a mockery of a smile. "Best night of my life." My sarcasm was thick enough to wade through. Maybe those whiskeys had started hitting me after all. "You?"

"Me?" He flashed me a blinding smile, and my pulse raced in reaction. He was fucking stunning, model-level beautiful with a strong jaw dusted with scruff and dark lashes any woman would kill for. "Nah, I'm celebrating. Can I buy you a drink?"

A grin curved my lips despite my shitty mood. "Sure." I gave a small signal to the bartender, silently ordering another of the same, then nodded to the handsome man beside me to indicate he was paying. He asked for the same as I was drinking and didn't speak again until our drinks were delivered in front of us in beautiful cut-crystal glasses.

"Cheers," he murmured to me, clinking his glass gently against mine, then downing his whole drink in one mouthful. He ordered another, then slid his gaze back to meet mine.

His eyes were a pretty mix of green and blue, and I found myself smiling at him.

"So, what are we celebrating?" I asked, letting my words drawl in a clear indication I didn't actually believe him. Based on the way he'd thrown that drink back, his night was going about as well as mine was.

The model-handsome man let his own lips curve in an answering smile. "My new job," he announced. His gaze flicked away from mine for a second, sweeping over the busy club and pausing briefly on the podium dancers. Both of them were down to their underwear, and the girl was climbing the pole with admirable ease. Totally mesmerizing.

"Oh yeah?" I prompted, suddenly curious about my new drinking buddy. He was ballsy enough to approach me; maybe he could cure my shitty mood tonight. Best way to get over a guy was to get under a new one, right? "Congratulations. What's your new job?"

His perfect face flashed with tension for just a second, then cleared into an easy smile again as he nodded to the male dancer on the podium. "That."

I choked on my drink. Just a little bit. Just enough to shock me and flood my cheeks with heat as I dabbed my lips on a napkin.

"That?" I repeated in a strangled voice, indicating the gorgeous Black man gyrating his hips in nothing but an electric-blue G-string. "You're a stripper?"

My new friend grinned wider, turning back to me and sipping his new drink. "Male entertainer," he corrected with a small nod. "Yep, sure am." There was pride in his voice, but also an edge of something darker. Disappointment?

Curiosity shoved aside my shock, and I ran my gaze over him as subtly as I could. He was pretty enough, no doubt, and the way he filled out his shirt spoke to a well-built frame. Yeah, he could definitely make good money taking his clothes off. Great money, when combined with that mischievous look in his eyes and the pure-sex way he brushed a droplet of whiskey from his lip and then licked his thumb.

"That's cool," I commented. "So, which lucky club snapped you up? I bet you're going to be in high demand."

His smile turned suggestive. "Did you just call me sexy?"

I snickered a laugh. "Was that too subtle? You're scorching. I'm not surprised you got the job. So…?" I really, *really* wanted to know which club had picked up this diamond.

The easy smile on his face faltered a split second as he answered. "This one, of course. 7th Circle is the hottest club in Shadow Grove, everyone knows that. And they pay their dancers better than all the other shitty clubs in town. I wouldn't even consider anywhere else, given the choice."

I almost choked on my drink again. As it was, I needed to take another large gulp, finishing my glass, and motion for another.

Apparently, I was going to drown my sorrows tonight and pay for it with a hangover in the morning. Fuck it.

"Wow," I replied. "That's…"

"Not true," he admitted on a heavy sigh, dropping the smile like he was shedding a coat. "I *wish* it was… It was supposed to be. I guess tonight's just not my night." He drained his glass again and reached for the fresh one the bartender had already made for him.

One of my favorite things about the bartenders at 7th Circle was that they were perceptive and often two steps ahead on drink orders.

"They didn't hire you?" I asked in confusion. "Were you being auditioned by a blind man? Actually, that's no excuse. I reckon even a blind man could sense your sex appeal a mile away."

My drinking buddy snorted a laugh. "Cute. Compliments will get you everywhere." He shot me a wink that went *straight* to my pussy, which throbbed in response. Goddamn.

"Here's hoping," I muttered into my drink, watching him from under my lashes. He was young…but so was I. If he was legally drinking, then the age gap couldn't be more than two years, since I'd celebrated my twenty-third birthday just a few weeks ago.

He'd heard my comment, based on the way a faint blush touched his cheeks, and he rubbed a hand over the back of his neck. "Well, I didn't even get an audition. The manager came out to meet me and announced that the interviews had been canceled. No explanation or anything, just…*go home.*" He sighed heavily, then grimaced. "Can I tell you a secret?"

I bit back the smile that wanted to cross my lips and nodded. "Of course. I'm a total vault."

It was a bit adorable, seeing as we hadn't even exchanged names or…*anything* else, and he was acting a little like a twelve-year-old girl about to spill the details of her crush. Totally adorable. Don't get me wrong, I still badly wanted to drag him into one of the private VIP rooms and fuck his brains out. But I also wanted to pat his hair and have him tell me all his problems.

"I really needed this job," he confessed, his voice losing all the joking it held earlier. "I've got some…family troubles. The money these dancers get paid would have really helped, and now I'm not really sure what to do."

Sympathy turned my stomach, and I reached out to touch his hand where it rested on the bar top between us. "So, will you try and get another interview?"

He wrinkled his nose and sipped his drink but didn't move his hand from under mine. "I don't really have the luxury of waiting around indefinitely for another shot here. I'll probably have a few more drinks and then go try my luck at Dick's."

I cringed. Hard. "Please don't."

Swinging Dick's was exactly what it sounded like: a seedy, disgusting, low-rate male strip club that horrifically exploited their dancers and ran a completely unsafe, unsupervised brothel in the basement. It was the type of business that was a carryover from the *old* Shadow Grove, and one that badly needed to be shut down.

"Trust me," he replied with a bitter laugh, "it's the last thing I *want* to do. But I'm confident the tips for dancing—and extras—will pay better than any other jobs I can get on short notice, and I need the money. Badly. As of this morning, only two clubs in town were hiring, and 7th Circle apparently no longer is. So…I'm fast running out of options."

Questions burned on the tip of my tongue, but they were questions I had no right asking this total stranger. Shit such as what had put him in such a desperate position that he'd even *consider* Dick's? Or why the hell hasn't he already made a fortune modeling or acting or something less nefarious?

"You know, this place isn't all it seems," I told him slowly, watching him carefully for a reaction. When he spoke about the money 7th Circle dancers got, did he actually mean the dancers?

Or was he talking about the "dancers" who only stripped as an advertisement for a darker, less legal menu behind the closed curtains of the VIP booths?

He arched a half smile at me. "I know." His hand turned over under mine so we were palm to palm, and his thumb traced a slow circle on my skin.

I pursed my lips, mulling that over. Maybe that was why the manager had sent him away without an interview. He had a total "good boy" vibe about him, despite looking like sex in jeans, an air of innocence that would be totally destroyed in the shadows of 7th Circle.

I hated to admit it, but I was glad he hadn't been hired. On the other hand, I also didn't want him to end up in the filthy, cum-stained underground of Swinging Dick's.

"Well…" I was being selfish. I was being totally selfish. But with the way my blood stirred at his touch, I knew he would be exactly what I needed to get over my embarrassing blunder from earlier, just a hot, nameless fuck to clear *him* from my mind and help me find my own steel-coated lady balls once more.

I was a force to be reckoned with, and that rejection had knocked me around. But this guy…this guy could help me fix it.

Maybe in return, I could find him a job. One that didn't involve actual sex for money.

"Well?" he prompted, and I realized my voice had trailed off as my thoughts ran wild.

I bit my lip, debating how I could make tonight swing in my favor without sounding like a total slutty whore. But really, all I could focus on was getting impaled on his cock, which I was pretty sure wouldn't disappoint.

"How about you just have fun tonight, and if you still want to try Dick's tomorrow…well, deal with that then. But you look like you need to just cut loose for a bit."

He looked tempted but undecided, like he'd already resigned

himself to his fate and was just working up the courage to go through with it. God knew why—I certainly wasn't known for my compassion or empathy—but I badly didn't want to see this gorgeous guy throw his life away at Dick's. Even if that meant breaking all my own rules.

"Look, I know some people," I offered, remaining vague. "I can probably get you a job that pays twice as much as Dick's ever would with considerably fewer sexual assaults and STDs."

His brow creased in suspicion. "What sort of job?"

I snorted a laugh. "Seriously, does it matter? You were about to quite literally sell your body." Then something occurred to me that put a damper on my mood. Maybe this gorgeous guy wasn't even into chicks.

But then, the way his fingers linked with mine as he pulled our hands from the bar top to rest in his lap told me that wasn't necessarily true.

"Fair point," he conceded with a grimace. "So, I guess I should be asking what you want in return."

My mood instantly soured, and I tugged my hand free of his grip. "Okay, this was a bad idea." I finished my drink and placed the glass back down just a touch harder than necessary. "Forget I offered."

Because I didn't fuck my employees. Ever. And if I gave this guy a job—out of some weird, passing sense of pity and compassion—then fucked him in the bathroom? Yeah, that'd make me a total sleaze.

Thank fuck I'd come to my senses before *that* happened.

I slid off my stool and started walking away from a potentially terrible decision. No matter how hot I found that random guy, it wasn't worth the headache later.

"Wait," he called out, hurrying after me and snagging my wrist before I could step out of the bar area and onto the dance floor. It was the quickest way out of 7th Circle, and I was officially ready to call my shitty night *done*.

I glanced down at his hand on my wrist, but he wasn't gripping me tight enough to hurt. It was just a gesture, not a demand. I gave a small headshake to the huge bouncer across the room who was scowling at my new friend like he wanted to toss his ass out on the curb.

"I'm sorry," the pretty guy apologized when I didn't yank my arm away and leave. Instead, I turned back to face him and tipped my head to look up at him. He was taller than I'd first thought... and that only made me more attracted to him. Damn it.

"It's fine," I lied. "It was a terrible idea. Sorry. But good luck with your job search."

I tried to leave again, but his fingers tightened on my wrist, and a spark of renewed interest shot through me. Maybe he wasn't as innocent as I was writing him off as.

"No, it's not. That was totally rude and presumptuous of me," he pressed on, tugging at my arm to turn me around once more. "I only meant I'd be crazy grateful for any help in getting a job that *doesn't* require me to book weekly STD checkups." He cringed at that, and I couldn't bite back my smile.

Goddamn it. Why did I want to help this guy so much? I never usually gave two shits about anyone outside my inner circle. I'd lost all faith in humanity a long time ago and generally treated anyone and everyone with a clear fuck-you attitude. It kept me alive, and it kept me in business.

"How old are you?" I asked him on a whim. Based solely on his looks, I might have placed him anywhere under twenty-eight. But there was just something about him that gave off a younger vibe.

He frowned slightly. "Twenty-one."

So maybe that was why. He didn't seem to have any obvious ink, so he probably wasn't mixed up with the Shadow Grove gangs. He likely had no idea what he was getting into.

"Look, I didn't mean to insult you," he continued as if I hadn't just deviated off subject. "Can we pretend that never happened?

You don't need to help me with a job, and we can just hang out tonight."

Suspicion pricked at my senses. "Why?"

He shrugged and gave me a shy grin. "Because you're easily the most beautiful woman I've ever met, and I would never forgive myself if I fucked up this opportunity."

"What opportunity?" I replied, frowning. Maybe I'd totally read this guy wrong. There was a reason I never picked up random strangers in bars.

The handsome guy just gave a small shrug, looking nervous for about a split second before making his mind up about something. "This one," he replied, bringing a hand up to the back of my head. His fingers threaded into my deep-copper hair and tilted my face up to meet his kiss.

The second his lips touched mine, I threw caution to the wind.

I needed this. I needed a gorgeous, nameless man to make me feel more like the badass bitch I knew I was and make me totally forget the tattoo-covered, scarred drug dealer I'd thrown myself at earlier in the night.

My lips parted, and I draped my arms around the beautiful guy's neck, pulling him to me as I kissed him back. I knew eyes were on us—on me—but I officially gave no more fucks. I needed this... and if word got back to Cass, then so much the better for it.

It was about damn time I moved on from my stupid crush.

CHAPTER 2

Whiskey warmed my veins, and the fact that I was so thoroughly smashing all my own rules made me dizzy with excitement. But still I retained enough presence of mind not to fuck the beautiful stranger right there in front of the bar.

Reluctantly, I released him and took one step away.

"Feel like heading somewhere else?" I suggested with a grin. I'd made my point at 7th Circle, but now I wanted some anonymity.

His blue-green eyes were glassy, and his lips held a blush from our kiss that only made me want to kiss him harder. "Where did you have in mind?"

My phone buzzed in my pocket, and I held a finger up to indicate I needed to check who the call was from. A thrill rushed through me as I wondered if it was Cass. But that would mean he cared who I was sleeping with, and he'd made it abundantly clear he *didn't*.

I wrinkled my nose when I saw the caller ID. "Sorry, I need to take this," I told the guy, whose name I hadn't even bothered to ask.

Answering the call, I brought my phone to my ear. "What?" I snapped, irritated that I was being interrupted.

A long-suffering sigh sounded down the phone at me. "You know what."

"Save it," I replied, turning to the nearest security camera and staring directly at the lens. "We're heading over to Murphy's anyway." I'd turned away from my new friend to glare at the all-seeing eye, and he slipped his arms around my waist in a forward but totally welcome gesture.

My employee on the other end of the phone was quiet for a long moment before replying. "You're being reckless. If this is about—"

"It's not," I bit out, cutting him off. But fury burned through me with the knowledge that he'd overheard Cass rejecting me earlier. How fucking embarrassing. "I'm a grown-ass woman, Zed, and right now I want to take this pretty man to Murphy's and probably let him fuck me against the wall of the accessible bathroom stall."

The guy behind me jolted with shock, clearly having heard what I'd just said, and then his grip on my hips tightened with enthusiasm.

Zed let out another frustrated sigh, but I wasn't in the mood for a guilt trip. "Just fucking relax, Zed. Take a break and get Amanda to suck your dick or something."

"Her name is Annika," he growled back at me, and I rolled my eyes. Whatever her name was, I hated her skanky ass. But I couldn't exactly tell Zed why, so I settled for passive-aggressive bullshit.

The guy behind me swayed to the dance music, his hips moving against mine and his crotch grinding against my ass. Yeah, he had moves...moves I'd like to take somewhere a whole lot less public.

"I've got to go," I told Zed, distracted as fuck by my new friend's wandering hands. "Also, you canceled a meeting earlier. Reschedule it for tomorrow."

A string of curses flooded over the phone at me. "I fucking *knew* that pretty boy groping you looked familiar—"

I ended the call before he could go on and on at me about what a bad idea this was. I knew perfectly well that it was stupid. But I also had no intention of this thing becoming anything more than exactly what it was.

So who fucking cared?

"Come on," I told my new friend, linking my fingers with his to pull him through the crowd, just in case Zed decided to really rain on my parade and turn up in person.

"Wait, we need to fix the bill," my friend protested, but I just shot him a grin over my shoulder.

"It's fine," I told him. "They'll just add it to my tab."

He gave a small frown but let me hurry him out of the bar. It was a converted warehouse on the outskirts of Shadow Grove, but it was popular enough that there were always taxis lurking outside to ferry drunken partygoers home.

"That wasn't my point," he murmured when I all but shoved him into a waiting cab and jumped in beside him. "I was buying *you* a drink. Remember?"

I smiled, amused by the whole lawful, good thing he had going on. Most guys I met wouldn't blink twice at getting free drinks from a chick who'd just openly announced she wanted to fuck them.

"Yeah, but I wanted to get out of there," I replied, vague as fuck. I gave the driver our destination, then turned my attention back to Pretty Boy. "What's your name?" I asked on a whim, then immediately gave myself a mental slap. So much for a nameless hookup.

The guy grinned. "I wondered if you were going to ask." He ran his thumb over his lower lip in a gesture that I couldn't help but follow with my eyes. Fucking hell, everything about him was mesmerizing me. "It's Lucas," he told me after a beat.

"Lucas," I repeated, testing the name on my tongue. It suited him.

"What's yours?" he asked me back, and I couldn't help the grin spreading over my face.

"Hayden," I said, shocking myself. I didn't give anyone my

real name. *No one.* So what the fuck had just possessed me to tell a random hookup?

He didn't even bat an eyelash, though. He really had *no clue* who I was, and it was totally adorable.

"Hayden," he repeated like I'd done to his name. "Can I ask you a question?"

"You just did," I replied, teasing. Where the hell *that* came from I had no idea. I didn't tease. I barely even joked. What the fuck had gotten into me?

Lucas gave me a smile. "I meant *another* question." When I nodded, he ran a hand through his hair, like in a nervous gesture. Why would he be nervous, though? I'd made it pretty damn clear I was interested. "What you said on the phone to your friend…"

About wanting to fuck you in the bathroom at Murphy's?

The cab rolled to a stop outside the packed dive bar then, cutting short our conversation. I quickly handed over about three times the cab fare and pushed Lucas out before he could object to me paying. But seriously, he'd just admitted he was broke enough to consider a job at Swinging Dick's. I wasn't going to let him pay for *anything*.

I linked our fingers together and led him straight past the huge line of people waiting to get in and up to the broad-shouldered bouncer guarding the door. Murphy's was a live-music venue, grungy and dirty, but a favorite among visiting rockers. Whenever there was a big name playing, the queue stretched halfway down the block, and lots of those waiting wouldn't even make it inside.

"Ma'am," the bouncer greeted me with a respectful nod as he unhooked the barrier rope for us to pass through.

I didn't respond. I wasn't obliged to, and I had a reputation to maintain, whether Lucas knew it or not.

"Are you some kind of big deal I'm supposed to know about?" my sexy companion joked as we made our way to the bar. The inside of Murphy's was packed way past the fire code capacity, and Lucas dropped his hands to my hips as I led the way.

I gave him a hollow laugh and shook my head. "Nah," I lied, "just a regular."

We ordered drinks, which no one was charged for—I had an account—then made our way through the crowd to the dance floor. Music boomed all around us, and people needed to yell to be heard by one another. There was no real chance to chat and get to know each other, and that was exactly why I'd chosen this bar.

Well…that and the fact that it was owned by the Reapers. If I fucked Lucas here, it would immediately get back to Cass—the head of the Shadow Grove Reapers.

Yeah, I was a petty bitch. But he wanted to call me a child? I'd damn well act like it. If he truly had no interest in me as a woman, then he would have nothing to complain about.

Lucas and I danced together until we were sweaty, panting, and crazy turned on. Eventually it got to the point that I was about to explode right there on the dance floor—because holy shit, he had *moves*. When Zed managed to pull his head out of his ass, he needed to hire Lucas for 7th Circle. Talent like his was wasted at Dick's.

"You weren't lying about being a dancer, huh?" I asked as we left the dance floor under the pretense of getting another drink. Neither of us headed toward the bar, though.

Lucas gave me a smirk. "I think I'd do well if anyone gave me the opportunity."

I couldn't agree more. I also couldn't wait to see what *other* moves he had. The moment we hit the side of the dance floor, I spun around to face him and linked my arms around his neck. I was drunk enough and *definitely* horny enough to throw caution firmly out the window.

The way Lucas kissed me back, I'd say he agreed.

He backed me against a wall that was covered in peeling band posters, and I groaned as his hands roamed my body. His hard length crushed against me, and I wanted nothing more than to climb him like a tree. There were way too many clothes between us. Way, *way* too many.

"Bathrooms," I murmured as his lips left mine and trailed down my neck, sucking and biting at my pale skin. "Come on," I grabbed his hand and basically dragged him down the short corridor that led to the grungy bathrooms. The accessible stall was occupied, much to my irritation, but Lucas read my mind and dragged me around the corner into a supply closet instead.

"Is this okay?" he asked me, looking around at the stacks of beer cases and cleaning supplies with a small frown, like he'd just realized where we were and what we were about to do and was having second thoughts.

His back was against the door, so I reached past him and flipped the lock on the inside. Now no one could walk in and catch us, and as an added bonus, the closet didn't smell like shit.

"It's fine by me," I told him, holding his gaze as I reached for the hem of my tank top and slowly raised it. "Is it okay with you?" I lifted the dark-gray fabric over my breasts, revealing my sheer lace bra, and then took the top off altogether.

Lucas's eyes flashed with heat as I dropped my shirt to the floor, and the next thing I knew, it was my back against the door while he kissed me like I was his oxygen.

"Hayden," he breathed when I deftly unbuttoned his shirt and exposed his muscular chest. It was a shock, hearing my real name on his lips. But I also kind of liked it. "This is… I don't do this."

I smiled as his face dipped back down, his lips kissing my neck as his hands cupped my breasts. "Do what?" I asked, breathless with desire as his shirt joined mine on the concrete floor. I smoothed my hands down all the hard ridges of his body and bit back a groan at how gorgeous he was.

"Any of this," he replied, then rolled one of my nipples between his fingers and made me groan. Tremors of desire shot through me with every touch of his skin on mine, and I was growing impatient. I unbuttoned my jeans and wiggled out of them, then kicked the stiff fabric aside, along with my high heels, which only increased the height difference between us. Lucas was going to have a hell of a sore neck in the morning if he kept leaning down to kiss me like that.

I made quick work of his belt and his fly, then gasped as his hot flesh filled my palm. And I really mean *filled* it. He was huge. No wonder he'd decided to get into stripping and prostitution in order to make the money he so desperately seemed to need. The boy was *blessed*.

"You mean you don't pick up random women in bars and fuck them in supply closets?" I teased, wrapping my hand around his shaft. I sucked in a short gasp when my fingertips didn't even touch. I was going to hurt in the morning. In only the best way.

Lucas groaned, his hands stilling on my breasts as I gave him a few test strokes. "Uh, yeah. I've never…" He sucked in a sharp breath and rested his forehead against the door beside my head. I swirled my thumb over the tip of his huge cock, smearing the bead of pre-ejac around like lube. "Hayden, this is a first for me."

I grinned, strangely pleased that he'd never picked up a chick for a random public fuck before. "Please, don't keep me waiting," I replied, my voice breathy and desperate. "Dancing with you out there damn near drove me out of my mind."

Lucas grinned and hitched his hands under my thighs to lift me up and pin me with his hips. "Like this?"

I nodded like a bobblehead, incapable of words for a second as his massive erection ground against my lace-covered pussy. I didn't want him to put me back down, even to take my panties off, so I just reached between us and hitched them to the side.

"Exactly like this," I replied in a moan as I grabbed his length and brought him to my core. It was reckless, exactly like Zed had accused me of being. It was also a bit fucking stupid not to use a condom. Not that I had any pregnancy fears—my IUD took care of that—but this guy could have *anything*. I could only hope that when he said this was a first for him, that also meant he hadn't picked up any diseases from an ex-girlfriend. Or boyfriend.

Too late now.

I let out a small scream as he pushed into me halfway, and he immediately withdrew with a concerned look on his face.

"Are you okay?" he asked, legitimately worried, and I couldn't help but laugh.

"No," I replied on a rough growl. "I won't be okay until you quit teasing and fucking fill me up." I grabbed him by the back of the neck and kissed him hard. My ankles crossed behind him and I pulled him closer, begging for him to fuck me properly.

He only hesitated a moment, then gave me exactly what I wanted. His next push was hard enough to fully seat him within me, and my cunt quivered with the beginning of an orgasm already. He was so, so much more than I was used to, and I had no doubt I'd be ruined for all other dicks after this one-night stand.

"Oh my god," he groaned, pausing for a second with his cock fully inside me and my muscles clenching him like they never wanted to let go. "Hayden, holy shit. Wow." Whatever else he was going to say disappeared in a moan as his hips started to move, and I turned to jelly in his arms.

He didn't need guidance, not after those first few instructions. Lucas seemed to read my body cues and deliver exactly what I wanted in exactly the right way, pounding me into the door hard enough to shake the shelves of liquor to my left.

I came way too soon, faster than I'd ever come before from dick alone, and my climax seemed to push him over the edge as well. He let out a dismayed sort of groan as his cock thickened against my spasming walls and his hot seed filled me in a couple of hard spurts.

For a moment the only sound within the supply closet was our combined heavy breathing, and he held me there with his dick still buried inside me and his hands on my ass holding me up.

"Hayden…" he whispered in a rough voice after he'd caught his breath. "That was… You're… I…" A panicked look crossed his face as his words all tripped over each other, and I grinned.

Tugging on the back of his neck, I pulled his face back to mine for another long, lingering kiss, and his dick twitched inside me.

"Lucas, that was incredible." I smoothed away the worried crease in his forehead with my thumb. Some of the tension seemed to ease from his face when I said that, and he gently set me back on my feet.

Thankfully, we were in the supply closet, so I grabbed a roll of spare toilet paper to clean up a bit of the mess between my legs before pulling my jeans back on.

"So, uh," he started to say as we both found our clothes once more. As much as I'd have happily gone on to round two—or three—with him, we'd already pushed things a bit far while in public. Not to say we couldn't continue this back at my apartment though. "I feel like a total idiot asking this, but…could I see you again?"

I tilted my head to the side, considering him. There was that innocence again. "Do you have plans for the rest of the night?" I replied with a sly smile.

His brows shot up. "Oh. *Oh.* I thought… Yeah, I mean, no. I mean I do now? I hope?" His hands went back to my waist, and his neck bent to meet me in another heated kiss. "This is actually turning out to be the best night of my life, I think."

I laughed and swatted him playfully as I stuffed my feet back into my heels. "Come on. My place isn't far."

Again, what the fuck had come over me? I didn't bring guys back to my place. Not even Cass had been to my apartment. Apparently, my subconscious had decided that I was throwing *all* the rules out the window when it came to Lucas.

I unlocked the closet door, and we exited together as Lucas checked a message on his phone.

"Oh shit," he swore, and I paused to see what the problem was. He looked from his phone back to me. "I got a message from the manager of 7th Circle."

My brows rose, but irritation at Zed's timing curled through my chest. "What did he say?"

"He wants me to come back for an interview," Lucas replied with a stunned smile. "But…he wants me there now. Like *now*. He asked me to be back there in half an hour, and he sent the message twenty minutes ago."

I ground my teeth together and vividly imagined all the ways I wanted to kill Zed. I told him to reschedule but I sure as fuck didn't mean *tonight*. "Well then, we'd better hurry."

Lucas and I hurried out of Murphy's with our hands linked like teenage lovers, and I cut the taxi line, taking the first available. It was only a five-minute drive from Murphy's to 7th Circle, but I was seething that Zed had tried to cockblock me like that.

Well, fucking joke was on him. Lucas was going to make it back for his bullshit interview, *and* I'd still managed to come harder and faster than in my entire life.

Who said I couldn't have it all?

———————

The manager of 7th Circle—Zayden De Rosa—was personally waiting at the front of the club when our taxi pulled up, and I shot him a sharp glare behind Lucas's back.

He just smiled pleasantly back at me, like the totally infuriating shithead he was.

"Mr. De Rosa," Lucas greeted Zed, totally oblivious to the silent conversation between us. "Thank you so much for reconsidering." He held his hand out for Zed to shake, but my old friend just looked him up and down, then sighed.

"Lucas, right?" he asked, like he didn't particularly care what this applicant's name was. "Come this way. We can talk in Hades's office."

Lucas's brows shot up in surprise. I instantly regretted getting out of the damn taxi. I should have just dropped him off and continued home. Then again, I was making all kinds of dumb decisions tonight, it seemed.

"Hades is here tonight?" Lucas asked Zed, looking vaguely worried.

Amusement flooded the venue manager's face, and his grin stretched so far across his lips that I imagined what it'd be like to cut it fucking off. Prick.

"Oh dear," Zed commented, his tone a step away from actual laughter. "You must be new in Shadow Grove, Lucas."

My new friend frowned slightly, shooting me a confused look before answering. "Yes, I just moved here from Colorado a few weeks ago."

Zed let out a bark of a laugh, shaking his head. "Come on this way." He indicated Lucas should follow him as he headed inside the club once more.

Lucas hesitated, though, looking at me with concern like he didn't want to leave me out there alone while he attended this interview. It was such a sweet display of consideration, and it killed me that all his good qualities would probably be stomped out of his soul before he'd survived a year in Shadow Grove.

I stifled a sigh, ruffling my fingers through my dark-red curls. I knew full fucking well what was coming next, and the only reason I'd allow it to happen was because Zed was one of my oldest friends. Still...he'd pay for this later.

"You coming, Hades?" the bastard called out to me, smug as fuck. "Or have you already conducted all the *auditioning* you need?"

It took a second, but when Lucas clicked the pieces together, I could have died. The hurt and anger that crossed his gorgeous face were almost enough for me to shoot Zed in the fucking kneecap. Mother. Fucker.

Gritting my teeth, I rolled my shoulders and adopted my normal, harsh resting-bitch face once more. "Lucas is here for a front-of-house job, Zed," I snapped, brushing past both men with my spine ramrod straight. "Nothing more. Come along, then."

The skin across my shoulders prickled with Lucas's accusing glare as I led the way through the club and up a narrow set of stairs to my office. I didn't let it affect me, though. I couldn't afford to. We'd had a fun night and shared a great fuck. That's where our personal interaction ended. If he wanted this job—and I knew he did—then that was *all* we would ever have.

I didn't sleep with my employees. Not ever.

Not until tonight.

Dammit. I needed to get my shit together. I was a successful twenty-three-year-old businesswoman and the head of a crime syndicate. I was a cold-blooded killer and a merciless bitch to anyone who crossed me.

To everyone who'd met me or heard of me in the years since my family's near massacre, I was all of those things rolled into one intimidating, fear-inducing name.

Hades. The leader of the Tri-State Timberwolves.

CHAPTER 3

My office wasn't anything fancy, just a small room with a desk, some chairs, and some filing cabinets. Hell, it wasn't even really *my* office. I only worked on-site for new openings, and when they were on their feet with all the teething pains ironed out—usually around six months after opening—I'd move on to my next project.

It'd been almost a year since we opened 7th Circle, but since I was running into all kinds of setbacks with the next club, I still used my office in the mezzanine of 7th Circle.

I sat down at the chair behind my desk, not saying a word. Years ago, I'd discovered how easily intimidated people could be by silence and an unblinking stare. I didn't *need* to threaten, insult, or curse. My silence did all the work for me in unnerving people.

Zed—that infuriating fuck—knew how I operated. He was the one who conducted interviews and auditions, not me. He just wanted to ruin my damn night by outing me when Lucas *clearly* had no clue who he was getting involved with. Had he known, he never would have hit on me in the first place. I was too damn scary.

"Take a seat, Lucas," Zed offered, indicating to one of the chairs in front of my desk.

The model-gorgeous man just stood behind the chairs, glaring at me with accusation and betrayal clear across his face. He'd need to work on that.

I let out an annoyed sigh. "Sit down, Lucas." My voice cracked with authority, and his face tightened in anger. But still, he did as he was told and slowly sank into a vacant seat.

That was a point in his favor, at least. He recognized when he needed to obey a command.

Zed didn't take the spare seat, instead opting to perch on the side of my desk. His designer suit was as impeccable as always, but his tie was missing and the top button of his shirt was undone. No doubt he'd been about to head off with whatever girl he was seeing this week before he decided to fuck up my night instead.

He reached over to the pile of employment applications in the middle of my desk—applications I hadn't even gone through yet—and pulled Lucas's from the top.

"Okay. Lucas Wilder," Zed started in a dry tone, "let's see. Twenty-one years old, recently moved from Colorado, no criminal history, no dependents, and"—Zed paused, dramatic as hell—"no prior work experience. Can you tell me why you want to work at 7th Circle?"

Lucas didn't respond. His eyes remained locked on me, burning with anger as if I'd somehow deliberately misled him. Okay, sure. That's what I'd done. But so fucking what? He'd gotten to screw the infamous *Hades* in a storeroom. There were wannabe gangsters—and fully blooded ones—all over this side of the country who would cut their own fingers off for a chance to get in my panties.

But that was the problem, wasn't it? Lucas *wasn't* a gangster. He was just a nice guy who needed money desperately enough that he'd consider whoring.

"Okay, this is going well," Zed muttered, throwing Lucas's application back down on my desk and turning to give me a meaningful glare. I just met his eyes with a cool gaze, and he turned back to our prospective employee. "Can you even dance?"

23

Lucas pushed his chair back abruptly, surging to his feet.

"This was a bad idea," he spat out, but the way he met my eyes implied he meant more than just applying for the job. Ouch. If I still had my soul, that one might hurt.

He started to leave the office, and I let out a small groan of frustration. I was about to do something stupid again.

"Lucas, don't be an idiot," I snapped, the sound of my voice freezing him with his hand on the doorknob. "You need the job. Stripping at 7th Circle pays double what whoring for Dick's does, so swallow your fucking pride and take the job."

"Who says he *has* the job?" Zed muttered under his breath, but I shut him up with a scathing glare.

Lucas hadn't moved from his position, and I knew he was in a bad situation. Damn it all to hell, I genuinely wanted to help him. What the fuck was wrong with me? Had someone spiked my drink?

"Lucas," I said again. "You won't get a better job in Shadow Grove. Not with that résumé."

His shoulders rose as he drew a deep breath, and then he turned back around to face us with a look of hard determination on his face. "I suppose I should be grateful, then? Is that how you audition all your new employees?"

Zed let out a small sound, like he was almost impressed by this guy's balls. No one spoke to me in that tone, then lived to tell the tale.

Yet here I was, not even mad about it. Fucking hell, maybe that rejection from Cass had broken something in my mind.

"Zed, give us a minute." My voice was cool and calm, unemotional.

My oldest friend and most trusted associate slipped off the edge of my desk without a question and clapped Lucas on the shoulder as he passed. "It was nice knowing you, kid. You'll make a pretty corpse." He chuckled at his own dark humor as he left the office, closing the door firmly behind him.

Lucas's determined expression faltered a moment, showing a flash of fear, and I swallowed an irritated sigh. Fucking Zed was such a shit stirrer, and he was getting worse by the day, always pushing my damn buttons the way only he could.

"What did he mean by that?" Lucas asked into the silence filling the room. "Are you going to kill me now or something?"

I let one of my copper brows rise as I sat forward, my fingers linked on the desktop. "It wouldn't be the first time I shot someone for disrespecting me."

Fear flickered across his face, and for the first time in forever, that emotion gave me no satisfaction. I just felt like an asshole, and I *hated* that feeling. Fuck me, what had I been thinking, scratching my orgasm itch on this innocent petal?

Oh yeah, that's right. I'd been thinking that Cass embarrassed the hell out of me, making me feel like a stupid, lovesick little girl, and I wanted to get back at him. I wanted to take back control and remind Cass exactly who he was dealing with. I was *Hades*, not some drugged-out gang whore.

The only downside to that plan? The stricken look on Lucas's gorgeous face right now. *Fuck.*

I heaved a sigh, rubbing a hand over my face. I was too drunk for this bullshit—and the earful Zed would no doubt give me when Lucas was gone. Maybe the solution was to drink *more.*

Reaching into my desk drawer, I pulled out a bottle of scotch and twisted the cap off. Not looking at Lucas, I took a long swig straight from the bottle, then closed my eyes and prayed for some sanity. But if there was a god, he or she had abandoned me a *long* time ago, so it was no surprise to receive no response.

"Lucas," I tried again. I let my long lashes flicker open and found him staring straight at me. Damn, that was unnerving. He didn't look at me with the wary respect I'd grown used to. He looked at me like I was a woman who'd just punched him in the balls for no good reason.

"Hayden," he replied, his voice soft and hurt.

My heart squeezed, and I shook my head. "Don't ever call me that again," I told him in a quiet voice, hating myself all the more. "It's Hades and nothing else. Got it?"

His brow creased, but he jerked a nod. "Got it." His tone was full of bitterness and anger.

I took another sip of scotch, but there wasn't enough liquor in the world, it seemed. "I'm giving you a job, Lucas. Don't be a fucking idiot and throw it away over your hurt feelings. Believe me when I say you *don't* want to work at Dick's."

His expression hardened. "Is that how you interview all your potential staff?" he asked, his tone scathing. "You take them all for a test ride and only give them the job if they make you come?"

I slammed my bottle down on the desk with a crack and gave Lucas a hard glare. "Watch your fucking tone, Lucas. You have no clue who you're dealing with."

Fury flared in his eyes, and I could practically smell the desire to snap back at me. But his better sense won out, and his lips tightened, holding his insults at bay.

Smart boy.

"For your information, tonight was a one-time lapse in judgment after a shitty day, and it won't happen again. Once you're an employee of Copper Wolf Enterprises, you'll barely even see me again, let alone…anything more. I don't screw my staff. Not ever." I was firm on that rule. My position of power was strong, but even the strongest of leaders had been toppled after trusting the wrong person. Just ask my father, buried with my blade in his back.

Lucas's brow dipped with a frown. "I won't ever see you again?"

I shrugged. "I'm moving on soon to work on one of my new clubs. Zed will run this one until he appoints a manager. I'll still come in occasionally to meet with business colleagues, but I certainly won't be here in any capacity as your boss, if that's what you're concerned about. I won't leverage my position to abuse yours."

His lips tightened as if that assurance had just angered him further.

I sighed, out of ideas. "Right, well. You're an adult, Lucas. You can make your own choices. Take the job or don't. But you won't get a better offer, and you damn well know it." I pulled a standard dancer contract from my filing cabinet and slapped it down on the desk in front of him. "Read it over. If you want the job, fill it in with your details and sign it. Simple as that. Zed will be back in ten minutes to see what you've decided."

I stood up from my desk and headed for the door, then turned to look at him over my shoulder. "A colleague always tells me: *Make smart choices.* I feel like you need that advice right now."

Lucas looked up at me, one brow raised. "What if I want to take the night to think on this? Can I sign it tomorrow?"

I gave another shrug. "If that's what you want."

A wicked smile crossed his lips. "So, if I'm not your employee until tomorrow...does that offer to go back to your place still stand?"

Surprise jolted through me. He still wanted to fuck, even knowing who I was? Or *because* of who I was? Ugh, this was the whole problem with my notoriety; it was impossible to know who was interested in me, *Hayden*, and not me, *Hades*. So I just used men and cast them aside before feelings could get involved.

Biting back a smile, I shook my head. "Sorry, that offer dissolved the second Zed outed me." I nodded to the contract. "Make smart choices, Lucas."

Leaving my office, I found Zed waiting in the hallway. He arched a brow at me, but I ignored him and made my way back downstairs to the bar. I needed more alcohol to numb all my bad decisions of the night.

"You know that's a fake name, don't you?" Zed asked as he followed me. "Lucas Wilder. Total fabrication."

I snorted a laugh, slid onto a barstool, and patted the one beside me for Zed to sit down. "Of course it is," I replied. "Just like Aphrodite up there." I smiled and waved to the beautiful blond working the stage in a glittery G-string and a pair of devil wings.

Zed huffed but picked up the drink our bartender placed in front of him. "Was he a decent fuck at least? He's pretty enough to work upstairs."

I choked on my martini. Fuck. Why did the idea of Lucas whoring in my VIP rooms turn my stomach so much? It wasn't like I was ever revisiting that avenue, and he'd make bank with that massive dick of his.

"Front-of-house *only*, Zed," I growled. "Don't fucking test me."

My second just gave me a wry smile. "Yes, sir. You're the boss."

I rolled my eyes and took another sip of my drink. "Damn right." Not that Zed ever offered me the same fearful respect as everyone else. Not when we were alone, anyway. We'd known each other too long, and he knew I'd let him get away with almost anything, including calling me *sir* in that teasing way of his. No one else ever knew he was mocking me; they just assumed it was what I wanted to be addressed as. It'd caught on way too effectively.

Apparently executing a brutal, bloodthirsty massacre and personally slitting my father's throat hadn't done shit to change the teasing dynamic between my best friend and me.

Well, not drastically, anyway. Zed and I were a long way from the close friends we used to be. He held a certain level of caution around me now, knowing how easily I killed. Everyone did.

Neither of us spoke for a few moments, then Zed ran his fingertip around the rim of his glass. "So. Cass, huh?"

I cringed. "Shut up." Of course he wasn't going to let that embarrassing blunder be swept under the rug.

Zed's lips tilted in a teasing smile. "I just never picked him as your type. He's old and a gang leader."

28

I gave him a glare. "He's not old. He's only eleven years older than me—eight years older than you—and in case you forgot, I'm *also* a gang leader."

"Well, yeah. Exactly my point. You start fucking Cass, and the Reapers are going to start getting too big for their boots, you know? We've got a good balance going with the Reapers and the Wraiths." The *don't fuck it up* was implied.

Those two gangs had owned Shadow Grove for two generations, and normally having my Timberwolves moving in on their town would be cause for an all-out gang war. Luckily for me, I owned all their asses. The Timberwolves held a tight stranglehold over all money laundering across three states. Without keeping favor with me and mine, they'd have a shitty time trying to clean their dirty money.

Obviously, I knew it wasn't smart to rock the boat now that we'd established a balance in power. But I also couldn't help the fact that I'd been fantasizing about licking Cass all over for way too damn long.

"Besides," Zed continued, clearly not finished berating my stupidity just yet, "he's so foul-tempered all the damn time. In five years, I don't think I've seen him smile once."

I had, though. Once. The first time I met him, when he didn't know who I was. He'd checked out my tits and smiled. Then I'd introduced myself as Hades and that was that.

"He looks like he'd be crazy rough in bed," I murmured, then cringed when I realized it hadn't stayed inside my own head.

This time it was Zed's turn to choke on his drink. "What?" he asked, blinking at me like I'd grown an extra head.

"What?" I shrugged. "I don't judge you for your kinks." Like how he loved fucking women in wildly public places where they could easily be seen. And *were*.

Zed just stared, then shook his head in disbelief and sipped his drink. "I never picked you for a sub, Hades. You legitimately ooze big-dick energy worse than any gangster I've met. I can't imagine you giving up control in *any* situation."

I sighed. "Sometimes, Zed, I get tired. Sometimes I need a break from being me." I paused, then added, "Doesn't make me a sub, though. Only makes me want Cass to throw me around his bedroom."

Zed grinned, saying nothing back.

"What happened to your pretty, young blond of the week anyway?" I asked him, turning the tables. "Anastasia, right?"

He glared back at me. "Annika."

"Same thing," I teased. Of course I knew her name; I knew *all* of their names. But it annoyed Zed to no end when I pretended otherwise, so I kept doing it. "So? You're usually out with her at this time of night, aren't you? How come you're still here?"

Zed gave me a sideways glance. "Reasons. Besides, I'm getting bored with her. She keeps making noises about wanting to move into my place, so I think that relationship has run its course."

I snickered. If Annika moved into Zed's place, she'd pretty quickly work out that Zed didn't actually understand the concept of monogamy.

"Fuck me," I groaned when my head swam a bit. "I'm drunk."

"No shit," Zed replied. "Want me to drive you home?"

I started to nod, then remembered Lucas was still in my office. "Nah, you'd better deal with our newest dancer. I'll grab a cab and come back for my bike tomorrow."

Zed just shook his head and indicated for our bar manager, Joanne, to come over. "Jo, there's a new employee up in Hades's office. Can you please collect his paperwork and get him added to the roster? Thanks, doll."

The thirtysomething woman assured us it'd be taken care of, and Zed slid off his stool, then waited for me.

I sighed, finished the rest of my drink in one gulp, then followed him out to the parking lot. He popped open the door to his low-slung black Ferrari for me, then closed it after I was seated.

Typical Zed: He never missed an opportunity to play white knight. Some things never changed, and I would never want them to.

CHAPTER 4

I barely even remembered getting into my apartment, but the aspirin and bottle of water beside my bed told me Zed had tucked me in. He and Seph were the only ones with keys to my place, and I doubted my bratty teenage sister gave two shits about my hangover.

Groaning, I scrubbed at my gritty eyes, then reached for my phone. It was plugged into my charger, and I smiled at Zed being so thoughtful. He'd even taken my shoes off for me but left my clothes intact. Smart man. He might be the closest thing I had to a best friend, but I wouldn't hesitate to kill him if I ever felt threatened.

"How much did I fucking drink?" I mumbled to myself, swiping my phone open, then cringing at how bright my fucking screen was.

Then I remembered all the events of the night—starting with my *stupid* idea to make a move on Cass, the hotter-than-hell hookup with Lucas at Murphy's, then Zed outing me as Hades like a little bitch.

My breath rushed out in a huff. I owed Zed a solid junk punch for that stunt because I could have been waking up to an honest-to-god Adonis right now.

"Cunt-blocking fucker," I muttered, dropping my phone on

my chest to rub my temples. It was already midmorning, and I was surprised no one had woken me up already. More often than not, *something* happened on a Saturday night that needed my intervention on Sunday.

Maybe Zed was feeling guilty if he was handling it all himself for once.

My phone buzzed against my chest, and I sighed. There it was.

Cracking an eye, I sat my ass up and took the painkillers before addressing my messages. Something told me I'd need them.

Swiping a hand through my tangled hair, I keyed open my phone once more and dragged down the notifications bar. Sure enough, there was a handful of messages from Zed, politely asking me to call when I surfaced. He had specified it was nothing urgent, so I deleted them and moved on.

Yep, there it was. I knew something in my messages would make my headache a million times worse.

Cass: We need to talk.

That was it. Fucking infuriating man. If he were anyone else…

But he wasn't, and that was the whole reason he'd evaded my bullet in his brain at least a hundred times in the past few years. Goddamn him and those sexy, soul-fucking eyes.

Still, I was stinging over his rejection way too damn hard to keep it professional, and I quickly tapped out a reply before I could let my better judgment take over.

Hades: You know the drill. Make an appt with Zed.

I closed his thread with my heart in my throat and moved to the next message on my notifications. It was from a number I hadn't saved, which made me sit up straighter. No one should have my number who I hadn't given it to personally. So who the fuck…

33

Unknown: I can't stop thinking about you.

A cold wash of fear rushed through me, closely chased by anger. If someone wanted to play mind games with me, they were about to learn exactly how I'd gotten my damn name.

Before I could reply to the unknown number, a new message from Cass lit up my screen, and my pulse raced.

Cass: Fuck that shit. Meet me.

I rolled my eyes. Meet him so he could tell me again how *not* interested he was? How he *doesn't fuck children*? Yeah, if I was being honest, it was that implication that I was a goddamn *child* that had spiked my temper the worst. Reject me as a woman, sure. Reject me as a valid, extremely dangerous player in the criminal underworld of the West Coast? Fuck *that*. He was goddamn lucky I hadn't shot him on the spot. Possibly all that'd stayed my hand were my hurt feelings—because I made it a rule not to shoot while emotional.

Hades: Trust me, only one of us will walk away breathing today, Cass. Talk business with Zed and lose my damn number. For your own good.

Rather than wait for his reply, I scrolled back to that unknown number.

Hades: Who is this?

Neither one of my message threads replied for a moment, so I tossed my phone back onto the bedside table. I needed a shower, clean clothes, and a lobotomy.

As it was, I barely managed the first item on that list before my little sister came bursting into my room without so much as knocking. Little shit.

"Dare, don't forget you said you'd get my car fixed today," she announced, using my old nickname in a way that set my nerves on edge. As if they weren't already. Hayden Darling Timber was my birth name, and for all my legal businesses I was Daria Wolff, CEO of Copper Wolf Enterprises. But only a handful of people had ever been close enough to use a playful nickname like *Dare*. Seph was one, and she still insisted on using it. Her newest best friend had briefly used it, but only because my asshole sister had introduced me as *Dare*, rather than *Hades*. No one had filled the poor girl in until she'd known me a good four months.

Zed hadn't called me by that nickname in over five years now, not since the massacre. That was the night I'd truly become *Hades*.

I tucked my towel tighter around my breasts and glared at her. She looked so much like me that we could be twins—even with the five-year age gap.

"I told you not to call me that, *Stephanie*." Yeah, I wasn't above playing dirty when it came to my little sister.

She gasped like I'd just called her a gutter slut, pressing a hand to her chest in mock outrage. "Wow, someone's in a bad mood this morning. Zed must be pretty shitty in bed if you're this bitchy."

I wrinkled my nose in confusion as I hunted for fresh underwear in my meticulously arranged dresser. "What the hell are you talking about, Seph? I'm not fucking Zed."

She snorted a laugh. "Uh, okay, sure. So I *didn't* see him creeping out of your room at the crack of damn dawn?"

I whirled around to face her with my satin panties in my fist. "I'm *not* fucking Zed, Seph. You know we're not like that." Much to my disappointment as a teenager when I'd developed *feelings* for my best friend. "But more to the point, what the hell were you doing up at the crack of dawn, huh?"

My sister's face flushed, and her lips worked as she hunted for a plausible excuse. I just rolled my eyes, knowing full well she hadn't been up to anything too dangerous. I had eyes on her pretty much twenty-four seven so she'd never get the *chance* to get into trouble.

"Whatever," I muttered, dropping my towel and pulling on my underwear.

Seph just pouted and glared at my tits as I hooked my bra on. "So not fucking fair," she sulked. "How come you got a rack like that and I'm still stuck padding my bra at age eighteen?"

I snorted a laugh and ignored her question. She was constantly griping to me about how no guys ever wanted to ask her out because she was too flat-chested. Far be it from me to clue her in that they won't ask her out because I'd fucking kill any punk-ass douche who tried to touch my sweet little sister before she graduated. It wouldn't be the first time, anyway.

Before deciding what I was wearing, I figured I should call Zed. He could give me an idea whether I could wear my jeans for a casual Sunday or if I needed something to intimidate and hide blood.

Except before I could dial his number, I spotted two new messages.

Crap.

Unknown: Lucas.

What in the actual fuck? How the hell did he get my number? Why?
My eyes went back to his first message, reading it again. *I can't stop thinking about you.*

Shit. *Shit.* Had I just fucked the enemy? Why else would he be messaging me again if not to mess with my head?

Hades: How did you get this number??

Ignoring my sister's intense stare—like she wanted to snatch my phone and read the screen herself—I flicked over to Cass's reply.

Cass: You owe me today.

I frowned.

Hades: For fucking what?

The little bubble popped up to show he was writing something back, but when I had to wait longer than a second, I became annoyed and flipped back to Lucas, who'd just replied.

Unknown: I found it in your desk drawer.

He finished his text with a winking tongue-out emoji that made my brain short-circuit. Was he flirting? What the fuck was going on?

Cass: For wiping the security footage at Murphy's.
Cass: *video attached*

Oh *shit*.

Biting my lip and barely breathing, I clicked on the video link. Sure enough, there was a security camera in the supply room at Scruffy Murphy's. Cass had just sent me my very own sex tape with Lucas.

Crap.

"Is that *porn*?" Seph squealed, sitting up on my bed and snatching for my phone. I dodged out of her reach, hitting the close button on the side of my phone to cut both audio and video, just in case. "Dare! Show me!"

"Hell fucking no," I exclaimed, dancing away from her and

pointing at my door. "Now get out of my room. I need to call Zed."

Seph stood up, her fists on her hips in outrage. "Zed was here all night. You could have talked then." Her brow creased, then she gasped. "Oh my *god*, is that home porn? Did you and Zed—"

"Seph!" I barked. "Quit it. Zed and I are *not* fucking. Now get the hell out of my room before I lose my shit." I totally ignored the heat in my cheeks at how close to the truth she was and let my eyes flash with anger.

She glared back at me for a moment, then let out a frustrated huff. "Whatever. Don't forget to fix my car today, or you're driving me to school tomorrow."

I just rolled my eyes and ushered her out my door, then slammed it after her. "Fucking brat," I muttered under my breath, crossing over to my bed and flopping down on my back. My phone wasn't leaving me alone, though. It buzzed again in my hand, and I groaned.

"What the fuck now?" I whispered at the universe, then peered at my screen with dread.

Unknown: Don't be mad.

I blinked at the message a couple of times before saving his number and replying.

Hades: You went through my desk? I didn't peg you for suicidal, Lucas.

The invasion of privacy should have made me more irritated, but there was nothing particularly confidential in that desk—aside from my mobile number, apparently, which I'd be having words with Zed about later.

Lucas: I want to see you again.

Huh, okay, he was bolder than I'd thought. Then again, this was the same guy who hadn't hesitated to fuck a girl he'd just met in a bar supply room, so maybe *bold* was just in his personality. Or maybe it was a trap.

And yet, now that Cass had sent me that unexpected sex tape, it was all so very fresh in my mind…and other places. I let my fingers tap out a reply faster than I could talk myself out of it.

Hades: Did you sign the paperwork?

There was a pause before his reply came.

Lucas: Yes.

My stomach sank. Dammit. Why'd he have to sign the fucking paperwork? He'd be great for business, no question, but fuck if I didn't regret not getting a second round out of him first.

Hades: I don't fuck employees.

His reply came quickly enough that he had to have thought about it in advance.

Lucas: Jo couldn't get me on the schedule until Tuesday. I'm not technically employed by you until that shift starts.

My lips parted in surprise at his forwardness, then curved into a grin. Fuck it straight to hell, I was tempted. So goddamn tempted.

Lucas: Please? You owe me, anyway…

I scoffed a laugh, my thumbs flying over my screen as I wrote my reply.

Hades: You think? I seem to remember getting you a damn good job offer from one of the hottest clubs in town.
Lucas: That's mutually beneficial. You know I'll be great for business.

I rolled my eyes but couldn't disagree on that point. If his moves on the dance floor at Murphy's were any indication, he was quickly going to become a main attraction on the stage at 7th Circle.

Hades: So, what do I owe you for?
Lucas: You used me to make someone jealous.

My brows shot up. Before I could reply to Lucas, though, another message popped up on my screen, and my stomach clenched.

Cass: Noon. Dogwood Lake, south side.

Anger burned away my anxiety, and I narrowed my eyes at his message. Who the fuck did he think he was talking to?

Hades: My office at 22. Eleven a.m.

That barely gave me half an hour to get there myself, but it would be more of a push for Cass to make it in time. If he was at his home—and I was banking on the fact that he was—it was a solid forty-five-minute drive to Club 22. And he knew how much I despised being kept waiting.

Part of me expected him to argue that fact, so I was surprised to see his reply ping through a second later.

Cass: Done.

I groaned. Now I really did need to get dressed and sort out some makeup. I needed my whole game face on to deal with Cassiel *fucking* Saint so fucking soon after being coldly rejected by the sexy bastard.

Lucas: So? Can I see you today? I keep replaying last night in my mind…

Biting my lip, I shook my head and tossed my phone on my bed without replying. Lucas was a distraction of the worst fucking kind, and I needed to get my head back on straight before dealing with Cass. I still needed to call Zed back and chew him out for that bullshit he'd pulled as well, but he could wait. My ever-loyal second wasn't going anywhere while I got my shit together.

"Dare!" Seph called out, making me grit my teeth in frustration. "I'm heading out to meet MK for brunch. Don't forget my car, yeah?" She shoved my door back open and gave me a pointed look with her arms folded under her breasts. Fucking kid had way too much damn sass. It was my own fault for spoiling the crap out of her over the five years since I'd slaughtered almost our entire family. A guilty conscience does crazy things.

I nodded, rubbing moisturizer onto my face at my dressing table. "You already reminded me, Seph," I muttered as I started my makeup. "Have fun but don't get into trouble."

If it were any other friend, I'd send a protective detail with her. But Madison Kate Wittenberg was one of the only people I trusted to actually keep my little sister safe. It helped that she was surrounded by three of the most dangerous bastards in the western states…aside from me and mine, that was. They wouldn't let a lick of danger touch Seph, and my sister was a happier person for that true friendship, so I was happy for her.

"Whatever." Seph rolled her eyes. "Don't say I didn't warn you when I wake you up for a ride to school tomorrow."

I flipped her off, sassy brat, and she blew a kiss back at me. That in itself summed up our dynamic. She was all sweetness, innocence, and light, and I… Well, I was a borderline sociopath with more blood on my hands than most convicted serial killers.

For that reason alone, I should steer clear of Lucas. Even if he had been considering a career as a male prostitute, he seemed… *innocent*.

CHAPTER 5

I arrived at Club 22 right at eleven o'clock, knowing full fucking well I'd beat Cass there. More often than not, I turned up late to meetings because it gave me the upper hand. When *they* had to wait for *me*, it put me in the position of power. There was never any question about who had the biggest dick in the room, regardless of anatomy.

But this time, I deliberately arrived on time so I could make the Reapers' leader sweat it out over how bad my temper would be at being made to wait for him.

I breezed through the staff entrance, pushing my dark sunglasses up onto my head and using them to hold my wavy copper hair back from my face.

"Morning, Boss!" the bar manager of Club 22 called out as I crossed the club floor toward the door to my office. He was an older guy with a generous streak of gray in his beard, and fast becoming one of my most valuable employees within the bars. He'd been with 22 since it opened and had never done wrong by me or my legitimate company—Copper Wolf.

Some people might assume that because I also ran the Timberwolves, all my staff were involved in that aspect of business too. They weren't. As much as possible, I liked to keep my legit businesses exactly what they seemed: legit. Sure, there were crossovers. There always would be, as my illegal business was conducted on the same premises for the most part.

"Good morning, Rodney," I replied, deviating over to the bar where he was taking inventory on his liquor. "How was last night? The bachelorette parties all have fun?"

"Yes, ma'am," he confirmed, inclining his head, then tucking his pencil behind his ear. "Cass is waiting in your office for you. He got here about five minutes ago."

My brows shot up in surprise. Motherfucker must have already been nearby. No wonder he'd been quick to accept a meeting here.

"Thanks, Rodney," I murmured, then sighed. "Actually, can I get a drink before I head in there?"

He gave me a wry smile but nodded and pulled out a cut-crystal rock glass for me. "Usual?"

I nodded, but he was already pouring a healthy nip of Writers' Tears Red Head whiskey into my glass. He dropped two ice cubes in, then handed it over with a smile.

"Buzz when you need another. He looked like he was in a foul fucking mood when I let him in." Rodney jerked his head in the direction of my office, and I shrugged.

"It's Cass. He's permanently grumpy." I took a gulp of my liquor—Dutch courage—then crossed the club to my office.

With my face carefully schooled into the perfect, ice-cold mask of Hades, I shoved the door open with the toe of my shiny black Louboutin pump and made my dramatic entrance.

Cass was used to my shit by now, though. He'd only been in charge of the Reapers for a year and a half, but he'd been Zane's second for years prior to that. Why the fuck he'd been content to second that slimy piece of shit I'd never know, but suffice it to say Cass had sat through plenty of unpleasant meetings with me and my boys.

He didn't speak as I rounded the desk and hooked my designer handbag over the back of the chair before sitting down. My favorite gun, a Desert Eagle, was not even vaguely concealed in an underarm holster, but just for good measure I took my blazer off. Underneath I wore just a thin, red silk camisole, black lace bra, and a gun. Sexy dangerous was my whole vibe…especially when I knew I'd be seeing Cass.

I badly needed to get over my crush on him. It was making me look foolish, and that was something I didn't have time for in my day.

"Cassiel, you look like shit," I told him, my voice like cold steel. "Rough night?"

He glared. That was new. No one glared at me. Not if they valued their balls—and their lives.

"You could say that," he rumbled, his ink-covered fingers drumming a pattern on the arm of his chair as he stared. As fast as the glare had come, it'd cooled down to a simple stare, and I was kind of disappointed. He was backing down from this fight, and it made me sigh internally.

Some days I seriously hated the reputation I'd built for myself. It made men afraid of me, which didn't work wonders when a girl just wanted some rough aggression from a lover every now and then.

"Cops were sniffing around Anarchy last night," Cass informed me when I said nothing, giving nothing away. If he thought I was going to address the awkward situation from last night, or the fact that he had a sex tape of Lucas and me, well, he would be waiting a while. I never showed my cards.

Except, of course, when I'd had one too many drinks and made a move on a man who held zero interest for me as a woman. Stupid, stupid mistake. One that would never be repeated.

"Nothing new," I replied, voice ice-cold and clipped. "The police presence in Shadow Grove has been a pain in all our asses

45

ever since that mess at Madison Kate's wedding. Why'd this require a face-to-face meeting?"

Cass let out a breath that sounded suspiciously like a frustrated sigh and ran a hand over his short beard. I hated beards on guys, but fucking hell, Cass made it look good.

"Because two of my boys got picked up after leaving the fight." There was an edge of accusation in his voice that got my hackles up.

I quirked one brow, my gaze steady. "And that's my problem how? I allow your *boys* to sell product in my venues for a cut of profit, but we're not partners, Cassiel. The safety of your low-level street dealers has nothing to do with me."

His glare darkened. "You and I both know the heat is on *you* right now, Hades. If my boys get picked up, it's an attempt to gather intel on your organization."

If he was trying to piss me off, he was succeeding. Holding his eye contact, I raised my glass and took a sip. Then I licked my scarlet lips and was rewarded by Cass's gaze darting to my mouth ever so quickly.

Then again, he was probably just remembering that awkward-as-fuck kiss from last night when I'd totally misread the situation for the first time in my life.

"They can try all they like, Cass. The Timberwolves are airtight right now. I trust your boys were clean when they were picked up?" Because there was no way in hell they were *leaving* a fight at Anarchy with excess stock.

Straight up, people in Shadow Grove liked to party. Only an idiot would try to run a clean venue with no drugs; it just wasn't happening. Either I worked *with* the street gangs to ensure clean products in my venues and got a cut of the profit, or I risked dirty, cut-rate drugs being distributed under my nose.

I was many things, but an idiot wasn't one of them.

Cass made a rumbling sound that was way too close to a growl for a human man. It did all kinds of delicious things to my insides, but none of them showed on my face. I hoped.

"They were supposedly found with a bag of angel dust." He all but spat the words, and my spine stiffened with shock. "Before you shoot first and ask questions later, my guys do *not* deal that shit. It was clearly a plant."

I hadn't even realized my hand had moved to the butt of my gun until Cass's eyes gave it a cautious look. He was right to be nervous. If I found out *anyone* was dealing angel dust in my venues—hell, in my entire damn city—I'd paint my walls with their blood. No, it wasn't the worst drug on the market, but my personal history with PCP made me issue a blanket ban on the sale of it within my territory.

"You took one hell of a risk bringing me this information, Cassiel," I told him in a deathly cold voice. He knew. He fucking knew my stance on that drug and what I'd do if I caught it back in circulation within the tristate area. If he'd been anyone else, I'd already have issued a punishment for him and his gang.

His scarred brow rose a millimeter, and his dark eyes held mine. "I know. But I also know that information needed to come from me and not some ladder-climbing shit trying to gain favor with the big bad Hades."

I drew a deep breath through my nose, my lips tight, with fury vibrating through my whole damn body. Someone deliberately planted angel dust—PCP—on the Reaper punks? That was too specific to be a coincidence.

"Why should I believe you, Cass?" I asked instead of voicing my dark fears and suspicions. "There could be good money in dealing angel dust to an untapped market. I bet Zane thought about it."

There were only a few things that I wouldn't permit within my territory, and disobedience garnered an instant death sentence if I found out about it. Child sex trafficking was one. Dealing PCP was another.

Cass shifted in his seat and cleared his throat, but to his credit he didn't break eye contact with me. I had always appreciated his balls of steel, compared to his skeevy predecessor's tinfoil ones.

"I think you know me better than that, Hades." His voice was low and careful, and my brows rose in surprise at the subtle subtext.

Against my better judgment, the corners of my mouth tugged into an echo of a smile. "Are you *seriously* playing that card right now, Cass? You're that suicidal?" Because fuck me, if he really thought he could manipulate my crush to get his gang out of trouble, I really might shoot him.

He blew out a long breath, leaning forward to rest his hands on my desk. Damn, he had nice hands, inked up and strong with prominent veins. Why was that so damn sexy on guys?

"I'm not playing shit. You know I'm better than that. The Reapers *aren't* dealing angel dust, not now, not ever. You're a good enough judge of character to know I'm not bullshitting you over this." His tone was earnest, with a tight edge of frustration. "Someone is gunning for your throne, though, and you need to be prepared."

From anyone else, that'd sound a whole lot like a threat. But not from Cass.

I pursed my lips, thinking over this new information. More and more over the past year, Shadow Grove PD had been growing their force with transfers and new recruits. It was no surprise, too, given the sheer volume of bloodshed the city had seen. But I'd fully expected the heat to cool off when the excitement died down, and it hadn't.

If anything, it was getting worse.

"Well then, thank you for informing me." I paused, then added, "Did this really require a blackmail threat, though?" Because I sure as fuck hadn't forgotten the sex tape he'd sent me this morning.

The corner of his mouth tugged up in a half smile. Most people probably wouldn't even know that was what it was meant to be, but I'd spent enough time around the grumpy fuck to know a smile when I saw one. Rare as they were.

"I thought you might need a little convincing for a face-to-face," he confessed, "rather than just sending Zed to deal with me."

My traitorous heart actually *liked* that he'd blackmailed me into seeing him in person. Surely that meant…something.

"You could have given this information to Zed," I countered with a shrug. "I trust that you've already wiped the camera footage and deleted the copy on your phone." It wasn't a question, because he had no choice here.

He dipped his head in acknowledgment, sat back in his chair once more, and swiped a hand over his half-shaved head. Tattoos continued all the way up his exposed scalp, like he'd run out of skin space anywhere else, and goddamn, it was a good look on him.

"So, who was he?" the big guy rumbled like he hated himself for even asking. "Random hookup?"

It was said so casually, but the sharp way he watched me from under heavy lids made me suspicious. Or paranoid. Or…pissed off.

"None of your business, Cass. You made it pretty clear that we're business associates and nothing more, so I'm certainly not going to chitchat about the incredible dick I got last night." I quirked a brow at him, then knocked back the rest of my whiskey in one mouthful.

The warm burn of it distracted me enough that I didn't show the flash of panic on my face. But what the *fuck* was I thinking, opening that line of conversation? What happened to pretending nothing had happened?

Cass let out a husky sound that was his version of a laugh. "Cut the bullshit, Hades. I saw the tape. He came in about three minutes. If that's your idea of incredible dick, then you need to get out more."

Shock rippled through me at his *sass*, and for a hot second I was rendered speechless. Since when was Cass comfortable enough to talk to me with such casual disrespect? Oh right, since I'd shown him my cards in making my interest known. *Idiot.*

Clearing my throat, I stood up from my chair and placed my hands on my desk, fingers splayed as I leaned forward. It'd offer a hell of a view down my red silk camisole, and if Cass were interested, he'd get a close-up view of the sexy black bra I wore beneath.

"Some might argue that it takes a talented man to make a woman come that quickly," I informed him in a voice dripping with sex and sarcasm. "You watched the tape, Cassiel. I'm sure you know exactly how hard he made me come."

His eyes narrowed, but they didn't leave my face. Disappointment rippled through me that he hadn't taken the bait to check out my tits, so I straightened up with a sigh.

"You're dismissed."

Cass clenched his jaw so hard his cheek twitched, but he slowly got to his feet. The sexy fucker towered over me, even in my stiletto heels, but we both knew who was the bigger threat in the room. Spoiler alert: It wasn't him.

"Next time you try to blackmail me, Cass, I won't be so forgiving."

He paused with his hand on the doorknob, turning slightly to give me an amused look. "Next time you try to make me jealous, pick a guy who can make you sleep through your messages the next day." With a pointed look, he gave me a sarcastic two-finger salute, then exited my office with a swagger.

Mother*fucker.* Yeah, he'd won that one.

I stood there seething for several minutes, then pulled my phone out of my bag. Ignoring all my unread messages and missed calls, I sent one of my own.

Hades: I'll be home in half an hour.

I followed it with my address, then turned my phone off. Fuck dealing with street gangs and stripper catfights like I normally did on a Sunday. I was taking the afternoon off.

CHAPTER 6

It took me longer to get home than I'd anticipated. Traffic had been heavy and I'd left my motorcycle at 7th Circle, so I couldn't just nip between cars like I usually did.

So when the elevator doors opened to my floor, I found Lucas already waiting outside my apartment door.

"You're here," I commented, completely unnecessarily. Obviously, he was; he was right in front of me, leaning against the wall like he'd just been posing for *GQ* or something.

His brow rose slightly, and a smile touched his full lips. "I'm not an idiot, Hayden."

My pulse quickened. *Fuck.* "Don't call me that," I reprimanded, but it lacked heat. There was something about hearing my first name on his lips that I liked way too damn much.

"Sorry," he replied with a smirk, sounding anything but. Fucking *hell*. His blatant disregard for danger around me was such a turn-on.

Holding his gaze, I swiped my magnetic key over the lock on my door, then pressed my thumb to the biometric screen that lit up. It took two seconds to analyze my print, then it flashed green and the door clicked open.

"That's very secure," he murmured as I stepped inside and held the door open for him to follow.

I raised one brow, letting a tiny smile touch my scarlet lips. "Sort of necessary when you're me." Even though I'd never invited anyone home—until today—it would have been supremely foolish of me to have an easily picked lock on the door. As it was, the biometric scanner was also linked to an alarm system that only Seph and I had access to. No one could enter our space without one of us allowing them.

The door closed with a nudge from my red-soled stiletto, the locks reactivating instantly.

"So, what made you change your mind?" Lucas asked, taking a couple of steps into my home and letting his gaze sweep around the room. The slight rise to his brows and the widening of his eyes told me he was impressed by what he saw. My home was a huge open-plan apartment with double-height ceilings and craploads of floor-to-ceiling windows with soft gauze curtains draping all over the place.

I brushed past him, closer than I needed to, stripped my black blazer off, and dropped it over the back of a chair on my way to the kitchen. "Your first shift at 7th is Tuesday?" I asked, ignoring his question. There was no way in hell I was opening up my personal life to this total stranger with the angelic face and godlike dick. Okay, no *more* than I already was by letting him into my home.

Crap. I was going to live to regret this decision, I could already tell. A huge old ass-biting was just looming on the horizon, waving at me like a bastard.

I unclipped my shoulder holster and placed it on the counter along with my heavy handgun, then rolled my shoulders to ease some tightness.

"Uh-huh," he replied, casually propping a hip against the kitchen counter as I pulled a bottle of wine from the temperature-controlled wine fridge underneath. It was barely past noon, but

I really felt like day drinking was acceptable in my line of work, especially to cure the hangover still plaguing my brain and loosen the knot of tension Cass had managed to tighten up again.

"Good," I murmured, pulling two glasses out, then pausing. "Do you drink Barolo?"

His intense green eyes flicked down at the bottle in my hand, then he gave a small shrug. "I've never tried it," he admitted.

I hesitated only a second longer, then poured a glass of the rich red wine for each of us. "If you don't like it, I have pretty much anything else." I slid his glass over to him, and his fingers brushed mine when he took it.

Such a small, innocent gesture, yet it sent a shock wave through me and made my breath catch. Maybe I was just hormonal or something, but I'd never craved someone as badly as I did Lucas. Not even my crush on Cass could compare to the fire building inside me with every smile and glance from this stranger.

He held my gaze as he raised the glass to his face and smelled the wine before taking a sip. His tongue dragged across his plump lower lip, and I watched like some kind of sex-starved freak, groaning inwardly when he made a hum of approval.

"I like it," he told me. "Tastes like cherries or something?"

Cute. He had a good palate. I took a long drink from my own glass and licked my lips to savor the taste. It really did have subtle cherry and black plum notes, and it was one of my favorite wines out of northern Italy. The winery was owned by my favorite aunt, Demi, and her wife, Stacey. They always talked about retiring there one day, but so far both of them were far too married to their work.

"So, I'm guessing you told me to meet you here for a reason?" Lucas prodded, curiosity burning in his emerald eyes. "When you stopped replying earlier, I thought I'd pushed too hard."

Nope. Just hard enough, pretty boy.

I couldn't just ignore his questions all afternoon. That would lead to a fairly awkward sort of encounter. So I took another sip of wine and drummed my fingernails on the marble countertop. He deserved a small amount of truth from me, especially as it concerned him.

"I had a meeting with…an associate." Yeah, I kept that vague. It was bad enough that Zed had witnessed Cass rejecting me; I sure as fuck wasn't filling Lucas in on the whole sorry story. "He owns Scruffy Murphy's bar."

Lucas's brow creased slightly. "The bar we were at last night?"

I gave a small nod. "The very same." I bit my lip, inwardly cringing. "Turns out there was a security camera in the storeroom."

His eyes widened. He immediately understood what I was saying—that our whole encounter had been taped.

"He deleted the footage before his staff saw it," I told him before panic could set in. "But it's certainly not ideal."

Lucas didn't immediately respond, taking another sip of his wine as he watched the way my fingernails tapped an anxious tune on the stone counter. Then he reached out and placed his hand over mine, stopping me.

Also damn near stopping my heart. How the fuck was he affecting me so hard? This wasn't a sappy vampire romance novel.

"I'm going to guess the guy who helpfully deleted the tape was also the one you intended to make jealous in the first place," he said softly, not accusing but…

"I didn't know there was a camera in there, Lucas," I snapped, pulling my hand free of his and reaching for my wine simply for something to do. "I'm not that much of an asshole."

"That's not what I said, Hayden, and I think you know it." He gave a casual shrug, not even slightly worried about pissing me off. Such a turn-on. Anyone else would have been basically licking my shoes at that mere hint that I was irritated.

Cass flashed across my mind, quickly followed by Zed. Okay, maybe not *everyone* else. But Zed had known me long enough to read when he was in real danger, and Cass…was Cass.

"That was a Reaper-owned club, wasn't it?" He sounded so casual, but there was a thread of fishing in his voice.

I cocked a brow. "And here I thought you were totally ignorant of Shadow Grove gangs, Lucas."

His lips curled in a grin. "I might have done some studying this morning. Seemed like a smart thing to do when I'm about to start working for the infamous, terrifying Hades herself."

I couldn't stop my eyes from rolling. "You're not," I corrected. "You're working for Copper Wolf Enterprises. I just happen to be the sole director of that company."

He nodded slowly, actually taking note of this information. It was public knowledge, though, so I wasn't risking anything by filling him in.

"And the Timberwolves?" he asked, vaguely confused.

"Are mine too. But Copper Wolf will be your employer because you're front-of-house staff." I tilted my head to the side, letting that information soak in.

Understanding dawned. "Ah, and Timberwolves run things *back of house,* then?"

I smiled. Copper Wolf owned and ran all the legitimate businesses—like my vodka brand and the bars and the strippers within them—while the Timberwolves ran everything else, taking a cut of all drug sales within Copper Wolf venues and running what were easily the most high-class and exclusive escort services in the country, among other, less glamorous aspects of gang life. I liked to keep my fingers in every pie possible, with the exception of those I'd traded to Archer D'Ath for his help five years ago.

Yes, both entities were run by me, but keeping them separated on paper was what had let my wolves fly under the radar for so long. For the better part of five years, people have thought the Timberwolves were extinct, but I've always known that can't last forever.

Silence extended between us, but for some reason it wasn't

uncomfortable. Neither one of us felt the urge to fill the gap with idle chatter, and he seemed just as content as I was to soak in the building sexual tension.

Lucas pushed off from the counter where he'd been leaning and took just one step closer, eliminating almost all of the space separating us. "Well, whoever he is, he's a fucking idiot."

It took me a second to follow his train of thought back to the Reaper-owned bar and the man I was supposed to be making jealous by fucking Lucas in the back room.

He wasn't wrong, though. That had definitely been a motivating factor.

"How so?" I murmured, gripping the counter behind me and tilting my head back to look up at him. Damn, he was tall or I was small or…both. Even with my stilettos on, I was craning my neck with him so close.

He brushed his fingertips over my décolletage, then gently gripped my chin as he bent closer. "Because only an idiot would say no to you, Hayden. But I'm glad he did."

My breath caught as he touched his lips to mine. It was a gentle kiss, like he was asking permission, yet the way he still held my chin in his grip said he wasn't *actually* asking. And I was more than okay with that.

The second my lips parted, he deepened the kiss. His fingers released my chin, but only so his hand could cup my face, holding me captive as he kissed the breath out of me and left me trembling with need.

"Sorry," he murmured in a husky voice, his huge palm still cupping my face and his lips only an inch from mine. "I needed to do that."

I let out a small laugh. My hands were still gripping the edge of the marble at my back, but my whole damn body was pressed up against him like a magnet. "Needed to?"

He nodded. "I haven't been able to stop thinking about you

57

since the moment you walked out of your office last night. Just now, standing here and talking to you, I thought I was going to die if I didn't kiss you soon."

"Well, fuck," I teased on a low chuckle. "I've killed men plenty of different ways, Lucas, but that'd be a first."

His lips curved in a wide grin, and his eyes seemed to take in every millimeter of my face. "Don't joke. I'm serious. The need to touch you is..." He let his voice trail off, sobering as he shook his head. "Sorry, I'm probably freaking you out now." He dropped his hand from my face and took one tiny step backward, creating a vacuum of air between our bodies.

Weirdly, though, he wasn't freaking me out in the least because that was exactly how I was feeling, too.

My red lipstick was faintly smeared over his mouth, and it only seemed to make him even sexier. I *had* only invited him over for one thing, and it sure as fuck wasn't conversation. So I reached out and started unbuttoning his shirt, slowly, holding his heated gaze as I worked.

"I wouldn't want to risk you dying on me," I informed him with a tiny smirk. "It'd be way too hard to explain to my cleanup crew, and I'd rather not have them inside my personal space."

His shirt was a soft linen thing, rolled up casually at the sleeves and not tucked into his jeans. So when I finished the buttons, it was easy enough to push it off his shoulders and leave his whole upper body bare.

Lucas caught my hand as I trailed my fingers over his chest, tugging me closer once more and bringing his lips back to mine.

"You're something else, Hayden," he murmured against my mouth some moments later when we were both breathing heavily and his jeans strained tight between us.

I let out a low chuckle. "I'll take that as a compliment, Lucas."

"It's *definitely* intended as one," he replied before kissing me again hungrily. His hands ran down my body, tugging at my clothes, then stripping my red silk camisole off in a smooth motion that barely even paused our kiss a second.

As badly as I was tempted to fuck him right there in my kitchen, I *really* didn't want to run the risk of Seph coming home early and walking in on us. So I pried myself away with monumental effort and shot him a wild grin.

"Come on. I'll show you my room." It was such a teenager thing to say, but it amused me. I'd been largely robbed of my teenage years. My father had sent me to a training camp for killers before I even hit puberty, and then I foolishly ended up engaged to my first boyfriend before I was even fifteen. I grew up way too fast, but something about Lucas made me feel young again. Carefree and impulsive. I loved it.

He followed eagerly as I led the way through my huge apartment. With a flourish, I pushed open the double doors to my suite and indicated for him to enter. He didn't hesitate, heading directly across to my Alaskan king bed—easily as large as two normal king-size beds—while I closed and locked my bedroom doors. There was no way I was letting my little sister mess with my afternoon fuck date.

"Is this why you wanted me to come over this afternoon?" Lucas asked with a lopsided smile. He sat on the foot of my bed, leaning back on his strong, tanned arms as I unzipped my skirt and let it pool at my feet.

I tilted my head to the side, admiring the sight of him on my bed. Zed was the only guy who'd ever been in this room, and that had been purely platonic.

"Would you be offended if I said yes?" I stepped out of my skirt, walking toward him in just my matching black lace lingerie and shiny Louboutin heels.

He watched me like a starving animal, and his breath sped up as I stopped between his spread legs. "No," he answered in a hoarse voice. "Not at all. I hate that some other guy is under your skin, but I'm happy to reap the rewards."

I barked a sharp laugh, shaking my head. "This level of honesty is refreshing, Lucas." I threaded my fingers into his brunet hair, quietly loving that it was just long enough to tug. "But while we're being honest, we've got to be clear on something."

"I know." He gave a resigned groan. "This can't be a regular thing because you don't fuck employees."

I nodded, firm on that. Or…firmish, considering the position we were currently in. But he hadn't technically started work for 7th yet, so…

Lucas gave a small shrug. "Tuesday is two days away, Hayden. Maybe I'll get a nice barista job at the new Starbucks across town instead."

I couldn't fight my grin. "And waste all your god-given talent for a fraction of the pay? Wash your mouth out, Lucas."

He sighed but sat forward to clasp my hips in his hands. "Fine, then I'd better make this an afternoon you'll never forget so every time you see me dancing on one of your stages, you'll know I'm really thinking about all the things I wanna do to you…but can't."

I groaned at that thought. Fuck. I could *never* go back to 7th Circle while Lucas was working. My willpower was strong, but Jesus fuck, not *that* strong. No one's was.

His fingers hooked under the band of my panties as his lips caressed my breast, and I shoved all those worries aside. No doubt this was a terrible idea, one that I'd regret later. But I might as well regret it *after* a few orgasms, not before.

The soft lace of my thong slid down my legs, and I reached around to unhook my bra. When I was totally naked, I kicked my shoes off and pushed Lucas flat onto my bed. His jeans were straining so tight around his huge erection that it took me a bit of effort to unbutton the fly, but it was effort well spent. He was even bigger than I remembered from the back room of Murphy's, and I sucked in a sharp breath as I took him in my hand.

"Holy fuck, Hayden," he hissed as I tightened my grip,

marveling at the fact that my fingers and thumb didn't even connect around his girth.

"I'm sure I told you not to call me that," I murmured, stroking his shaft slowly.

His hips surged, pushing into my hand harder as his breath hitched. "Yeah, but you didn't mean it." His lips held a lazy, teasing smile. Fuck, he had a great mouth. Totally kissable.

So I did just that. Placing one knee on either side of his hips, I leaned down and claimed his mouth in a lingering kiss. His hands found my face, then threaded into my hair in a possessive, slightly controlling way that lit my whole body up with arousal.

His hard length ground against my core, and I gasped into his kiss. All my plans to take my time and toy with him flew out the window. If I didn't get his thick dick inside me immediately, I was likely to explode.

"Fuck," I muttered, placing my hands on his muscular chest to push up a scarce inch. "Condom. Don't fucking move."

Even though we hadn't bothered with protection last night, it seemed like a supremely bad idea to simply continue in kind. Not even IUDs were one hundred percent effective, and pregnancy was most definitely not in my plans.

I climbed off Lucas and left him lying there looking like an angel as I grabbed a condom from my dresser. Just because I never brought guys home didn't mean I didn't have condoms ready to throw in my handbag when I went out. Okay, so my casual hookups were rare, but they happened occasionally.

Lucas watched me with heavy-lidded bedroom eyes as I returned to him and ripped the packet open with my teeth. He tucked his arms behind his head, his gaze following my every movement as I straddled his thighs and smoothly rolled the condom down his impressive length.

"Holy shit," I muttered with a laugh, "I need to get some bigger condoms."

His brows hitched, and a smile danced over his lips. "Oh yeah?"

I cringed, then shook my head. "Nope. No, I don't because this is not going to be a recurring thing."

His grin just spread wider, and he grabbed my hips. "We'll see."

In a swift movement he rolled us, taking charge and settling between my spread thighs. His lips moved over my throat as he reached down to position his tip at my cunt and pushed inside ever so slightly.

"Is this okay?" he asked in a breathless whisper, pausing for... *consent*? Fuck, he was adorable.

I nodded quickly. "Yes, fuck yes." I parted my legs wider and pushed against him, begging for more.

With that permission, Lucas gave me what I wanted. He didn't force his way inside with one swift motion; instead, he rocked in with small thrusts, getting deeper with each push until I was panting and thrashing under his body.

"Hayden," he whispered with all the reverence of a prayer. "Holy shit." He buried his face in the crook of my neck, kissing my skin and shifting his position to carry his weight on his bent elbows.

I just moaned and writhed under him, hooking my ankles together behind him to pull us closer together. I was so full, so stretched, but it was the most insanely exquisite feeling. So, *so* much better without the haze of drunkenness dulling my senses.

"Lucas," I groaned on a sigh, "please..."

He bit my neck gently, his hips moving in shallow thrusts—enough to drive me wild with anticipation but not give me the rough, hard fuck I wanted.

"I don't want to hurt you," he confessed, his lips capturing my earlobe.

I let out a low chuckle, digging my fingers into the flexed muscles of his back. "Trust me, Lucas, you can't hurt me."

He pulled away just far enough to give me a skeptical look, but I held his gaze steadily. He had no clue what I'd been through, the shit that had shaped me into the cold, merciless killer I was now. Pain barely even registered on my radar these days, and even if it did, this kind of pain would still be welcomed.

"I feel like there's so much more to that statement," he murmured with a small frown, "but if you're sure—"

"I'm sure." Just to prove my point, I bucked my hips against him and tightened my legs around his waist. "Please, Lucas? Fuck me like you mean it. Break my bed."

He let out a bark of laughter, but a challenge flashed in his gorgeous green eyes. "Yes, ma'am."

Oh man, this guy was hitting *all* my buttons. When his mouth met mine again, I knew he was taking me at my word. His tongue tangled with mine, demanding and forceful. A fraction of a second later, his dick slammed into me just the same way. Forceful as fuck.

I screamed into his kiss but tightened my fingernails against his back before he could panic over hurting me. I *wanted* everything he had to give, even if it did mean I'd be walking funny tomorrow. *Especially* if that's what it meant.

It didn't take long for him to work into it, and soon my headboard was banging against the wall loud enough to annoy the neighbors—if I had any. There was no way he'd actually break my bed—it was a seriously solid build—but goddamn, he was giving it a good try.

Sweat glistened on his body over me, and I couldn't stop touching him. It was like an addiction, and with every second that passed, every thrust of his perfect cock inside me, I knew it was going to be a rough withdrawal to quit him.

My orgasm built steadily, not even needing any extra attention on my clit—practically unheard of—and I clung tighter to his body. "Lucas," I gasped as his teeth found my neck again. "Fuck, I'm gonna come already."

"Good," he whispered back, his voice dark desire in my ear.

A hard shudder rippled through me. Somehow, hearing his

deep voice was all it took to push me over the edge, and my every muscle stiffened. My climax rolled through my whole body, making my back arch, my muscles clench, and my fingers flex on his tight butt. I moaned, long and low, as the ecstasy shuddered through me, making my head spin and my heart race.

"Holy fuck," Lucas breathed, his neck and shoulder muscles bunched tight with tension like he was desperately holding off his own climax. "Shit, Hayden, you're a goddess."

I laughed, my body turning to liquid in the wake of my orgasm. But still, I didn't want to be done yet because when I let Lucas walk out of my apartment, I would have to stand by my word. Nope, I wasn't ready for that yet. So I rocked under him, wordlessly showing I wanted him to keep going.

He groaned, then found my lips again and kissed me breathless as he started fucking me hard once more. Then he broke away, breathing hard, and bit his lip.

"Turn over," he told me, his chest and biceps flexing as he pushed up.

Internally, I screamed a protest when his dick withdrew from my aching core, but I quickly did as he wanted, flipping onto my belly, then pushing up on my hands and knees. Excitement fluttered through me at the idea of taking his massive cock from a different position. I was already soaking from my orgasm, so I doubted it would be a problem.

"Shit," he cursed as he shuffled to his knees behind me. "Uh, that condom broke."

I snorted a laugh, totally unsurprised. "Told you I needed bigger ones."

He coughed a chuckle in response, stroking his hand over my butt cheek, then sliding a finger into my pussy. "I'll grab another one."

"Don't bother," I said quickly, then gasped as he slid a second finger into me. His thumb reached forward, finding my swollen clit and teasing it. "I've got an IUD and I'm assuming you'd have said something last night if you had a known STI."

He didn't immediately respond, fucking me with his hand for a couple of moments, and I got the feeling he was undecided.

"Just come on my back," I told him, "or grab another condom from my dresser. But decide quick, babe."

He let out another soft laugh, taking his fingers from my cunt and gripping my hips. "Yes, ma'am." His decision was clear when he thrust into me, filling me up with one smooth motion and making me moan.

"Thank fuck," I whispered, my hands tightening in the bed-clothes as he gripped my hips and pulled me harder onto his dick. The new angle was doing *incredible* things for me, lighting me up in ways I'd never even known were possible, and within no time at all, I could feel sweat trickle down my spine as another climax built.

My bedroom was filled with the sounds of our rough breathing, small groans and grunts, and the delicious slap of flesh on flesh. When Lucas released one of my hips and reached around to rub my clit, I exploded. I came harder than I could ever remember, and my arms shook, threatening to dump me on my face.

"Holy crap, Hayden," Lucas exclaimed as I moaned and writhed, my whole body quaking with wave after wave of pleasure. "Shit, I'm—" He swiftly pulled out, and a split second later his hot load spilled all over my lower back.

I let my shaking arms give out then, and the two of us collapsed onto my mattress in a tangle of sweaty, sticky limbs. For a moment, neither of us spoke or even moved. Then Lucas shifted us around until I was cuddled in his arms, totally impervious to the fact that I was slick with his cum.

Fuck it. If it didn't bother him, it didn't bother me. We could shower when we got up.

"Sorry," he murmured against my hair after we'd lain there for the longest time.

I tilted my head back to look up at him. "For what?"

His cheeks pinked slightly, and he dragged his lip through his teeth before replying. "Nothing, it's…nothing." His gaze dodged away, like he was embarrassed about something.

I didn't push the issue, though. We barely knew each other, nowhere near enough for me to try to force pillow talk out of him. But my chest tightened at the thought that I'd made him uncomfortable about something, so I shifted onto my side to face him, propping my head on my hand.

"You're different from other guys around here, Lucas. Why is that?" I didn't mean it as an accusation, more a compliment, but I was genuinely curious about this angelic man who'd fallen into my lap when I needed him the most.

He gave me a wry smile. "Because I'm not from around here?"

I rolled my eyes. "All right then, smart-ass. Where are you from? I haven't had a chance to snoop through your employment application yet."

"Most recently? Colorado," he told me with a small grin. "Dinosaur, to be exact."

I frowned. "Excuse me?"

He laughed. "Dinosaur, Colorado. Not even joking, that's what it's called. Tiniest town you've ever seen."

"That's legitimately the best thing I've heard in a long time," I told him with a chuckle. "So, why Shadow Grove, then?"

He wrinkled his nose, and it was one of the cutest things I'd ever seen. *Fuck,* why was I so fascinated by this man?

"Uh, long story," he said with a sigh. "In a nutshell, my uncle—my mom's brother—used to live here. He didn't like the way I was always moving around with my mom and offered to pay for my education if we moved here to Shadow Grove."

Surprise rippled through me. "You live with your mom, then?"

He stiffened, and his expression shuttered. "She's…not well. About a week before we arrived here, *after* my uncle paid for my schooling in full, he died from a heart attack. My mom hasn't taken it well." He paused, seeming uncertain about telling me more, then gave a sigh. "She's got MS, and it's been getting worse. Just after my uncle died, she deteriorated to the point of needing a wheelchair. So everything that was left in our savings went toward installing accessible ramps in the house."

Understanding dawned, and I nodded. "So you're attending Shadow Grove University during the day and stripping at night to pay for your mom's medical expenses?" I was absolutely in no way judging. In fact, it was admirable of him.

Lucas's cheeks pinked, and he dragged that lush lower lip through his teeth again before nodding. "Yeah, something like that."

I reached out, trailing a fingertip over one of his warm cheeks, then impulsively pressed a kiss to his lips. It was out of character for me in that it wasn't a kiss to initiate sex... It was just a kiss because I *liked* him.

"I'm glad you came to 7th Circle, then," I murmured. "You'll earn good money there. What's your major?" He was twenty-one, so if he'd been caring for his mother for a while, it was possible he'd been doing online courses until starting at SGU.

His gaze ducked away from mine, and he ruffled his fingers through his hair. "Uh...undecided. So far my only real talents are in dance and gymnastics, and without any aspirations to take that professional, I don't really know what I want to do with my life."

"You're still young. You've got tons of time to work it out," I told him with a grin. "But in the meantime, those skills will pay well in my clubs, that's for sure."

He snorted a laugh. "You say that like you're *so* old."

Smart boy, he didn't actually ask my age. Not that I cared, but it was bad manners to ask a lady her age. Or that's what Demi always told me.

"I'm twenty-three," I said with a bitter laugh, "but I feel like

I'm sixty-three. Criminal life is stressful, Lucas. Don't get mixed up in that shit if you can avoid it."

His expression sobered, and he gave a small nod. "I'll keep that in mind."

I bit my lip, suddenly feeling all kinds of vulnerable, like I'd somehow revealed a deep secret by admitting how tired I was of my life. Shaking it off, I wriggled out of bed and started toward my bathroom.

"You coming?" I called over my shoulder. "My shower is big enough for two…"

CHAPTER 7

Against my better judgment—and my usual practice of hit-it-and-quit-it hookups—I didn't kick Lucas out after our shower. Mainly because it ended with him fucking me against the wall, then over the vanity, then somehow we found ourselves back in my giant bed with me riding him like my own personal pony.

Even so, after a full afternoon of quite literally the best sex of my life, I still didn't show him the door. Despite *knowing* I should. Come Tuesday, he'd be on the books as a 7th Circle employee, and I refused to cross that line. I knew too many sleazy club owners who leveraged their power and authority to "sample the goods," and the idea of becoming one of them turned my stomach.

Sex for sale was part of the Timberwolf empire I'd inherited, and all of my back-of-house staff were there willingly and happily, earning damn good incomes for their work. I wasn't my father. Everything was run with the utmost professionalism now.

So why, then, did I find myself falling asleep in Lucas's warm embrace later that evening?

A loud knock at my front door jerked me out of that half-asleep daze, and I sat up in alarm. Who the fuck was knocking on my door?

I blinked a couple of times in confusion, looking down at Lucas. But he just shrugged as if to say *It's your apartment. How would I know?*

The banging continued, and I sighed heavily. Not bothering to get dressed, I just grabbed a thin satin-and-lace robe and threw it on as I went to find out who in the hell was at my door—even though I already knew, as there was only one person it could be.

"What the fuck, Zed?" I snapped as I jerked the front door open. I wasn't a total fool. The video display beside the door had showed me it was him before I opened it. And he was the only person who would dare bang on my door like that.

"What the fuck, *me*?" he replied, his face pure fury. "Me? Are you kidding right now, Hades? Where the fuck have you been all day? I called you at least a hundred times."

He started to push past me, but I stopped him with a hand flat against his chest. I was barefoot—seeing as I was totally naked under my robe—and it put me at a significant height disadvantage to Zed. Luckily, he was all too well aware that height did not reflect danger, and he froze.

"Zed, you're going to want to check that bullshit attitude right there at the door before you really piss me off," I told him in a cool tone, my glare hard and uncompromising. "Who the fuck do you think you're talking to right now?"

His jaw clenched and his teeth ground hard enough for me to hear, but he took a step backward nonetheless. "My apologies, sir," he growled, his eyes flashing with anger. "I didn't mean any disrespect."

I folded my arms under my breasts to glare harder at him, but the effect was ruined when the shoulder of my robe slipped down and halfway exposed my left boob. Zed's attention immediately shifted to my chest, and I cleared my throat in a pointed way as I tugged my robe back up.

He didn't even have the grace to look apologetic when his cold blue eyes met mine once more. Shithead.

"Get in here," I snapped, indicating that he enter my apartment. "Sit your ass down and explain what's got you in such a fucking mood."

He took my offer, coming inside and waiting while I closed the door and the locks slid into place. As I turned back to him, I caught the way his gaze trailed over my exposed legs. Then he frowned at the two half-empty glasses of wine sitting on my counter. And the man's shirt on the floor beside my red camisole. Yeah, no prizes for guessing what I'd been busy doing all afternoon.

"Did I interrupt something?" he asked with an edge of sarcasm to his voice.

"You damn well know you did," I muttered, grabbing my bag from where I'd dropped it to fish out my phone, "or I would have answered my phone."

Oh yeah. I'd turned it off after my meeting with Cass.

I held down the power button to turn it back on and gave Zed a questioning look while it booted up. "So? What happened?"

Zed slid onto one of my barstools, only half sitting on it in a weirdly *him* kind of way with one foot still on the floor. "You know about the Reaper kids getting picked up with PCP on them. Cass told me you met this morning." The look he gave me implied so much more than he was saying. I fucking hated that he'd witnessed my moment of weakness with Cass last night.

"And?" I prodded, not in the mood for his bullshit.

"And then you dropped off the fucking radar all afternoon," he snarked back at me with an accusing glance in the direction of my bedroom. "Who is he?"

"None of your fucking business, Zed, that's who." My voice was like a whip, and he jerked with surprise. "You didn't come here to tell me what I already know, so what *else* has happened?"

He paused a beat, studying my face before replying. "Sonny-boy was killed last night."

Those words hung in the air between us, and for a hot second

I was totally speechless. Of all the things he could have come to tell me, I hadn't expected that. Not because my Timberwolves were such upstanding individuals, lord no, but because Sonny-boy wasn't even working right now. His wife was expecting their first baby any day now; he was officially on leave from all business, both Copper Wolf and Timberwolves. So there was no way in hell he'd been killed in the line of duty, so to speak.

"What happened?" I asked after swallowing heavily. For all my cold, heartless reputation, I wasn't a damn robot. I cared about my people, and I cared when they were hurt or killed.

Zed shook his head, clearly still furious, which told me it was nothing innocent. "He was shot full of holes like he'd been in front of a firing squad, over in one of the old abandoned houses in the old west side."

My brows hitched, and alarm rippled through me. "That's Reaper territory."

Zed jerked a nod, his expression grim. "The body wasn't found until early this afternoon. Cass didn't know about it when you met."

Well, that was something at least.

"Who discovered him?" I asked, trying to click the pieces together in my head. What the fuck had Sonny-boy been doing in Reaper territory last night?

"Cops," Zed told me with a grimace. "Anonymous tip, apparently. They got there before any of the Reapers' boys even, locked the whole scene down too."

"Excuse me?" I exclaimed, half-convinced I'd just heard him wrong. Not only had cops been tipped off before the Reapers themselves, but they'd been cops *not* on the take? The odds of that happening were too low for it to be coincidental.

Lucas chose that exact moment to exit my bedroom, looking next-level gorgeous with his hair messed up and his jeans slung low on his hips.

Zed's brows hitched, and I caught the way his hand shifted to the gun at his hip. Fucker.

"I should probably go," Lucas murmured, picking up his shirt from the kitchen floor and pulling it over his perfectly formed arms.

If I'd been any less distracted, I'd have probably told him to stay. After all, we still had all of Monday before he started work at 7th Circle... But the murder of one of my Timberwolves trumped anything else. Worse yet, I'd been so distracted that it'd all happened right under my nose.

Distracted. So fucking distracted. I couldn't afford that weakness.

Lucas had to go.

As if he could sense the murderous tilt to my thoughts, Lucas threaded his fingers into the back of my hair, tilted my face up, and kissed me. It wasn't a casual peck, either. It was one of those deep, possessive-level kisses that told me he was flipping Zed off.

Fucking hell. As if Zed gave a crap who was warming my bed; he barely even saw me as a woman most days.

"I'll text you," Lucas told me when he released my hair.

"Don't," I replied, my voice hard. "Delete my number."

Lucas just flashed me a wide, mischievous grin, then gave a nod toward Zed. "Boss. Sorry, didn't see you there."

Zed snorted. "Sure you fucking didn't." His hand was fully resting on the butt of his gun now. "Fuck off, kid. The adults are talking."

I bit my tongue, refusing to entertain that little comment. Lucas was two years younger than me, hardly a *kid*, but whatever. We really did need to talk business, and I wasn't comfortable doing that with Lucas around. Not until I knew whether he could be trusted.

Zed's attitude didn't seem to bother Lucas, though. He just finished buttoning his shirt and sent me a lust-filled glance on his way out the door.

Silence reigned as the door closed behind Lucas and the locks reactivated. Then Zed's eyes narrowed at me in an accusing glare.

"Really, Hades? You're fucking strippers now? You can do better than that." His tone was total judgment, and my temper flared cold within me.

"Oh, fuck right off, Zed. You've screwed *how many* of our girls over at Club 22? Quit throwing stones from inside your glass house, my friend, it makes you look jealous." I was just taking swipes to piss him off, but his eyes flashed with a darkness that I didn't expect. Maybe things had gone sour with his flavor of the month already and I'd struck a nerve.

His jaw clenched, and he gave an angry shake of his head. "I'm not throwing stones, Hades. But you haven't even done a background check on that guy, and he's *here*? Inside your home, where Seph lives? What the hell is going on with you this weekend?"

Guilt rippled through me at the truth in his words. I was acting reckless. Stupid. Distracted. It wasn't good enough. I needed to be better than that, above it all.

Fucking hell. I needed to kill Lucas.

"I'm getting dressed," I announced, ignoring Zed's pointed comments. "Tell me the rest of it, then call a meeting with all the heads in the area. It's time we all had a chat."

He followed me through to my bedroom, eyeing the mess of tangled sheets on my bed with thinly veiled rage. Whatever had his panties in a bunch, it had nothing to do with me. He could take all that baggage elsewhere because I wasn't interested in becoming an outlet for his personal drama.

I crossed over to my huge walk-in closet and pulled out some fresh clothes but blew out a frustrated sigh when nothing but silence followed me.

"Talk, Zed. Fill me in on everything you know." Anger colored my own tone of voice now, and every passing second had me feeling more and more murderous.

Sonny-boy had to have been killed sometime last night—while I was busy sulking about my rejection from Cass or fucking Lucas in a supply room. Or maybe while I'd slept off all my many drinks after Zed dropped me home. Either way, it had been while my back was turned, and that simply *couldn't* happen.

"We don't know all that much," Zed said after a moment's pause.

I shrugged off my robe right there inside my closet, even though I'd left the door wide open, and pulled on some fresh underwear. There was no time to shower, but it hadn't been all that long since my last shower with Lucas, so…fuck it.

Irritation pricked at my skin, and I had to take a calming breath before responding to him. "What *do* we know, Zed?"

I glanced out of my closet and found him with his back turned to me. I expected nothing less, given how carefully respectful he was around me these days.

"Just that he'd been shot all up, riddled with bullets. Same with the room he was found in, so it's likely that's where he was killed." He scrubbed a hand over his short hair, and I could tell he was frustrated as hell. We were used to being in charge in *every* situation. This lack of information must be burning him as badly as it was me.

I took a moment to consider it as I dressed in skin-tight leather pants and a black lace top that showed my bra underneath.

"Why did no one hear the shots?" I asked, grabbing a pair of high-heeled ankle boots from my shoe wall and coming out of the closet.

Zed stiffened a fraction of a second *before* he turned around, and I gave him a suspicious look, then looked past him to my dresser…and the mirror above it. Had he been watching me?

"You look—" he started, then caught himself and clamped his mouth shut tight.

I gave him a confused scowl as I sat on the end of my bed to put my shoes on. "You're acting fucking weird, Zed. What gives?"

He let out a long exhale, shaking his head. "I know. It's this shit with Sonny-boy. It's got me all fucked up, Boss." He paused again, rubbing the back of his neck as I zipped up my ankle boots and stood up. "The cops claim they found PCP on him."

I blinked several times. "Excuse me. Fucking *what* did you just say?"

Zed grimaced. "They—"

"I heard you the first time," I snapped, stalking across to the hidden panel beside my closet. Pressing the release, I opened my weapons safe and loaded myself up. Not that I needed a huge amount of firepower on my person—that's what I had Zed for—but it didn't hurt to get my own hands dirty every now and then. It reminded anyone who might be eyeing my throne exactly *why* I'm Hades.

"It's not what we think, Boss," Zed told me firmly as I slammed my weapons safe shut again and made my way back to the kitchen. I'd left my Desert Eagle there, and there was no way I was leaving the apartment without it. Not now.

I stuck it in my shoulder holster, then gave Zed a hard look. "Of course it's not. That's not even remotely possible. But *someone* wants to send us a message, and that in itself is bad enough."

Angel dust had been wiped out of my territory for five years, and now it was resurfacing in the most suspicious circumstances? Not a coincidence. No freaking way. But the most likely culprit, the one who might want to send a message to me… He was dead. I'd shot him myself.

So who the fuck was playing the part of his ghost?

CHAPTER 8

Zed drove and I sent out summons from my phone on the way to my chosen meeting point. It was an old church and had been the Timberwolves' base of operation when my father was in charge. It was also a solid three-hour drive away from Shadow Grove in the heart of old Timberwolf territory.

When I had confirmations from all the gang leaders in the general vicinity—including a terse message from Cass asking why I'd been uncontactable all afternoon—I sent a quick message to my aunt Demi.

Aside from being a kickass lawyer, she was also heading my information department. She had access to some of the best hackers in the world, and with enough time and money, there wasn't much she couldn't uncover for me.

Zed glanced over at my phone while we were stopped at a red light, then arched a brow at me. "What are you texting Demi about?"

I scowled. "None of your fucking business." Then rolled my eyes. I had no reason to keep secrets from Zed. "I'm asking for a full background check on Lucas, okay?"

Both brows raised. "I thought you didn't care about his clearly fake name?"

I glared at the side of his head. "I don't. But like you said, he's been to my home. With this weird shit going on and angel dust resurfacing in my territory... You know I don't believe in coincidences."

There was a note of bitterness to my voice that I knew Zed heard too. But so what? I was bitter. I'd finally met a gorgeous guy who seemed totally into *me*—not Hades—and it was starting to look like a setup.

Fucking hell. I really was going to have to kill him.

"You gonna kill him, Boss?" Zed asked with curiosity.

Was I? My natural instinct was to eliminate the potential threat, and if Lucas turned out to have *any* ties to Chase Lockhart, then he was already a dead man walking. Yet somehow, it just wasn't sitting right in my gut.

I breathed out a long sigh. "Probably. I dunno. I'll wait and see what Demi comes back with on him, I guess." I let my gaze wander out the window and chewed on the edge of my nail as I thought about it. Lucas *seemed* so innocent, so totally unrelated to all these gangs and feuds and bullshit. But that in itself was too good to be true. Wasn't it?

"Stop that," Zed scolded, tugging on my wrist to pull my nail out of my teeth. "Talk to me about what you're thinking. It's not the Lockharts, we know that."

I snorted a bitter laugh. "Not unless he's risen from the dead."

Zed shot me a frown, his eyes returning quickly to the road in front of him. We were in his Ferrari, driving almost double the speed limit, but he was fully in control as per usual. "It has to be someone associated, though. Doesn't it?"

I wasn't so sure. It could just be an opportunistic shit coming in from another state who saw a gap in the market for selling PCP. It certainly wouldn't be the first time someone had tested my laws within the tristate area. But Zed was clearly thinking the same as I was...that this was more than someone breaking my rules. They were *flaunting* their disobedience in a way that deliberately sent a message to me.

"Yeah." My sigh gusted out, and I rubbed my temples. "It sure feels like it. But who? We left no one alive to seek revenge." The Timberwolf massacre had taken out more than just my father's dirty, low-life followers. It'd also cleaned up anyone he'd been colluding with in the sale of young girls stolen from their families and traded to equally depraved men—and women—who used them in ways no human should be treated.

The entire skin-trade operation had been eliminated in one blood-soaked night, and within that had been a small crime family who'd made their name primarily in the import and sale of PCP. It was a drug I particularly abhorred thanks to my own personal experience with it and the state I'd found Seph in after she'd been forced to take it.

"The Lockharts are all dead," I said out loud, needing to hear those words. "Every single one of them. You and I know that better than anyone else."

Zed was silent, but his knuckles whitened on the steering wheel. He and I had personally delivered the killing shots on the key players of that family, but the ones we'd intended to spare, the innocent children of the Lockhart family, had been collateral damage when the Lockhart mansion exploded from a damaged gas line.

We had a lot of blood on our hands and didn't regret much. But those kids… That was a guilt Zed and I both carried with us even now, five years on.

"Yeah," he murmured after a long time. "Yeah, I know. Hopefully some of these other assholes have more clues for us to piece together."

I grunted a sound of annoyance. "If they don't, they're fucking lying. There's no way Sonny-boy's death was the first incident. No way in hell. Our little rats have been keeping things from me, Zed."

He gave me a sidelong look, the corners of his mouth pulling up in a grin. "Should I have lined up a cleaning crew in advance?"

I just shrugged and ruffled my fingers through my loose curls. "Probably."

Because as a woman holding as much power as I did in a man's world, I could never show weakness or vulnerability. I could never let anyone think my rules were negotiable or optional. The punishments for disobeying me were swift and bloody; it was the only way I could stay on top. It was the only way I could confidently keep Seph safe and give her the future she deserved.

I'd do fucking anything for my little sister. Anything.

The old church was a mess of construction when Zed and I walked in, but we bypassed the scaffolding and drop cloths, heading straight for the basement door. Timberwolf headquarters had been where my father had acted like a god, playing with his subjects' lives like they were no more than an amusement for him, things to be owned and used as it suited him. The fact that he'd chosen a church was the epitome of his arrogance, but I, weirdly, hadn't been able to get rid of the building itself since taking over.

It wasn't until recently that I'd accepted the fact that it was still a pillar for my organization, and I should treat it as such. So we had started work to renovate and rebrand. Soon, the old Timberwolves HQ would reopen under Copper Wolf branding as Timber, a hot new nightclub with a dark and sexy lower level for high-stakes poker games.

Nothing laundered blood money easier than a *successful* business. None of this dodgy laundromat bullshit for my crew.

"New roof is looking good," Zed commented as he followed me down the staircase to the basement. We'd needed to replace the entire cathedral roof over the sanctuary because my father hadn't believed in regular maintenance and it'd leaked like a sieve.

"It does," I agreed. "I'm excited for this club. It'll be our best one yet, I think."

We shared a grin, the buzz of our new project tingling through my body. Zed and I had come up with the idea to open bars and nightclubs about a year before taking over the Timberwolves, back when I was still in high school and sneaking out to dance clubs with Zed and Chase. It had turned into a passion project for us just as much as a front for our Timberwolf finances.

We walked through the main basement room, the one that would turn into a bar with lots of seating areas and low lights, then passed through a short corridor to the back room. The crypt. The room that would become our high-roller room.

Four dangerous-looking men covered in ink already waited at the table set up in the middle of the old crypt, and they watched us cautiously as we entered. Or me. They watched me because I was the one who held their lives and their gangs in my grip. Part of my Timberwolf inheritance had been a whole stack of leverage, documented crimes that could see most of the men running the local crime world put away for life, should it be sent to the right people.

Better than that, I controlled all the money laundering through my territory. The one thing all these fuckers valued more than their pride was their money. When I couldn't kill the people who pissed me off—for whatever reason, usually because they were too useful—I simply taxed their respective gangs as punishment.

Given the choice, though, I'd rather just shoot them. It was easier that way; people understood death.

"Gentlemen," I greeted them in a cool tone, "thank you for coming on such short notice."

The oldest of the group grunted an annoyed sound that made my eyes narrow. "Did we have a choice?" he asked and met my glare with his beady-eyed gaze.

I held his eye contact as I made my way to the head of the table, and he looked away before I'd even sat down. Pussy.

"No, Maurice, you didn't." My voice was glacial and my glare withering. "But it doesn't hurt to use our manners every now and then, does it?"

The leader of the Riverstone Vipers was an older guy, somewhere in his mid-fifties if I were to guess, and had never been particularly pleased to be beholden to a *woman*. But, as he'd learned very quickly, if that was a problem, he could kiss my perky ass. I wouldn't stand for *any* disobedience in my zones, and sadly for him, Riverstone was within Timberwolf territory. The only reason I—and my father previously—allowed other gangs within the entire tristate area was that they served a purpose by doing the shit I had no interest in doing and paying me a tithe for the privilege.

He gave me a tight, bitter smile, but ducked his head in acknowledgment. "I suppose not, Hades."

The other gang leader who'd arrived before me—Vega of the Dogwood Death Squad—snickered a laugh, shooting Maurice a mocking smile. "A man your age should know better, Maurey. What would your old lady say if she heard you disrespecting Hades like that?"

Maurice was old-school crime, with his Vipers closer to an MC than a gang, and had some real deep-seated misogyny to overcome. So he just glared daggers at Vega across the table for implying his wife had any say in what he said or did. There was no love lost between them, but hell, none of us were friends. We just maintained a careful tolerance for one another as long as it was beneficial to all parties. Sooner or later, one of them would get greedy and start shit, but right now everyone was behaving.

Before Maurice and Vega could get into an argument, though, another inked-up gangster walked in with his backup. I sighed inwardly, recognizing Skate, the leader of the Shadow Grove Wraiths—a real piece of work. I almost missed Charon D'Ath when I had to deal with this slime bucket. But for the most part he'd been smart enough to stay off my radar, so he was still alive.

For now. At least he'd made good on the tax I'd imposed on the Wraiths after Zane double-crossed someone I liked.

Skate paused at the far end of the table, glaring at me like *I* was the one who'd killed his mentor and father figure last year. He was barking right up the wrong tree on that, even if I had given protection to the real murderer.

"Sit down, Skate. I don't have time for theatrics." My tone brooked no arguments, and I all but dismissed him from my mind as I shifted my gaze to the backup he'd brought. I didn't recognize this gangster, and that in itself set my warning bells ringing.

I made it my business to recognize anyone important enough to *possibly* attend one of my meetings, but this punk was a total stranger.

"Who's your friend, Skate?" I asked in an empty, emotionless voice. They'd get no tells from me.

The Wraiths' leader just sneered as he leaned back in his chair. "Does it matter? We're all permitted to bring an associate per your own rules, Hades."

The silence that fell over the room was so thick I was actually a bit surprised when Vega shifted awkwardly in his seat and let out a nervous laugh.

"Been sampling a bit of your own product, Skate?" he joked weakly, shooting a curious glance over at me, then back to the Wraiths' leader. "Attitude like that could see you walk outta here with one less finger."

He wasn't wrong.

Skate just glared at me, fuming, and I raised one brow. It was the only chance I would offer him before providing a physical reminder that I was in charge for a *reason*.

"My apologies, Hades," he finally growled out. "This is Joseph."

The unknown guy met my gaze unflinchingly as he gave me a nod of greeting. Instantly I knew Joseph was no normal Wraith. Fuck no. His eyes were too sharp, too calculating, and I'd already caught the way he'd assessed and cataloged every square inch of the room.

Either Joseph was a cop or he was a spy. Or both. Either way, Skate had brought a snake into my lair.

"Joseph," I repeated.

The dude just shrugged, exuding way too much confidence. "Never got around to picking a cool gang name."

Bull. Shit.

Before I could poke the snake with my verbal stick, the rest of my guests entered the room and took their seats around the table. There were only enough seats for gang leaders, their backups left to stand against the walls behind them as they always were.

"Ezekiel, you made good time," I observed, giving a small smile to the most unassuming of the men around the table. He looked, for all appearances, like a mild-mannered accountant. I knew better, though. Ezekiel ran a syndicate of muscle for hire. He had aspirations of one day rivalling the mercenary guild, but he had a long way to go yet. Still, he was smart enough to have a real shot at it. Aim for the stars and land on the moon, my mother used to say.

He was also located the farthest from Timberwolves HQ, so must have taken a helicopter to make it here in time.

"Wouldn't miss a summons from you for anything, Hades," he replied with a wide, slightly lecherous smile.

I respected Ezekiel as an asset to my territory and a formidable ally, but goddamn, he needed to stop leering at me. He'd never tried to take it any further, though, so I ignored it.

A deep, rumbling grunt came from Cass, who sat directly opposite Ezekiel. Based on the way he was glaring down the unassuming assassin, he wasn't a fan.

I ignored him too. Instead, I turned my focus to the last man who'd taken a seat at my table. While not technically a gang leader, Archer D'Ath held enough power in Shadow Grove to be granted a place in this room of criminal kingpins.

"Archer, good of you to come." I gave him a pointed look, silently conveying the question I couldn't ask. He hadn't brought anyone else with him, which was a power move in its own way. He was showing the other players that he was unafraid.

He gave me a small nod in response, and I knew he was answering my look and not my words. Yes, Seph was safe. She'd been at his house visiting Madison Kate when I'd put out the summons, and she'd be safe there until we were done.

We had plenty of history, Archer and me. After all, I never could have usurped my father's throne without his invaluable help. Out of everyone in the room, Archer and Zed were the only ones I trusted not to put a knife in my back the second it was turned. Not even Cass—no matter how badly I wanted to fuck him—had earned that trust from me.

"Let's get down to business, then," I announced. Zed shifted slightly behind me, a subtle move to reassure me that he was fully ready for anyone who wanted to test my authority. It was something that happened more often than I'd like, but was not all that surprising considering my lack of male genitalia.

Apparently, it could be triggering for the old-school gangsters to take orders from a woman. It had taken a few dead backup gangsters before they finally got the point that I wasn't to be pushed. Zed's trigger finger was just as twitchy as my own, and he was a deadly quick shot.

"Someone has been breaking my rules, and I want to know what you all know about that." I cast my eyes around the table as I said it, and the silence that followed was deafening. "Let me elaborate for you, seeing as we're all playing dumb today. Someone has been importing and, I'll guess, *selling* angel dust within my zones."

Ezekiel's brows rose, his thin-framed glasses moving on his face with the gesture. "That sounds like a supremely bad idea, if I might say so, sir. I assure you, I haven't seen or heard anything of the sort in my area. Sounds like someone wanted to diversify their portfolio." He cast his eyes over the other gang leaders, giving pointed looks at Cass, Skate, and Vega. Their gangs were the ones who ran the most recreational drugs.

Archer just kicked back in his chair, watching everyone with guarded curiosity. I knew he didn't have anything to do with it, but he would want to know what was going on, if only to keep his family safe.

Then again, considering I'd previously handed him a forty-nine percent share in the import-export company that facilitated literally all of the drug trade in Shadow Grove, maybe he had heard something I hadn't.

"You already know everything I know," Cass rumbled, his hand balled in a fist where it rested on the table. "I actually had the balls to own up when I found out about angel dust in Shadow Grove." He arched a brow across the table at Skate.

"Screw you, Cass," the rival gang leader spat back at him. "One of these days you'll kiss Hades's ass so hard your head will get stuck up there."

"You wanna pretend there's no dust floating around Wraith territory, Skate?" Cass all but sneered the Wraith's name. That was new. He was usually so stone-cold emotionless, but there was real disdain in his tone.

Skate's eyes narrowed as he glared back at Cass. "The fuck would you know about Wraith business? You got spies in my house, friend?"

Cass's lip curled. "I'm no friend of yours." But he also didn't answer the accusation… How curious.

But they could take their Shadow Grove bickering elsewhere; I didn't want this meeting lasting any longer than it needed to.

"Skate, this is your one and only chance," I told him in a flat voice. "Tell me what you know about who is responsible for this breach, or the Wraiths will be taxed for insubordination."

I couldn't *always* kill people who disobeyed. How would they ever learn if no one was alive to carry the lesson forward?

Archer, at the opposite end of the table, shot me a sly grin. He had a fair idea what I meant when I said the Wraiths would be *taxed*. It meant that the cost of imports on cocaine and MDMA—the Wraiths' primary money earners—would triple in price indefinitely, something that directly lined my pockets and Archer's. It also meant I would take a higher cut of any money they laundered through my businesses during the period of their punishments.

Where death and violence didn't always motivate obedience, threatening their bottom line usually worked.

Skate glared at me, his nostrils flaring with anger and indecision flickering in his eyes. It was a tiny movement, barely even noticeable for how quick it was, but I spotted the second his eyes flicked to the side. Like he was fighting the urge to look at Joseph for permission.

Mother*fucker*. I knew it.

My instincts had carried me this far in life. They'd kept me alive when the whole world had been against me. I trusted them, but if they ever steered me wrong… Well, too fucking bad.

So, acting purely on my gut feeling, I surged out of my chair. Skate started babbling some panicked bullshit, but I wasn't listening to his lies any more. He was no longer in charge of his gang; I'd stake my whole fortune on that.

My jaw tight and my resolve hard, I pulled my gun and fired a single shot. The bullet hit square between Skate's eyebrows, blowing out the back of his head in a splatter of blood and gore. His lifeless body toppled onto the floor as his chair tipped backward. My Desert Eagle packed a hell of a punch, especially in such close confines.

Immediately, Joseph made a break for it—predictable as shit. Zed was quicker, though, firing a shot through the back of the fake Wraith's knee.

Joseph fell to the floor, screaming in pain, and the sound echoed through the crypt in the most fitting way.

Zed paid the man's protests no mind as he grabbed him by the back of the neck and dragged him back to the table. He nudged Skate's body aside, and Vega's man, Diego, helped by righting the fallen chair again. A chair into which Joseph the snake was dropped unceremoniously and held in place by Zed's heavy hand on his neck.

"Well. It looks like I have a lead after all," I murmured, eyeing Joseph critically. He wasn't the one calling the shots, but I'd bet he knew who was. "Does anyone else have anything to tell me before I get on with this?"

I arched a brow at Vega and Maurice. Cass had already come forward about the angel dust found on his guys, and Archer was removed from suspicion in this.

"Now or never, gentlemen. I'm a busy woman."

Surprisingly, it was Maurice who cracked. "I might have heard something," he admitted with a heavy swallow. "One of my guys was picked up a couple of weeks back by the local PD. They claimed he was carrying dust, but there's no way. Not my crew." He shook his head firmly, perspiration beading on his brow.

I stared at him a long moment, weighing the sincerity of his words. My father had thought it was a cute trick to teach me poker as a seven-year-old, so I'd been reading body language a long time. Some people were harder to read than others, of course, like Cass, who was a closed and locked book. Maurice, though, was a pretty open one.

He also wasn't lying to me. Or he was telling me what he believed to be the truth.

"You think the cops planted it on him?" I asked. That would create a common denominator in all the instances of PCP I knew of. But why the fuck would law enforcement be doing the dirty work for a criminal with a vendetta? It didn't add up.

Maurice spread his hands wide. "There's no other explanation."
Yet.

I gave a small nod. "Next time you keep information from me, Maurice, you'll be joining Skate in my shark tank. Do you have anything else I need to know?" He shook his head quickly, his naturally bronzed skin ashen. "I expect you to send me the arrest details and to immediately contact me if it happens again. Is that clear? You're dismissed."

The leader of the Riverstone Vipers quickly scurried out of the crypt, his plus-one tight on his ass like hellhounds were snapping at their heels.

"Vega?" I tilted my head to the Death Squad president. He had been in his position for a long time, wisely making good choices after my father's fall from grace and surviving to tell the tale. He was no idiot.

"Nothing to tell, Hades. I can assure you, if that shit turns up in my turf, you'll be the first to know about it."

"I'll second that sentiment," Ezekiel offered, adjusting his glasses. "But if trouble does come knocking, my services are, as always, at your disposal, sir."

I inwardly snorted a laugh. Yeah, at a price.

Also, the fact that Zed's use of *sir* had caught on with other people was annoying the shit out of me. But it was better than *ma'am*, so I let it happen.

"Very well. You can both go. But keep your ears to the ground and your eyes open. Someone isn't finished making their point." I turned my attention back to Joseph, who was sweating and pale but watching me with an intensity that said he still thought he'd make it out alive to report back to his boss. Poor fool. He'd been a dead man the second I'd made him as a fake Wraith.

Vega, Ezekiel, and their men murmured pleasantries and left the crypt without even glancing at Skate's body. It was nothing new for our way of life.

"Thank you, gentlemen," I told Cass and Archer. "I trust you'll both keep me informed if you hear anything of interest."

Neither of them made any move to leave, despite the clear dismissal in my tone. Instead, Archer leaned forward and rubbed a thoughtful hand over his stubbled chin.

"You think this has something to do with the Lockharts." It was a statement, not a question. He knew full fucking well that's what I was thinking. What I *feared* was true.

Cass drummed his fingertips on the table. "The death of your boy last night was a definite message," he commented, his rough, gravelly voice too damn welcome in my ears. I'd truly thought my afternoon with Lucas had kicked my Cass addiction, but clearly, I was wrong.

"I'm aware," I snapped, a thread of anger evident in my tone. It was frustration at myself more than anything, though. "Zed filled me in."

"I could have run you through it myself," Cass pushed, not dropping the matter like he badly needed to. "My calls weren't going through though." His dark gaze caught mine, and I had to fight to keep my calm, emotionless, supreme resting bitch face in place. Fucking hell, when had my crush on him gotten so out of hand?

I wasn't playing games though, not when I had a slippery spy to torture and kill. "Thank you, gentlemen," I repeated. "You can go."

Archer knew when to back down and pushed away from the table. "I'll dig around a bit," he told me, despite me not asking for his assistance on the Lockhart matter. "Maybe someone survived."

I shook my head. "They didn't."

He gave a one-shouldered shrug. "All the same." He gave a nod to Zed, who returned it. The history between us all had Archer sitting awfully close to *friend* status for both Zed and me.

Cass was slower to rise from his seat, and I breathed a small sigh of annoyance.

"Actually," I said before he got to the door, pausing him in his tracks, "I've had enough of the Wraiths. I don't think another change of leadership is going to do them any favors here."

Cass arched a dark, scarred brow at me. "What would you like done, Hades?"

"Absorb them into the Reapers or kill them. Your choice. But as far as I'm concerned, Shadow Grove belongs to the Reapers now." I gave a small smirk. "With the exception of my venues, of course."

Cass dipped his head in acknowledgment. "Of course. I'll get it done." His gaze remained on me for a beat longer than necessary, and then he left silently.

As the footsteps of all our guests faded away from hearing, I drew a deep breath and turned my attention back to Joseph.

"Hello, Joseph," I said with a saccharine smile. "I think it's time we got to know each other better."

CHAPTER 9

Several hours later Zed and I emerged from the crypt covered in blood and no better off for our efforts. Joseph had proved a harder nut to crack than I'd encountered in a *long* time and ended up taking his boss's identity to the grave with him.

The only useful thing we'd learned from him was that the Wraiths had been flipped over a month ago.

I grimaced as I peeled my blood-soaked gloves off on our way through the main bar's construction zone. They were leather fingerless gloves with metal woven into the knuckles, a Christmas present from Madison Kate last year, designed for maximum impact with minimal damage to my hands. They were easily my second favorite accessory, after my Desert Eagle.

"You feeling better, Boss?" Zed asked, leaning against the rough stone wall beside the main entrance. We needed to wait on our cleanup crew to arrive before we could leave. It wasn't the smartest thing to do, leaving bloody corpses unattended on my own property—especially not with the current state of cleanliness in the local law enforcement.

I frowned at Zed, tucking my gloves into the pocket of my jacket. "What's that supposed to mean?"

He gave a too-casual shrug. "Sure seemed like you had a lot of pent-up anger to work out there. I can't remember the last time you beat the crap out of someone that thoroughly without a weapon." He paused, scrutinizing me. "Wouldn't have anything to do with why you turned your phone off today and shacked up with a barely legal stripper boy, would it?"

"He's twenty-one, Zed, and what did I tell you about throwing stones inside your glass house? Pretty sure that perky blond you picked up in August was barely even out of high school." I gave him a judgmental grin, but I had worked off enough of my built-up tension that he wasn't irritating me. Not while there was no one around to hear us talk like this. Like friends.

Zed just rolled his eyes but gave a smug grin. He was a fucking manwhore and had zero qualms about who knew it. Hell, I was at least ninety percent sure he had an exhibitionism kink. He was also gorgeous, so it was no freaking wonder he picked up women so easily.

"So…did you fuck Cass out of your system, then?"

Ugh. Of course he knew exactly what I was doing. Goddamn fucker knew me way too well.

I breathed out a long sigh, giving a mournful shake of my head. "I thought I had."

Instead of making a smart remark like I expected, Zed just watched me from the corner of his eye for a long moment, then huffed a sound.

"Fucking shoot him, then. You don't need that shit taking up space in your brain, Boss. Plenty of other guys out there are more than willing to throw you around a room if that's really what you want."

I snickered a laugh. "Trust you to remember the shit I say while I'm drunk."

Zed just arched a brow at me, then pulled a rolled blunt from his pocket. He lit it up, took a drag, then handed it over to me.

He watched me with a weird look on his face as I placed the spliff between my lips and inhaled deeply. As usual, it was way more weed than tobacco, but that was how we both liked it. We never smoked enough to get properly high, but a light buzz every now and then, particularly after torturing and killing a motherfucker, was nice.

"You're acting weird tonight, Zed," I told him when I passed the cigarette back. His fingers brushed mine as he took it, and he frowned abruptly. "What gives?"

"Nothing," he replied, a clear lie. I squinted at him with accusation, and he grinned as he placed the cig back between his lips. "Nothing for you to worry about, Boss," he amended.

"If you say so," I murmured, noticing a familiar white van on its way down the street. "Robynne's here."

We made no move to leave, though, staying where we were to finish the shared spliff while our cleanup crew pulled into the loading zone and started unloading their equipment from the van.

The ancient woman who owned Rodent-Rid Pest Control hopped out of the driver's seat and followed her staff up the main steps as she pulled on a pair of industrial-thickness gloves. She was already neck to toe in a blue coverall, and I knew from experience that she'd pull the hood up and don a full face mask before entering the crime scene.

"Hades, Zed," she greeted my second and me. Her wrinkled lips pulled in a wide grin as she ran her gaze over me. "You look good, Boss. Red is your color." She cackled at her own joke, then passed us to get on with business.

"She scares me," Zed murmured as we made our way down the steps of the old church, heading for his car. "But you probably should clean up before you get in my Ferrari."

He popped the passenger door open, then pulled a packet of baby wipes from the glove box and tossed them to me with a smirk.

"Seriously?" I deadpanned.

"Seriously. I don't want to have my car stinking of blood, thank you. Just hurry up. I had a date with Emily tonight, and I'm already about nine hours late." The lazy smile on his face said that he was feeling the small amount of weed already.

I rolled my eyes and used the pathetic little wet wipes to remove the worst of the blood from my face and neck, then slid into the passenger seat of Zed's car.

"There's no way that girl is still waiting for you," I told him with a mocking headshake. "By the time we make it back to Shadow Grove, it'll be almost dawn."

Zed just gave an easy shrug and wide smile. "Perfect. I'll creep into her bed, wake her up with my face between her thighs, blow my load all over her perfect tits, and then leave before she goes to class."

"You're a class act, Zayden De Rosa," I muttered in a dry tone, relaxing back into my seat with a yawn. That easy, comfortable sort of chat between us was few and far between these days. Most of the time, I was so caught up in my Hades persona that I couldn't even let myself relax around my oldest friend. Most of the time, he treated me like a grenade with a loose pin.

But not now. I could almost picture us as we used to be. Before the massacre. Before I made the choice to become a mass murderer. Before *Hades*.

We drove most of the way home in comfortable silence, and Zed didn't even speed much. For a guy so eager to get his dick wet, he was really in no hurry. It wasn't until we were almost back to my apartment building that our idle chat turned back to business.

"Dissolving the Wraiths won't be an easy task for the Reapers, you know." Zed's comment was an echo of what'd run through my mind right before I'd made the decision.

I let out a long, tired sigh and nodded. "I know. But Cass has the experience necessary and the loyalty of his Reapers. He can handle it. And there were far too many cooks in my kitchen as it was."

95

"No disagreements here," Zed agreed. "I'll just keep a close eye on things to make sure it doesn't raise any unnecessary scrutiny from SGPD. Want me to offer any assistance if the Reapers need it?"

I snorted a laugh. "Fuck no. If Cass needs our help, then maybe we should dissolve the Reapers too."

Zed gave me a sidelong look. "So you're not killing him, then?"

"Cass?" I arched a brow at Zed. Then shook my head. "Not today. But fuck, he's on thin ice."

Zed slowed his Ferrari and glided to a stop directly in front of my building. It was an old one with no concierge to monitor people coming and going, but I loved it. I had enough security on my actual apartment; I didn't need anyone stopping people in the lobby.

"Speak of the ice-skating elephant himself..." Zed muttered, nodding across the road.

Sure enough, there was the Reapers' leader himself, seeming like he was just waiting for me as he leaned against his sexy fucking motorcycle.

"Fucker has a death wish," I commented, unbuckling my seat belt and climbing out of the low car. Zed started to follow, his gun already in hand, but I waved him off. "I can handle this alone."

My second snorted a laugh. "No doubts about that. I'll go make sure Seph is home safe."

He waited until I jerked a nod of approval, then disappeared into my apartment building while Cass crossed the street toward me.

"What's happened?" I asked as he got closer. I didn't miss the way his eyes ran over my exposed skin, taking in my crappy cleanup of Joseph's blood. Weird.

His dark brows knitted as he took a step closer than necessary, making me crane my neck to look up at him. Bastard was six foot five, so even in my high heels he towered over me.

"Nothing happened." His growly voice was in full effect, and I stiffened my shoulders to stop the thrill it sent through me. Goddamn moronic hormones were taking control of my life.

I folded my arms under my breasts, cringing inwardly as I felt the tightness of dried blood in my cleavage. "So, why are you here?"

His frown deepened, if that was even possible. "Can I come up so we can talk?"

I shook my head, firm. "Hell no. We're allies, Cass, not friends."

He scoffed a humorless laugh. "Bullshit. I'm as close to a friend as you've got outside of Zed and Archer's boys." He swiped a hand over his half-shaved head, and I couldn't help following the movement.

So damn sexy.

"You're a business associate at best," I snapped back, letting my anger get the better of me for a rare moment.

Fucking Cass must have been drinking from the idiot fountain, though, because he took another step closer. I was still standing beside Zed's car, and if I'd been inclined to back up, I would have ended up with my back against the Ferrari's door. I didn't back up for anyone, though, not even a sexy-as-sin mountain of a gangster.

"You make a habit of kissing all your business associates, Hades?" he asked in a low rumble, his neck bent so that his lips were right beside my ear. All I could see was the broad expanse of his black T-shirt, and the rich scent of his leather jacket filled my nose. I couldn't even be mad, because he smelled delicious.

Still, he was pushing his damn luck. "Maybe I do," I retorted, placing a hand against his chest and applying a little pressure to remind him that he was walking a tightrope with my temper. I'd already dissolved one gang tonight; I could easily make it two.

He didn't take the hint, though. Far from it. If anything, my hand on his chest was taken as an invitation, and his rough fingers grasped my hips as he pushed me into Zed's car.

"I don't believe you," he whispered, all husky and…

But his rejection from Saturday night was still fresh in my mind, barbing me with embarrassment every time I thought about it. No way was I giving him *more* power than I'd already provided.

"Believe what you want, Cassiel," I told him in a sultry sort of purr, "but if you don't take your hands off me, you'll find out real fast what I do to people that don't respect my personal boundaries."

He didn't immediately step away, not like he would have a week ago, *prior* to me making a move on him. Instead, his thumb teased the bare skin between my lace top and leather pants, and his breath warmed my neck as he sighed. Then, slowly, he released my hips and stepped back.

I almost wished he'd refused.

But that wasn't Cass's style. He was easily the most respectful-around-women gangster I'd ever met. It was half the reason I trusted him to keep Seph safe when Zed and I weren't around.

Still, my shriveled and pitch-black soul craved a bit of defiance from this man. I wanted the unpredictability and challenge that I *knew* he could provide.

With a small sigh, I shoved him a bit harder and brushed past to head toward my apartment entrance.

"No one likes a tease, Cass. It's just rude, especially after the night I've had." I tossed the words over my shoulder, not expecting a response at all, given how economical he tended to be with his voice.

So it made me pause when I heard his gruff reply. "Who says I was teasing, Hades? Maybe I just regret my choice the other night."

Get fucked. He did not just say that.

Then I remembered how he'd seen the security footage of me fucking Lucas in the supply room and how this was *probably* just male ego at play. He didn't regret turning me down; he was just… I didn't even know. Jealous? Annoyed that I could so easily replace him?

"Why are you here, Cass?" I asked again, ignoring that comment and spinning around to level a steady glare at the big inked-up fuck.

He didn't flinch away from my stare. Instead he held it, unblinking and confident. "I figured you might want eyes on Seph if you were going to be gone for a while." He nodded to the remnants of blood all over me. Yeah, torturing Joseph had taken longer than anticipated, so I was quietly glad he'd taken the initiative.

"Thanks," I said, my voice clipped. I wasn't in the habit of offering thanks, because it could so often be misinterpreted as a weakening in power. My mother would turn over in her grave at how infrequently I used my manners these days.

But Cass often looked out for Seph, making sure she got places safely and keeping an eye on her when she thought she was alone. It certainly wasn't his job to do so, but I *did* appreciate it. Maybe he just felt protective toward her, seeing as she'd taken a liking to the big grump when he'd first met her. Seph had been an annoying seven-year-old, and Cass hadn't stood a chance when she asked him to hold her doll during a meeting with the Timberwolves.

"If this is about the Lockharts, they'll target her," he told me, totally unnecessarily. I was well aware of this, and it was the reason the cold acid of fear had been sitting in my belly since he'd told me about the angel dust. I didn't give a fuck if someone took revenge on me for the Lockhart family deaths...but if they touched Seph, so help me I would burn the whole world down.

I drew a deep breath to calm my exterior, knowing there was no hope for the turmoil in my mind. "I know," I told him, my jaw tight and my spine stiff. "It'll be their own funeral."

Cass gave a small incline of his head, not breaking eye contact for even a second. "I expect nothing less."

Not sticking around for more confusing conversation that set my skin on fire and my pulse racing, I spun back around and headed inside my building without a backward glance at him. He was acting fucking strange, and I didn't have the emotional capacity to dissect his actions. Not now. Not while Seph could be in danger *again*.

CHAPTER 10

The sun was already on its way up by the time Zed left my apartment, and it felt like I'd barely been asleep for five minutes when Seph ripped my blanket off.

"What the *fuck*?" I groaned, fumbling around to try to find my stolen blanket without opening my eyes. "Seph, I swear to fuck if my blanket doesn't reappear in three seconds, I'll—"

"You'll what?" My little sister flopped down beside me, pushing my face until she could share my pillow. "Gonna go all big bad Hades on me, Dare? Ooh, I'm shivering in my boots."

The sarcasm in her voice was enough to make me crack an eyelid and glare at her. "Test me, brat. Fucking test me. You'll make Rapunzel look like a goddamn party girl by comparison."

She just poked me in the nose and smirked. "Fuck off, you love me too hard to lock me up and throw away the key."

Her sass levels had gone off the damn charts since she'd made friends with Madison Kate. If I didn't like that girl so much, I'd have labeled her a bad influence.

"Right now I'm thinking that nice Catholic boarding school in Alaska is looking like a really good option," I mumbled, cracking my second eye open to glare at her properly. "Why are you in my bed? What fucking time is it? Shouldn't you be at school?"

Seph rolled her eyes. Damn kid was too pretty for her own good. The number of teenage boys that have needed to be warned off her since we moved to Shadow Grove was insane. I had a feeling she was crushing on someone new too.

"It's eight," she told me, blinking those long, dark lashes of hers. Yep, she was wearing a touch more makeup than usual. "And I'm in your bed because *someone* forgot to drop off my car to be fixed yesterday."

She gave me a pointed look, and I groaned.

"This is your own fault, Dare. I could have taken it to the mechanic myself, but *no*. You insisted you'd take it, and now you have to drive me to school. Come on, get up. I don't want to be late."

There was no way in hell I was letting her anywhere near my mechanic, so yeah, I'd stick by my word on that one.

"Since when did you give a fuck about being late for school?" I grumbled. A long yawn pulled my jaw as I rubbed my eyes and shoved Seph off my bed. She landed on the floor with a yelp—she'd been *right* on the edge—then scowled up at me when I climbed over her.

"Since when did you complain that I was taking my education seriously?" she shot back, picking herself up and smoothing down the skirt of her Shadow Prep uniform. I gave her a suspicious look, trying to decide if her skirt had mysteriously gotten shorter since last week. Had she grown? Or just rolled the waistband?

"Besides," she hurried on before I could ask prying questions, "where were *you* all night? And how come Zed was leaving our place at dawn again if you're not fucking?"

Sneaky minx. Nothing quite like going on the offensive when you're feeling defensive.

"Because Zed is my second and we had shit to do all night," I told her with an eye roll, grimacing at my reflection in the mirror. I'd showered before falling into bed—no way did I want blood flakes all over my sheets—but my hair was still damp and looking a bit like a flame-red lion mane.

Fuck it. I was only driving her to school, then coming straight back to bed. I tugged my threadbare men's T-shirt off and wiggled my tits into a sports bra before throwing an oversized *Vampire Diaries* sweatshirt over the top. It'd been a joke gift from Seph a few years ago because it read *Mystic Falls Timberwolves*. But it was also super cozy, so I wore it way more than I should have.

"Come on, brat," I told her, stuffing my legs into a pair of ripped jeans. "You can tell me all about this boy you like on the way."

Seph's cheeks flooded with redness, and she gaped at me. "What? I don't... What makes you think... *Ugh,* shut up!"

I snickered a laugh as she stormed out of my room, leaving me to hunt for a pair of sneakers and tie my wild hair into a high ponytail. With no heels, no leather, and not a scrap of makeup on, I was virtually unrecognizable. I looked like Seph. Until you looked into my eyes, that was, and saw how truly dead inside I had become.

Yawning again, I made my way through the apartment while tucking a small pistol into my jeans and grabbing my Desert Eagle off the counter where I left it far too often. It was my security blanket to carry with me everywhere, even if it didn't exactly work with my outfit.

"Double armed for a school drop-off," Seph commented as we locked our apartment and headed for the elevators. "Something happen that I need to know about?"

I glanced at her sideways, then sighed heavily. "Maybe."

When I said nothing more, she stayed silent all the way down to our underground parking garage. Only when we reached my "family car," a soft blue Range Rover, did she reach out and give me a one-armed hug.

"I trust you, Dare. You'll keep me safe, like always. Just give me a heads-up if I should start carrying a weapon to school or something, okay?" She gave me a bright smile, and I forced myself to echo it, even if I was all messed up inside.

I rolled my eyes, shrugging off what could have been a heartfelt moment between my sister and me. "You should always carry a knife at least, Seph. You know that."

She let out a laugh as I peeled myself away from her hug and climbed into the driver's side of my car. It was the one I used when I was taking her places or showing up for meetings at her school and shit. The Timberwolves were still, for the most part, just rumor and legend. There was simply no need for me to show up in full Hades attire and scare the poor parents of Shadow Prep.

Seph hopped into the passenger seat, then unzipped her bag and pulled out the silver-black butterfly knife I'd given her on her fourteenth birthday. It used to be mine, but she needed covert weaponry more than I did, and it made me feel better knowing she could defend herself.

"Good girl," I muttered, turning on the engine and buckling my seat belt. "Now, about this boy..."

"Dare, shut up," she groaned, tucking her knife away and buckling her own belt. "There's no boy, so you don't need to go sending Alexi to pick me up again."

I snickered, remembering the last time a boy had asked my sister out. I'd had one of my upper management—a semi-pro MMA fighter—pick Seph up from school on his motorcycle. She'd been furious, but it'd served the purpose I needed.

"Sure there's not," I teased as we exited the parking lot. "You just get dressed up for the teachers' benefit, huh?" Then my eyes narrowed. "He's not a teacher, is he?"

Not that I had a problem with age gaps; I still wanted to fuck Cass, who was eleven years older than me. But I *did* have a problem with a man in a position of authority taking advantage of an eighteen-year-old girl.

"What? No! Ew, Dare, don't be gross. If I wanted to hit on an old dude, I'd be more likely to take Zed up on his offer." She shot me a smirk, and I slammed my foot down on the brakes.

I almost caused an accident. As it was, the car behind me leaned on their horn, and I just flipped them off in the rearview mirror.

"Fucking *excuse me*?" I demanded, staring at my sister in alarm.

"I'm joking," she replied with a wide grin. "Jesus, you *are* touchy about him. Pretty sure you guys are fucking."

Seething, I started driving again. "That's not fucking funny, Seph. I don't have the time or patience to find a new second-in-command right now." Not to mention it'd sting a bit to have to shoot my oldest friend for hitting on my kid sister.

"Oh my god, drama," she muttered. "As if Zed has *ever* treated me as anything other than a little sister. I'm just saying, that girl he was with two months ago? Candace? She's only six months older than me. She graduated from Shadow Prep last year."

I snorted a laugh, wondering if Zed knew that or not. Probably not. If he didn't plan on seeing them more than once, he barely even got their names, let alone their life stories.

"Nice deflection, brat," I told her with a grin. "I still wanna know who the boy is. I thought I'd scared off all the punks in your school already."

She glowered. "Yeah, thanks for that, by the way. I'm going to be the oldest virgin in the entire country at the rate you intimidate guys."

I just shrugged, not even feeling the slightest bit guilty. "You'll thank me one day, Seph. Guys should treat you like the queen you are, not get you drunk and fuck you in the back of their dad's Porsche after some rich douchebag's party."

"You'd know all about that," she muttered, sounding bitter as she looked out her window in a sulk.

My temper flared, but it wasn't her fault. She had no idea that someone was sending me reminders of my first love—the boy I'd lost my virginity to in the back of his dad's Porsche, only to find out later I'd been drugged. The same boy who, years later, I'd shot in the head.

Neither of us spoke for a while, and the tension grew thick and uncomfortable inside the car. Eventually, Seph sighed.

"I'm sorry," she whispered.

I nodded my acceptance but didn't trust myself not to be a horrific bitch if I spoke, so I kept my mouth shut. She had no idea what I'd dealt with over the weekend, and I wasn't about to clue her in. I wanted her to have a normal life...as normal as she possibly could, even with me as her sister.

"He's kinda new," Seph told me after another long pause, "and so freaking hot that he has the *whole* cheer squad falling all over him."

I wrinkled my nose. "So? You're hotter than those plastic bitches."

She just glared at me like I was making a *mom* statement. As if it wasn't true. The only reason Seph wasn't a cheerleader herself was because she couldn't dance for shit. I'd never seen a kid so out of tune with the music in my life.

"Doesn't matter, anyway," she said. "He's in my art class and has never even said two words to me. Pretty sure I don't exist on his radar."

"Then he's blind as well as stupid. Forget him, Seph. Plenty of better fish in the sea...after you graduate." I gave her a wide, slightly teasing smile, and she groaned.

"Yeah, as if you'll let me date even after graduation. I bet you'll still be chasing guys away when I'm thirty." She glared at me. But we'd just arrived in front of her school, so the argument was over already.

I just shrugged. "Probably. Only because I love you, *Stephanie!*" I sang her birth name loudly right as she started climbing out of my car, and the look she gave me could boil a lesser woman's blood.

My sister was the cutest. I was still laughing to myself as I pulled away and left her to all the high school drama of liking a boy who didn't know she existed. Although that, I'd bet, was far from the truth.

CHAPTER 11

Leaving Shadow Prep grounds, I made a snap decision to drive through Reaper territory on my way home. There was a kick-ass coffee and cake shop there, and I was curious to see the crime scene where Sonny-boy had been killed. Maybe there would be some clues that the stupid cops hadn't totally destroyed in their quest to become better police. Gag.

Their whole no-longer-taking-bribes policy was total crap and not something I believed for even a second. This recent spate of angel dust only proved it. They were still taking bribes, just not from me or any of the gangs under my rule.

Someone was paying better and blackmailing harder.

I parked in a covered lot a block away from the crime scene, not wanting to immediately announce my presence to anyone on the lookout, then walked to Nadia's Cakes.

The old woman who owned the store was the definition of hospitality, getting me coffee in a takeout cup and offering me a slice of apple pie while I waited. There was a cautious look in her eyes, though, so it was safe to bet she wasn't fooled by *casual Hades*.

Not wanting to be stared at while I ate, I politely declined the pie and took my coffee back outside with me. It should only be a short walk over to the house Sonny-boy had been killed in, if I was thinking of the right area.

I made some calls while I walked over, setting up a death benefit for Sonny's wife and unborn baby. There wasn't anything I could do to bring him back from the dead, but I could at least provide a college fund for his kid.

It wasn't hard to figure out which house was the crime scene. It was all sealed up with SGPD tape in some lame attempt at stopping people from accessing the area. Either the idiots who closed the scene were new to this town or they were just ticking boxes, but a bit of tape wasn't keeping anyone out.

Certainly not me, anyway.

I simply ducked under the tape and went on inside like I had every right to be there. And I did. The Shadow Grove Reapers were firmly under my rule, so I didn't need permission to go anywhere in "their" territory, including this abandoned house riddled with bullet holes and stained with Timberwolf blood.

The chances of there being any clues remaining after god only knew how many cops had tramped through the house were low. But I wasn't in a hurry to get anywhere, so I took my time looking around, sipping my coffee as I went.

"Find anything?" A low, rumbling question came from the front entrance about fifteen minutes after I'd arrived.

I shook my head, nudging an old, torn armchair with my toe. "Nope. Nothing. Except that my man was shot up by a firing squad in the middle of *your* territory and no one heard anything." I arched a brow at Cass. "Why is that?"

He shook his head, not rising to the bait. "Your guess is as good as mine, Hades. None of the local residents seem to have been paid off, either."

I narrowed my eyes at him, weighing whether he was bullshitting me or not, then nodded. "Silencers, maybe. Might have suppressed the sound enough that neighbors at a distance didn't notice it. The houses directly next door are vacant too, aren't they?"

Cass grunted a sound of confirmation. "They were bought up by Samuel Danvers during his rejuvenation project the other year. The ones opposite too."

I finished the last of my coffee, then shook my head in annoyance. I needed to access the written reports to get a better idea of what had gone down, but even then I couldn't trust the information—not if they wanted to claim my man was carrying angel dust. Even if we did sell PCP, Sonny-boy was a strip-club security guard, not a drug dealer.

"You look different," Cass observed, taking a couple of steps into the dim room.

I scoffed a sharp laugh. "Seriously? Fucking hell, Cass. *Now* you're taking a second look? Maybe I should have fucked a stripper under your nose years ago."

"That's what you think?" He sounded genuinely confused as he closed a little more distance between us with those long strides of his. "I've taken a hell of a lot more than a *second* glance over the years, Red," he told me in a low voice that went straight to my pussy like a lightning bolt.

Red? Where the fuck had that come from?

"But in case you haven't noticed," Cass continued, getting all up in my personal space again, just like he'd done in the early hours of the morning while I was covered in blood, "I'm too fucking old for you, and we're *rivals*."

In stark contrast to his words, his tattoo-covered fingers came up to my face and stroked a loose tendril of my very *red* hair away. His touch was almost reverent, like he was scared I might break or explode, but it made me shiver nonetheless.

"Don't flatter yourself, Cass," I told him, tilting my head back to meet his eyes. This time, when my palm flattened on his chest, it wasn't to push him away from me. "We're not rivals. I could flatten your entire operation with a snap of my fingers." His lips twitched with the hint of a smile, and my fingers twisted in the front of his T-shirt.

But he'd rejected me before; I wasn't running that risk again. Sorry, but this bitch learned from her mistakes.

I released his shirt and moved to step out from under his looming presence, but Cass had other ideas. He caught my wrist and jerked me back to him before I'd made it more than one step.

My instinct was to lash out. In the blink of an eye, my free hand pulled the gun from my lower back and pressed it to his ribs. But Cass just ignored it. He kept my wrist captive in his grip as his other hand wrapped around my ponytail, tugging it back and tilting my face up.

"Cassiel," I growled, anger and outrage thundering through my veins…along with some other emotions.

His dark eyes met mine with a glimmer of challenge, and the corners of his lips kicked up. "You gonna shoot me, Red? Do it."

Fuck. *Fuck.*

He tugged harder on my hair, lowering his head until his lips hovered a breath away from mine, and my index finger stroked the trigger of my gun.

"Shoot me if you want," he rumbled, "but I'm going to kiss you anyway."

"I thought you didn't fuck children," I snapped back, my voice all bitter anger.

He huffed a sound awfully close to a laugh, his breath warming my lips. "I don't."

He didn't elaborate on that. He didn't need to. His lips met mine in a bruising kiss that temporarily short-circuited my brain. Then I let out a small moan and kissed him back.

My gun was still against his side, my finger still on the trigger, but that seemed so very appropriate as we kissed like we were at war.

After a few moments, though, he released my wrist and shifted his hand to my waist. His fingers slipped beneath my loose sweat-shirt, meeting bare skin and sending shudders rippling through me. I needed to put my damn gun down before I accidentally shot one of us.

It seemed the universe was against us hooking up, because a second after tucking my gun away, the heavy sound of footsteps came up the front steps to the porch and an unfamiliar voice called out, "Hey!"

"Motherfucker," Cass growled, echoing my own feelings.

"Hey, who the hell are you?" the stranger shouted. "You can't be in here! This is a closed crime scene!"

"Fuck's sake," I huffed, pushing away from Cass's smoking-hot body to glare in the direction of the voice. It was an SGPD cop, and a nervous-looking one at that, probably fresh out of training and tasked with keeping an eye on the crime scene. He'd been doing a shitty job of it too, considering how long I'd already been poking around.

"Y-you're going to have to come with me," the rookie told us in an uncertain voice.

Cass just arched a brow at me, silently asking if I wanted to handle it. I appreciated the sentiment but shrugged and waved my hand as if to say *All yours, Grumpy Cat.*

He gave a short nod, then crossed the room to the baby cop in just a handful of long strides. The poor kid didn't stand a chance, barely managing to babble out a weak protest before Cass's fist met the side of his head and knocked him out cold.

The heavy thump of the cop's unconscious body hitting the floor seemed to echo, followed by the crackle of his radio.

"You okay in there, Simmons? Need backup?"

I rolled my eyes. "Great. He has a buddy."

Cass just shrugged. "I'm about fucking done with these bas-tards. They're reporting back to someone, and it's sure as fuck not the SGPD commissioner."

I was inclined to agree, but I was also curious what he hoped to achieve by assaulting an officer who wasn't under our control. I probably would have just told the poor kid who he was trying to arrest and let the fear of our names—*my* name—do its work.

"We'd better go." I sighed. "Dealing with law enforcement is pretty fucking low on my to-do list today."

Cass grunted a sound of agreement. "Or any day. Come on." He jerked his head to the back of the house. "I parked my bike around back. Your car is too far away."

"Stalker," I muttered, but followed him anyway. He pushed through a back door and strode down a short path to an alleyway behind. He swung a leg over his gorgeous motorcycle, then jerked his head for me to get on.

With absolutely no hesitation I climbed on, sliding in close until my throbbing core was firm against his ass and my legs bracketed his. I certainly wasn't the kind of girl to be any biker's bitch, but I could definitely see the appeal.

"Hold on," Cass told me as I wrapped my arms around his rock-hard abdomen. A cop car had just rolled past the end of the alleyway, and a second later, its lights flashed on. "Let's give this fucker a tour of Shadow Grove."

I could have sworn he laughed then—an actual laugh. But it was right as he revved the engine of his bike, so maybe I was imagining things. Either way, my grin was wide as we tore out of the alley, straight past the cop car with my ponytail streaming.

A high-speed chase was a much better use of my Monday than sleeping anyway.

CHAPTER 12

It was almost disappointing how easily we ditched the cop on our tail, but Cass didn't seem to be in any great hurry to deliver me back to my car. Instead, he took the mountain road behind Shadow Grove, racing around the tight corners with expert handling and speed.

He was getting no complaints from me, either, as his muscles bunched and flexed under me with each shift of the bike. I was definitely seeing the appeal of being a passenger rather than driver. Fuck me.

"What are we doing up here, Cass?" I asked when he slowed to a stop at Eagle's Rest lookout. He flipped his kickstand out, and I climbed off to shake out my limbs.

He swung his leg over the bike as well, then wrapped his hands around my waist. "This," he said, then instead of lowering his face down to mine—flat sneakers had me a full foot shorter than him— he picked me up off the ground to kiss me.

A flash of shock rippled through me, then I wrapped my legs around his waist to keep from being dropped as I kissed him back. He tasted of scotch and mint with a faint hint of tobacco and used his lips like a weapon—exactly what I'd been imagining since meeting him years ago.

But my phone started buzzing incessantly in my pocket, and I groaned with frustration.

"I need to check that," I told him, my hands on either side of his face and my face just an inch from his.

His eyes narrowed. "Do you, though?" Punctuating his point, his hands tightened where they'd slipped to my ass and his lips found mine again.

For a moment, I let him sway me, kissing him back as my phone stopped buzzing. But then it started again, and I unlinked my legs from around Cass, pushing away.

Pulling my phone from my pocket, I took a couple of strides away from temptation, then answered the call.

"Zed," I said in greeting.

"Boss," he replied without any hint of teasing in his voice. "I'm at the city morgue. There's something here you need to see."

I didn't ask questions. If Zed said I needed to see something with my own eyes, then he meant it. Dread curdled through my gut and I breathed a short sigh.

"I'll be there in half an hour. Do you have a copy of the reports yet?"

"Working on it," he said, sounding annoyed. "See you soon."

He ended the call, and I turned back to Cass. The sexy, inked-up bastard just stared at me with his arms folded over his impressive chest.

"Duty calls?" he guessed, his dark gaze running over my face and pausing on my mouth like he was still thinking about kissing me again.

I jerked a nod, shoving my arousal aside. Business first, *always*.

Cass didn't ask anything more, just got back onto his bike and waited for me to climb on behind him before revving the engine.

We didn't speak again for the whole drive back into Shadow Grove, and Cass took me directly to my car in the covered lot near Nadia's Cakes. Instead of just dropping me off and leaving, though, he parked beside my Range Rover and waited as I popped the trunk open and hunted out a change of clothes. It was one thing for Cass—who I wanted to get naked—to see me dressed so casually. But if I was showing up at the city morgue in official capacity, then I needed to look the part.

Luckily, I kept a bag of spare clothes specifically for times like this.

His eyes remained glued on me as I swapped my hoodie for a leather jacket—thankfully, my sports bra was black, so it worked as a "top" underneath—and my sneakers for a pair of black patent leather Louboutins. Then I slid into my driver's seat, leaving the door open as I flipped my mirror down and applied some heavy mascara, winged eyeliner, and bloodred lipstick.

"Just like that," Cass commented in a low rumble, "Hades is back."

I arched a brow at him, pulling my messy ponytail free to weave my thick hair into a tight French braid. He wasn't wrong, though. Changing my appearance went a long way toward focusing my attitude.

"You got a problem with me as Hades, Cassiel?" I asked in a cool tone, sliding back out of my seat and taking two steps closer to him. My heels clicked on the concrete floor, and I already felt different. Less emotional.

Maybe that was why I liked Lucas so much. He seemed to still see the real me through my Hades facade.

Cass just watched me with a wary cautiousness that stung a bit. He also didn't answer my question, and I didn't know whether to be offended or not. Then he ran his gaze over my body from head to toe and shook his head.

"See you around, Red," he rumbled, swinging his leg over his bike and kicking over the engine.

I turned my back on him, going back to my trunk to tuck a couple of spare ammunition clips in my pockets. The roar of his bike faded away as I got back into my seat and slammed the door, and I allowed myself a small spike of disappointment before pushing it all aside.

Business first.

Personal life…later. Maybe. If later ever came.

It was only a short drive over to the morgue at the county medical examiner's office, so I was only a couple of minutes later than I'd told Zed. He was waiting for me outside, not a good sign, and he was smoking. An even worse sign.

He straightened up when I got out of my car, dropping his cigarette to squash it under his boot. I didn't comment on it, though, just arched a brow at him as he fell into step with me. He gave me a grimace, then opened the front door for me to enter ahead of him.

The metal detectors beeped as we both passed through, but neither of us stopped to surrender our weapons. Enough of the city was still under my control that the guard on the door just turned the beeping off and pretended like it'd never happened.

"What am I walking into here, Zed?" I asked in a low voice as we made our way down the long corridor. We'd visited the morgue often enough that we knew where to go without needing someone to guide us.

He huffed a sigh. "You wouldn't have believed me if I'd told you, Boss. Better to see it for yourself."

Apprehension prickled my skin, but I didn't argue. It was pointless when I was about to find out. Drawing a steadying breath, I pushed open the swinging doors to the morgue itself.

A woman in a lab coat and glasses startled so hard she almost fell off her stool, then quickly recovered and strode over to greet us.

"Hades, ma'am, sir, sorry, uh—" She fumbled over her words, and I held a hand up to stop it before she panicked too hard.

"You must be Meredith," I said, giving her a quick once-over. Our old medical examiner had recently suffered a stroke. He was doing well, but he'd been forced to retire and appoint a replacement: Meredith Quay.

She was a pretty woman with tightly curled hair and a dusting of freckles across her nose. Her head bobbed in confirmation, and she held her hand out for me to shake.

"Yes, ma'am, uh, sir, uh, Ms. Timber?" Her panicked eyes shifted to Zed, who was hiding a smirk behind his hand as he pretended to scratch his cheek.

"Just Hades is fine," I told the new medical examiner with a cool smile. I knew it wasn't one that reached my eyes, though. They rarely did these days. "Zed tells me you have something to show me?"

Meredith bobbed her head again. "Yes, I mean, I probably wouldn't have noticed anything super suspicious about it on a body like this, but..." She paused, hurrying over to the metal gurney already set up in the middle of the room with a body on it. A sheet covered the whole corpse, but she quickly flipped the sheet down to reveal Sonny-boy. "I mentioned to Mr. De Rosa that the victim had a recent tattoo." Her eyes darted to Zed as she pulled a fresh pair of latex gloves on, then indicated I should come closer.

Not that I needed any encouragement. I was no stranger to dead bodies, and Sonny had *loads* of tattoos. But something about this one had alarmed Zed enough to call me down to the morgue in person, so I was burning with curiosity.

Meredith rolled Sonny's corpse slightly, lifting his shoulder off the table to show me the fresh ink in a small patch of previously un-inked skin.

Alarm ricocheted through my whole damn body when I saw the tattoo in question, and my eyes flew to Zed's. He gave a nod, confirming that I wasn't fucking imagining things, and I silently cursed.

"This looks like it was only done a day or so before he was

killed," I commented, keeping my tone carefully neutral and my face blank.

Meredith put the body back down and shrugged. "Yeah, I'd say so. Within a day or two, anyway. Does it mean something?"

Zed and I exchanged a quick look, then I shook my head. "Not that I can think of," I lied. "But thank you for showing me, anyway."

She didn't believe me, and I would have been disappointed if she had. Still, she took the hint and didn't push any further.

"No troubles, Hades," she chirped. "Also, Mr. De Rosa, Jenks made a copy of the file for you." She snapped off her gloves and hurried over to her desk where she picked up a thin folder of paper.

"Thank you, Meredith," Zed said as he took the file from her. "I really appreciate how helpful you've been today." His smile was pure charm, and I had to bite my cheek to stop from rolling my eyes at him.

Meredith blushed, though, despite being an easy ten to fifteen years older than Zed. Fucking hell, his appeal knew no limits, apparently.

I didn't hang around to watch him flirt with the new ME and stalked out of the morgue with paranoia pricking my skin with every damn step. Zed followed quickly, catching up before I'd even made it to the end of the corridor, but didn't say a word as we exited the building.

Once outside, I drew a couple of deep breaths, letting the fresh air ground me and calm me down. It didn't totally work, but the pressing sense of panic subsided slightly. I didn't feel quite so much like I was about to pass out.

"Tell me that wasn't what I think it was, Zed." My voice was a rough whisper as I continued toward my car in the parking lot. Zed was close enough to touch, though, so he heard me just fine.

"Can't do that, Boss." He grimaced. "It's exactly what you think."

Not wanting to believe him—or what I'd just seen with my

own two eyes—I swiftly grabbed him by the front of his shirt and slammed him into the side of my Range Rover. He didn't fight me as my shaking fingers tugged his buttons loose, parting his shirt to reveal the tattoo on his chest.

His chest rose under my touch, his breath gusting out as I ran my fingertips over the geometric design over his heart. It'd been years since I'd seen it this close and even longer since the day Zed had drawn it as a doodle in the margin of my economics workbook while he helped tutor me through exams.

"How is this even possible?" I breathed, tracing those lines over and over with my finger. It seemed like an intricate and possibly random design, but I'd watched him create it. It was my middle name. Darling.

Chase had seen him draw it too. Chase goddamn Lockhart, my first love and Zed's best friend. It'd been *his* idea to make it into a tattoo, and Zed had only gotten it done because Chase *Dared* him to do it. It was a stupid fucking game. *Dare.*

"I don't know, Dare," Zed whispered back, using my nickname for the first time in five years. It shocked me almost as much as seeing that tattoo on Sonny-boy. "We'll figure it out though. Whoever it is, they're just trying to get inside our heads. Don't let them." His index finger pressed under my chin, lifting my gaze to meet his. "You're Hades, remember? No one scares you. Not even a ghost."

I wanted to believe that so badly, but he was wrong. No one scared me *more* than this particular ghost.

CHAPTER 13

Zed and I headed back to my apartment from the morgue, not wanting to discuss sensitive topics out in the open. By the time we'd finished reading through the police report of Sonny-boy's murder and officially decided that a certain Officer Randall was our lead, I was running late to pick Seph up from school. And I still hadn't dropped off her car with my mechanic to be fixed.

"I'll take it in now," Zed offered when I said as much aloud. "I need to go back to the ME's to pick up my car anyway. I can drop hers at Rex's on the way."

He'd come home with me in my Range Rover, as if he didn't want to let me out of his sight for that amount of time. Silly really. I was scared and paranoid and wallowing in old guilt, but I was perfectly capable of driving alone. And yet I hadn't protested when he'd climbed into my passenger seat.

"You're the best, Zed," I told him with a genuine smile. "What would I even do without you?"

He rolled his eyes with a short laugh. "Let's never find out." He headed over to the hall table where Seph usually tossed her car keys when she came home. He found them straightaway, thanks to the fluffy pink ball hanging from them.

I groaned as I stood up and stretched, feeling all the kinks in my spine and regretting that I hadn't gone back to sleep this morning. With a yawn, I pulled my shoulder holster back on, shifting it until it was comfortable, then strapped a couple of slim but deadly blades to my thigh, right over my jeans. Fuck it. I gave less than zero fucks if stuck-up Shadow Prep parents saw me and screamed.

"Safety first," I told Zed with a smirk when I caught him watching me. He was probably thinking I was going overkill for school pickup, but I'd rather be over-armed than dead.

He gave me a tight smile, then opened the front door. "Shall we?"

We made our way down to the parking garage together, and my phone buzzed with a message just as we were getting out of the elevator.

I opened it, thinking—stupidly—that it might be from Cass.

Lucas: I tried not to message again. I tried. But you're all I can think about. Yesterday was incredible. You're incredible. Can I see you again?

The message surprised me enough that I stopped dead in my tracks and read it three times. When he'd left my apartment last night and I told him not to text me, I thought he listened. But I should have known better… He knew what he wanted and seemed to have a good read on when to push me.

"What is it?" Zed asked, giving me a wary look from a couple of paces away.

I shook my head. "Nothing." My fingers flew over the keyboard of my phone, sending a quick reply as I started walking again.

Hades: Lose my number, Lucas. I'm your boss.

His reply dinged before I opened my car door.

Lucas: It's only Monday.

I rolled my eyes, fighting a smile.

"You okay, Boss?" Zed asked, unlocking Seph's dented-up Camaro. She was a truly crappy driver and had collided with the back of a Jeep on her way home from school last week. Not bad enough to need a tow, but bad enough that she shouldn't be driving it around, hence why I was playing chauffeur. God knew I wasn't letting her drive my cars with her track record.

"All good," I told him with a smirk. It was so tempting to tell him Lucas was begging to see me again, if only to turn the tables on him. He was constantly telling me about his revolving bedroom door, so it'd be interesting to see the shoe on the other foot.

But for some reason I held my tongue. I had no intention of ever seeing Lucas again in a less-than-professional capacity, but I also didn't want to use him. Not like that. He was too genuinely *nice*.

Zed gave me a suspicious look but nodded and popped Seph's door open. "See you at 7th later?"

"Probably." If I didn't fall asleep first. Usually on a Monday night I spent a couple of hours hanging out with Seph, making sure she was completing all her homework and cooking dinner. Then when she went to bed, I headed into one of the clubs. My average night's sleep was around four hours, and I'd just gotten used to it.

Zed left the garage ahead of me, giving me a little salute as he drove out in Seph's Camaro. I took a moment to reply to Lucas, though.

Hades: I'm busy tonight.

It was important to me to try to provide *some* level of normalcy for my sister, so there was no way I'd be ditching her to get some dick. No matter how epic that dick happened to be.

123

Lucas: Then I quit.

I barked a laugh, shaking my head at his reply. He didn't mean he'd quit trying to see me; he meant he'd quit his job before even starting.

Hades: No, you don't.

He didn't reply quickly this time, so I inserted my phone in the car cradle and drove out of my building. Seph was probably already getting annoyed waiting for me to pick her up.

His response lit up my screen a few minutes later, and I smiled. It was just the broken-heart emoji.

A call from Seph came through when I was only about two minutes away from her school, and I answered it on Hands Free.

"I know, I'm late," I said as soon as the call connected. "I'm almost there."

"No, uh, that's okay," my sister said, sounding way too fucking perky.

Instantly my heart raced. "What's going on, Seph? Are you okay?"

She let out a forced laugh that only panicked me further. My foot pressed down on the gas.

"I'm fine, Dare," she replied with another fake laugh. "But, uh, um, I have a favor to ask."

Oh.

My foot eased off the gas again, slowing me back to normal speed.

"Go on…"

"So." Seph lowered her voice like she was trying not to be heard. "Remember that guy I told you about this morning?" She was practically whispering into her phone, so I was going to guess he was somewhere nearby.

I snickered a laugh. "Yeah, I remember. What about him?"

"Well, he's my new project partner in art class and he usually walks home and I kind of sort of told him that my sister would give him a ride and I don't know why I said that and now I can't take it back and—" It was all one long sentence with no gaps for breathing, so I cut her off.

"Seph, fucking breathe. You want me to give this kid a lift home? It's not a big deal." I shook my head, wondering where the fuck she got all her melodrama from. Sure as hell wasn't me.

"I want you *not to kill him*." She hissed those words at me, and I had to bite my lip not to crack up laughing.

"Seph, I don't *kill* boys for liking you. I just politely educate them on the consequences should they lay their dirty teenage-boy hands on you. Honestly, you make me sound like a monster." I grinned as I said it, not feeling even the slightest bit guilty for keeping my sister safe. She had her whole life ahead of her for bad romances, but she'd already lost so much of her childhood, thanks to our family.

She made a frustrated, slightly panicked sound over the phone. "I hate you," she muttered without conviction. "If you scare him off, I'm moving to Reykjavik and never speaking to you again."

I snickered. "Sure thing, brat. See you in thirty seconds."

She ended the call, probably frantically trying to think of a reason to rescind her offer to the new boy. But it was too late; I was already turning into the long driveway up to Shadow Prep.

I spotted her in the distance, waiting on the front steps of the administration building with her copper-red hair still in a perfect bun. She was standing on the bottom step, messing with the shoulder straps of her bag and talking to a boy who sat a couple of steps higher.

He sat in the shade of the building, so I couldn't make out what he looked like except that he wore the Shadow Prep uniform and had the hot-guy slouch down pat. Fucking player, I'd put my money on it. No way in hell was I letting him chase my sweet little sister without some severe warnings about what would happen if he hurt her.

I pulled up right in front of the steps, obscuring my own view, and waited patiently for Seph to get in. She took her sweet-ass time, too, popping open the passenger door as she chatted in a high-pitched, panicked voice.

"No, it's totally fine," she was telling him. "It's on our way anyway, and you shouldn't have to walk all that way. Besides, we need to talk about our art project, right?"

Her attention shifted to me as she paused with the door open, and her brow drew into a tight frown when she saw my thigh strap full of knives and shoulder holster holding my Desert Eagle in plain view.

"What?" I asked at her horrified expression. "Get in, Seph. I don't have all day."

Her eyes widened, her whole face *begging* me not to embarrass her as she slid into the front seat. The back door opened, and the tall boy she'd been flirting with climbed into my car.

"Hey, thank you so much. You—" His polite thanks cut off abruptly as our eyes met in the rearview mirror. My lips parted in shock, and he froze. Just *froze*.

Seph was none the wiser, though, pulling her door shut and buckling her belt as she rushed to introduce us.

"Lucas, this is my sister. She's not a very good 'people' person, though, so, like, just ignore her if she says anything rude or mean or generally threatening, okay? She'll just be joking. Right, Dare?" Seph gave me a hard glare like she wanted me to nod and smile, but I was too busy *freaking right the fuck out*.

Lucas was quicker than me to recover, breaking eye contact and clearing his throat before closing his own door.

"Really nice to meet you," he murmured, his eyes meeting mine in the mirror once more. This time his green gaze was full of apology and guilt, silently begging me for a chance to explain. "Dare, was it?"

I had fucking *nothing* to say. What the hell could I even say? Less than twenty-four hours ago he'd fucked me on just about every surface of my bedroom and bathroom. Now he sat in the back seat of my Range Rover wearing a Shadow Prep *school uniform*.

What the actual *fuck*?

"Dare," Seph hissed, poking me in the leg and damn near cutting her finger off on one of my blades. "Stop acting weird."

My attention snapped back to her, but I still couldn't think of anything to say. So I just shook my head and started the car. I couldn't exactly kick Lucas out without telling Seph that he'd spent the weekend with his dick buried between my legs.

Fuck. *Fuck.*

I'd known he was too good to be true. Now I was wishing he really had been a spy for a rival gang… That would have been infinitely better than this. Anything would have.

Seph chatted away, clearly trying to cover for my awkward silence as we drove back to town. Lucas responded to her in one-word answers, and every time I glanced at him in the mirror, he was staring at me. Just fucking *staring* like he didn't care if Seph found out.

Then again, she was sitting directly in front of him, making it hard for her to see him. She probably hadn't even noticed.

"Where am I taking you, Lucas?" I managed to grind out from behind clenched teeth as we got closer to the edge of town. My knuckles were white on the steering wheel, and it was taking all my willpower not to drop Seph at home and take Lucas somewhere to shoot him.

Actually, that was a lie. Even in a goddamn Shadow Prep uniform, he looked so gorgeous it hurt. I was too damn scared of what I'd do if I was alone with him…because chances were I wouldn't shoot him at all. Just like I'd failed to shoot Cass earlier.

Oh fucking hell. Cass. What was Cass going to say when he found out? Or Zed, for that matter?

I cringed internally, already anticipating their mockery.

Lucas gave me directions to his house, his voice low and soothing, like he was trying to apologize with every word. That wasn't going to fucking cut it, though.

The neighborhood he directed me to was an upper-middle-class area, and the house he pointed out was cute, in a slightly run-down way.

I stopped the car in the driveway and still had nothing to say, so I just waited for him to get the fuck out and let me erase the past three days from my brain permanently.

"So, did you want to call me later, and we can plan out our project?" Seph asked, spinning in her seat to beam at Lucas. Fuck me, she was totally crushing on him. Not that I could blame her; she had good taste. But this was one hell of a disaster just waiting to happen.

"Um." Lucas met my gaze in the mirror *again*, and I quickly looked away. I wanted nothing to do with this mess. "Yeah, sure."

Seph beamed even brighter. "Great! Pass me your phone. I'll put my number in."

He handed his phone to her, and I jerked. What if he'd left our message thread open? *Oh, fuck.*

Seph didn't say anything though, just typed her info in and handed the device back to him with a smile. "I sent myself a text so I'd have your number," she told him. "I hope that's okay."

Lucas's eyes widened—I was fucking watching him in the mirror again—but he nodded and gave my sister a tight smile. "Cool. I'll, uh, see you. Thank you for the ride home, Dare." His lips twitched with mischief as he said that, and I shook my head at him in the mirror.

Fuck right off with that shit, Lucas.

"Good*bye*, Lucas," I told him in a hard voice, meaning it.

His responding grin as he climbed out of the car was the same one he'd given yesterday after he'd kissed me in front of Zed like he was staking claim.

I pulled out of his driveway quickly, before I could change my mind and confront him right there. Seph didn't say anything for the longest time, then finally let out a long and very dramatic sigh.

"What?" I asked, side-eyeing her. "I didn't even *try* to kill him." Even though I should have.

"No, I know," she groaned, then gave me the worst kind of pouty face. "I think I know why Lucas hasn't really paid attention to the girls at school."

Shit. "You do?"

She nodded, the picture of unhappiness. "I think he's got a girlfriend."

I blinked a couple of times, refocusing on the road ahead as I swallowed. "Why do you say that?"

She huffed again. "When I sent myself a text from his phone, I saw the most recent message thread in his inbox."

Oh fucking hell.

"What? Seph, that's an invasion of privacy! You can't just read his messages!" Yeah, I had a vested interest in my little sister *not* being that rude. *Please let her not have read them.*

She just rolled her eyes and crossed her arms. "I didn't *open* it. Jesus, Dare, what do you take me for? But she's clearly his girlfriend. Her contact was saved as just *H* and a love-heart emoji."

What?

"Well..." I searched for something to say to that. Anything. "Maybe he has a *boy*friend."

Wow. That was the best I could come up with to deflect attention? Hopeless. Something about lying to my sister got me all twisted up in knots, and I definitely didn't use my best material.

Seph huffed again. "Yeah, maybe. Or maybe it's just an ex or something. I dunno. Argh, why am I even telling you this? You're probably already planning on sending one of your guys over with a gun and a threat later tonight. I'm doomed to graduate a virgin."

I smiled at her, not totally faking it this time. "Seph, if any guy *lets* me intimidate them away from you, then he's clearly not worth your time or attention. Think of it like that."

She didn't though. She glared daggers at me the whole way home and jumped out of the car the second we parked. Her timing was impeccable, too, because a split second later my phone lit up with a new message.

Lucas: We probably need to talk…

CHAPTER 14

Considering there was quite literally nothing Lucas could say that would adequately explain why he was a student at Shadow Prep, *not* Shadow Grove University like he'd led me to believe, I ignored his message.

I helped Seph with her homework like normal, cooked sweet chili chicken breasts with garden vegetables for dinner, watched three episodes of *Gossip Girl* with her, then made an excuse not to go to 7th Circle.

The next morning I had a half-dozen missed calls from Lucas, all of which I cleared from my call history. I dropped Seph off to school way earlier than she needed to go—paranoid I would see him—then drove over to Rainybanks to meet with the Timberwolves accountant.

As much as it sounded like fun to be the CEO of a multibillion-dollar hospitality company and the leader of an exceptionally lucrative criminal organization, it was really just a whole lot of work.

Thankfully, I'd always done well in school, as had Zed. We each had a degree in business administration, as well as postgrad degrees in event management and finance. Zed, being a couple of years older, had been able to tutor me through a lot of the coursework, which allowed me to get my qualifications through online learning rather than attending an actual college. Not as prestigious, but who gave a fuck?

That level of education meant that I wasn't relying on other people to tell me the truth. I could cross-check their work and know for myself if anyone was ripping me off, as our first three bookkeepers found out the hard way.

Thankfully, the fourth one had a bit more of a brain in her head and hadn't tried to screw me yet. She was also perfectly unflappable and didn't even bat an eyelid whenever I randomly dropped in to review the books and check end-of-night reports. Zed and I quietly joked that she was the Mary Poppins of the crime world. She was always so prim and proper, despite managing money from sex workers and drug deals.

"Good morning, Ms. Wolff," she greeted as I quietly let myself into one of the lush fifty-fourth-floor offices that Copper Wolf occupied. Here, in the bright light of day, I was Daria Wolff. Honestly, all my names used to confuse me, but now they came as easily as slipping on a coat when it was cold out.

"Good morning, Macy," I responded with a polite smile. "You look lovely today. Is that a new scarf?"

Her smile widened, and she touched her perfect, nude-manicured nails to the floral silk scarf around her neck. "It is, thank you. I was about to order coffee. Would you like one?"

"That would be great," I replied, passing her and pushing open the door to my own office, next to hers. Mine wasn't an office I used particularly often, but it was nice to have a work-space that wasn't in the dark bowels of a nightclub or on my own sofa.

I switched my computer on and leaned back in my high-backed chair with a yawn. Macy followed me into my office a couple of minutes later, placing two external hard drives down on my desk with a smile.

"Coffee will be up shortly," she told me. "Any questions, let me know."

She let herself back out, closing the door softly behind her, and I selected the first hard drive. Silver for Copper Wolf records, black for Timberwolves. Anyone who tried to say that it was too risky to keep digital documents was living in the damn past. Digital was a million times more secure than an antiquated paper-and-ink record just waiting to be stolen and used in court.

As long as you had a great security system, encryptions, and a self-destruct sequence to wipe the data if anyone unauthorized accessed it, which I was lucky enough to have, digital was the way to go.

I plugged the silver hard drive into my computer and went through the process of entering my passwords. There was a soft tap on my door before I'd even opened the first spreadsheet, and Macy's assistant silently delivered my coffee to my desk.

The next several hours disappeared in a flash as I cycled through the last week of spreadsheets across all my Copper Wolf bars and clubs—there were seven of them now—and then reviewed the profit and loss statements for my vodka brand.

When I finished on the silver hard drive, I took a break to pee, stretch, and check my messages. Then wished I *hadn't* checked my messages.

Lucas: Please don't ignore me. I need to explain. I had no idea Seph was your sister; she only ever called you Dare. Why Dare, by the way? Were you a reckless kid? I could see that.

Fuck me. Lucas Wilder—totally not his real name—had balls of steel. Any other guy would have already skipped town, changed his name seventeen times, and possibly looked into plastic surgery. Not Lucas, though. Nope, he still wanted a chance to *explain*.

I couldn't figure out if that irritated me or impressed me, but I seemed to be leaning toward the latter.

The reason I wished I hadn't read it was because I was having a hard time not replying to him. Christ, I'd known the kid—because that's exactly what he fucking well was—for all of three days, and he'd already got under my skin worse than anyone else since Chase's death.

It was so damn tempting that I sat there with a reply screen open for ages. Then a new message came through, and I breathed a sigh of relief that I had a distraction.

Zed: You okay, Boss?

I frowned, then tapped my reply.

Hades: Yeah, why? Something happen?

The little bubble that said he was typing popped up, then disappeared, then reappeared, and my eye twitched with irritation.

Right when I was about to call him, his response appeared.

Zed: Nothing new. Just checking in.

Weird. I frowned at his message for a moment, then hit Call at the top of the screen. It only rang once before he answered.

"What the fuck, Zed?" I asked in lieu of a greeting. "What was that about?"

"What? I just hadn't heard from you this morning." He didn't sound strange... Maybe I was overthinking things.

"So?" I wrinkled my nose in confusion. Then understanding dawned. "Oh, you're worried that seeing my Darling logo on Sonny's corpse has sent me into a dark place, huh?"

There was a long pause, and I knew I'd guessed right.

"I was just checking in, Boss," Zed replied eventually, his tone neutral. "Nothing more to it."

Bullshit.

"If you say so, liar," I muttered. "I'm at Wolf HQ checking the reports, but I'll call when I'm done here. The contractors for Timber ran into some city council red tape that needs to be lubricated."

"Understood. I'll wait on your call then." Zed was back to his usual polite respectfulness.

Annoyed, I ended the call without another word, then drummed my fingertips on the desk a couple of times. Seeing that tattoo had shaken me, no question, but it had also felt like something shifted with Zed and me. Like we were *us* again, for just a couple of hours. I missed that.

Releasing another sigh, I tossed my phone aside and plugged in the black hard drive. I might as well put my restless mind to good work staying on top of every facet of my income streams.

Timberwolves documents took a whole lot longer to wade through, thanks to every single folder being encrypted, but by the time I was done, I felt a whole crapload calmer. Control-freak coping mechanisms.

Macy was still at her desk when I dropped the hard drives back, and she politely bid me a good night as I left the office.

My phone rang as I stepped into the elevator, and I frowned when I saw the caller ID.

"Vega," I said on accepting the call.

"Hades," he replied, sounding grim. "Got news for you."

A groan rolled through my mind, even though I knew Sonny-boy hadn't been a coincidence. Still, did it all have to happen at once? Didn't mysterious bad guys ever take a break for normal life?

"Get on with it then," I snapped to hurry him the hell up. I despised dramatic pauses, unless I was the one using them.

"Couple of college kids over here in Dogwood were taken to the ER this weekend. Suspected PCP overdose." Vega sounded less than pleased to be delivering this information to me, but I had to give him props for calling me himself and not palming it off on his second.

I ran my tongue over my lips, wetting them as my whole mouth had gone very suddenly dry, and then I pulled my shit together.

"Send me copies of their medical files," I told him. "What condition are they in now? Lucid enough to talk?"

"They are. Already given a statement to my guys too. I'll include that for you to read. Nothing stands out to me as suspect, except that they got their hands on angel dust to fucking start with." The fury in his voice was clear, and I expected nothing less. Some other fucker selling banned drugs on his turf was a clear challenge to his authority.

"Get to cleaning up, Vega," I told him with a hard edge. "Whoever is doing this isn't working alone, and I don't believe for a second the Wraiths were the only street gang infiltrated."

He let out a frustrated sigh, but he knew I was right. "On it," he growled.

I ended the call as the elevator doors opened to the parking level and I stalked over to my car. My favorite mode of transport, my motorcycle, was still parked at 7th Circle where I'd left it on Saturday night, but I'd been feeling far too *Hades* this morning to drive my Range Rover. So I was in my hot red Corvette and loving how it matched the soles of my shoes and my lipstick.

Rather than calling Zed, I just drove straight back to Shadow Grove, knowing I'd likely find him at 7th Circle. He was officially the group's manager overseeing all the bars but was standing in as venue manager for 7th until we found someone who was a good fit for the role.

My phone pinged a few times along the way, and I knew it'd be Vega sending me the files he'd promised. While I appreciated his honesty in bringing me the information, it sure as fuck wasn't what I wanted to hear.

It was sounding more and more like a targeted attack across all my zones at once. Reaper dealers being arrested outside Anarchy, kids in Vega's town OD'ing, Sonny getting murdered…all in the same night.

I'd put money on it that Maurice had something to tell me, too, but was still searching for his balls.

It was late by the time I pulled into the parking lot outside 7th Circle, and there were more cars than usual for a Tuesday night— always a good sign for a profitable night at the bar and in the back rooms.

One of the reserved spaces beside my bike was free, so I parked my Corvette and frowned when I realized Zed's Ferrari was nowhere to be seen. Maybe he'd caught a lift in with Emily or Annika or Selena or whoever the fuck he'd spent last night with. Hoping I would find him, I headed inside anyway.

As I passed through the main doors, the buzz inside the club was electric, something more suited to a weekend than early in the week, and I frowned with confusion. What the hell had the crowd so worked up?

My silent question was answered a second later, when I entered the main bar area and stopped dead in my tracks.

There on the main stage, working the pole like he'd been born to dance, was a very sweaty, very sexy, very possibly *underage* Lucas Wilder.

Fuck. It was his first night, and I'd forgotten to fire him.

CHAPTER 15

Joanne, my 7th Circle bar manager and most likely choice to promote to venue manager, sidled over to me as I stood there frozen in shock.

"Bet you're glad you hired that one, Boss," she commented, her admiration for Lucas's skill on the pole evident in the way her eyes sparkled and her smile spread wide over her face. "This is the most worked up I've seen a Tuesday crowd since we opened. They're barely even paying attention to poor Destiny." She indicated the next stage over, where one of our full-time girls was shaking her tits for a group of sloppy businessmen.

Jo had a point; the attention was mostly on Lucas, from men and women alike. Damn, if that didn't make my blood burn like acid through my veins.

Lucas seemed to *sense* me watching because his eyes scanned over the crowd until they locked with my gaze. A slow smile curved his lush lips, and with a confident look in his eyes, he sent me a slow, deliberate wink.

The women watching let out a collective scream, each of them probably imagining it'd been sent to them, but I just gave a slow shake of my head. He fucking *knew* he was in deep shit, yet he didn't run. He didn't back down or cower away from the impending doom that was my anger.

I kinda liked that.

"Ho-ly damn." Joanne coughed a laugh. "I think I just creamed my pants, and he wasn't even looking at me."

I scowled. "He's half your age, Jo. Keep it professional."

The older woman just gave a small shrug. "Age is just a number, Boss. So long as he's legal, ain't no one got any reason to judge."

Fucking hell, hadn't I only recently thought a very similar thing when justifying my attraction to Cass? Why the hell should it be so different if Lucas was the younger one? So long as he was, in fact, legal. If I found out he was actually seventeen, I might have to put myself into witness protection from myself.

"Send him to my office when he gets offstage," I told Jo as Lucas performed some particularly jaw-dropping move on the pole that should have been straight out of the circus. He *had* said he was into gymnastics.

Jo grinned knowingly. "Yes, Boss. Can do." I leveled a flat glare at her, and she quickly wiped the smile from her face and cleared her throat. "Uh, sorry. Yes, absolutely, the second his set finishes. Can I get you a drink?"

"Yes," I replied, "a gimlet. Have you seen Zed tonight?"

She nodded. "Yes, sir. He left about half an hour ago to sort out a stock issue over at 22."

Damn it. I needed to tell him about the kids in Dogwood and read through the notes Vega had sent across. Jo was already heading back behind the bar to make my cocktail, so I decided to wait for it at the bar to save pulling a waitress away to deliver it to my office.

Yeah. That's why I stayed. To save a waitress from walking up a flight of stairs to deliver my drink. It had *nothing* to do with the stunning creature gyrating on the stage for a horde of screaming women. It definitely had nothing to do with the way his gaze kept coming back to me or the way his movements seemed to echo what he'd done to me in bed a couple of days ago.

Ugh. I was clearly getting bitten by karma for all the people I'd killed.

Jo handed over my cocktail way too quickly, but I forced myself to look away from the stage as I headed up to my office. At least I knew he'd be getting a good look at my ass in the tight lace-up pencil skirt I was wearing.

Even with the door to my office closed, though, I could hear the music booming up through the floor. I hadn't bothered sound-proofing this room, knowing it wouldn't be *my* office for more than a few months, but now I was regretting that choice. Especially when "Pony" by Ginuwine came on and the crowd went mental.

"Oh, come on," I groaned, then promptly turned my CCTV monitors on. Yes, I was that level of masochistic. No, I didn't care when there was no one around to witness me self-destruct.

Luckily—or unluckily—my phone started ringing with Zed's name flashing on the screen, so I switched the screens off again before answering.

"Trouble at 22?" I asked him after connecting the call.

"Minimal," he responded, the sound of live music playing in the background of his call. We often had a jazz band at Club 22 early in the week, and a local dance school had taken to dropping by after class to let off steam. It was a fun atmosphere.

"I'm at 7th," I told him. "How soon can you get here? Vega had some shit in Dogwood that we need to discuss."

Zed let out a small, frustrated groan, and I initially thought it was in response to my news. But then I caught the low, seductive sound of a woman's laughter and reassessed.

"Actually, never mind," I snapped, letting my annoyance take control of my tongue for a second. "I'll call if I need help."

"Hade—" His protest cut off as I ended the call.

For some reason my anger had spiked dramatically, so I carefully placed my phone down on the desk and drew a few calming breaths. As a teenager I'd taken a trip to Tibet and studied meditation with monks for a month. I was awful at it, but more and more these days I found myself remembering their lessons on control. Even if it only worked on the surface.

By the time I'd finished my drink—admittedly in just a few mouthfuls—there was a knock at the door, and my heart slammed into my rib cage harder than ever.

"Enter," I called out, already knowing who it would be. The quintessential male-stripper song had stopped playing downstairs, and the crowd was already more subdued.

When Jo had said she would send him up when he got offstage, she'd been literal. Lucas stepped into my office still glistening with sweat and wearing nothing but a black towel draped around his hips. I was going to assume he had a thong underneath, too, seeing as my strippers didn't go fully nude. Not front-of-house, anyway.

"You asked to see me, Hades?" he asked, all innocence.

Dammit. This had been a bad idea. Why had I asked to see him in my office *alone* again? Oh yeah, to fire his lying teenage ass.

"Close the door, Lucas," I told him in a curt voice, trying really hard to keep my eyes *off* his body. Had he gotten more buff since the weekend? My pussy clearly hadn't gotten the message that Lucas was now off-limits because it was throbbing with need just having him so close and so very undressed.

He did as he was told, then sat down in one of the chairs opposite me. He didn't look even the slightest bit worried that he might not walk out of the office alive, and I *still* wasn't sure if that was total ignorance or the biggest balls in the goddamn world.

"What are you doing here?" I asked before the tension could ramp up any higher. "Do you have some sort of death wish?"

One of his brows tweaked up, and he ran a hand over the back of his neck, swiping sweat away. The motion made his chest and biceps flex, and I clamped my lips tight to stop from drooling.

"I was on the roster for my first shift tonight," he replied, a tiny smile playing at his lush lips. "And no one told me *not* to show up, so…"

I glowered. He knew damn well he shouldn't have.

"My mistake," I seethed. "Consider yourself fired, Lucas. I don't take kindly to my employees blatantly lying to my face."

He let out a breath, some of that cocky arrogance slipping away. "I didn't *lie*—" He started to say, then cut himself off when my eyes narrowed further. "Okay, so I did lie a little bit," he amended. "But I had no idea who you were when I said I was twenty-one, and I *really* needed this job. I know your clubs don't usually hire anyone under the legal drinking age, so I had my ID tweaked…"

I said nothing, just glared, but he didn't flinch away. Not once. Balls of fucking *steel*.

"Look," he tried again, this time totally dropping the playboy bullshit in favor of what seemed to be sincerity. "I lied to you about my age and my surname, but that's it. Everything else was one hundred percent truth, and can you really blame me? You wouldn't have looked twice if you'd known I was eighteen."

Oh wow. Eighteen. Better than seventeen, I guessed.

"You're right," I murmured. "I'd have thrown your ass out of my bar for using a fake ID and risking my liquor license." He cocked a brow at me like he was silently calling me out, and I let out an annoyed growl. "Fine, I probably wouldn't have. But you can bet your ass—"

"That you wouldn't have dragged me into the supply closet of a grunge bar and let me fuck you against the door?" he finished my sentence for me. "Yeah, like I said, can you blame me? That was easily the best night of my whole damn life, only to be topped by the next day at your place."

My cheeks warmed at the reminder, and I scrubbed a hand over my face. This had definitely been a bad idea to bring him up to my office. All I could think about was how good he felt sinking into my cunt and the way he whispered my name like a prayer as he fucked me.

"You're a liability, Lucas," I told him, desperately fighting my baser instincts. "You distract me, and that's something I can't afford in my line of business."

Determined to extract myself from a situation that was fast slipping out of my control, I pushed back from my desk and stalked over to the door. Opening it, I turned back to Lucas with a tight jaw.

"Leave now, and I'll pretend this never happened. I'll even put in a good word for you at the Starbucks near Shadow Prep." Okay, that was a bit of a low blow, but my brain was misfiring all over the place.

He stood slowly from the chair, then gave a short, humorless laugh as he shook his head. There were only a couple of steps between him and the doorway, and for a hot second, I thought he was going to pass straight through without another word.

But then he paused, his fingers gripping the edge of the door and his sheer nearness making my skin prickle.

"So, that's it? I'm fired?" His tone was low and thoughtful, and I frowned.

"Yes. Do you need it in writing?" Anxiety was making me snappier than my usual cold, detached self, and my reply made him smirk.

His gaze met mine, his green eyes twinkling with victory. "Good."

He pushed the door, slamming it shut, then slammed his lips against mine. Shock held me immobile, but I really should have seen it coming. I'd said I couldn't fuck him because I was his boss. Then I'd fired him.

It didn't take a high school graduate to add those numbers up.

And yet I didn't immediately push him away. Why? Because holy god, he kissed like the devil, all sinful and intoxicating. Lucas Whatever-his-name-was hit my bloodstream like pure cocaine and lit me up like a fucking Christmas tree.

I groaned, kissing him back and letting him crush me against the wall as his towel dropped to the floor. The level of willpower I needed to summon to push him away was staggering, but somehow, I managed it.

Except with that space between us, and his towel on the floor, his little black thong was doing fuck-all to hide his massive erection.

My mouth watered and my pussy clenched. I'd officially lost my damn mind because I was already trying to work out the easiest, quickest way to get his dick inside me, considering how tight my damn skirt was.

"Don't push me away, Hayden," he pleaded in a rough whisper, his gaze burning with intensity. "Just give me a chance."

He drifted closer again, and when I didn't shove him back, his lips dropped to the bend of my neck and his hands clasped my hips. It was a bad idea. It was *such* a bad idea. But Jo'd had a point earlier… So long as he was legal, age was just a number. And I wasn't exactly a cougar. So was it really such a bad idea?

"Goddammit, Lucas," I groaned, sliding my fingers into his hair and gripping it tight as I brought his lips back to mine.

My desire for control flipped a switch, and a moment later I'd reversed our positions, crushing his gorgeous body against the wall—not that Lucas seemed to mind. His hands found their way under my black silk blouse, tugging it free from my skintight skirt and palming my breasts.

I gasped against his kiss as he rolled my nipples, sending wave after wave of pleasure shooting straight to my cunt. Mentally, I wrote a quick eulogy for my panties because they'd officially drowned.

One of his hands moved to my ass, groping it through the tight fabric of my skirt, and it was right on the tip of my tongue to tell him to rip the fucking thing off me.

Then the door opened again, and Zed's startled gaze met mine from a mere foot away.

CHAPTER 16

It was safe to say I couldn't remember the last time I'd seen Zed speechless. But the way his eyes widened and lips parted, I'd say that he was pretty damn close.

"Zed, fuck off," I snapped, shoving him out of the office with a hand to his face, then kicking the door shut once more.

Lucas let out a soft laugh, and it brought me back to reality. Crap. I couldn't fuck him again, if for no other reason than that he was my *baby sister's crush*.

Clearing my throat, I peeled my hands and body from him and took a couple of very deliberate steps away. The message was clear, and he let out a disappointed sigh.

"Hayden—" he started to say, but I held a hand up to silence him.

Turning my back—because he was painfully tempting standing there basically naked—I quickly tucked my blouse back into my skirt and counted to five in my head. Okay, I counted to twenty.

Then I turned back around, stooped to pick up his towel from the floor, and handed it to him.

"Your break is probably over by now, Lucas," I told him in a cool voice, deliberately opening the door to indicate we were *not* continuing what we'd just started. No matter how badly my thighs were quivering with need.

Zed was waiting right outside the office door, his brow drawn in a deep scowl, and I opened the door wider to indicate he could come in.

"Pretty sure Sisalee was looking for you, new kid. Something about a cowboy costume?" Zed arched a brow at Lucas, his quick gaze taking in all that naked skin and the small towel barely covering his dick.

Lucas ignored Zed—ballsy—and locked eyes with me. "I thought I was fired."

My teeth ground together; Zed would give me grief over this whole exchange later. "Did you lie about your mom?" I finally asked, my voice barely louder than a frustrated growl.

Lucas shook his head. "Not a word. God's honest truth, I wouldn't make something like that up."

I released the breath I hadn't known I was holding. "Then hurry up and get into costume. You get to keep one hundred percent of your tips on your first night."

Lucas frowned, his jaw tight with the need to argue with me. But at the end of the day, if he was telling me the truth about his mom's medical bills and the strain on their finances, then he wasn't going to take a barista job over this one. Not with the way those women were throwing cash at him downstairs.

So I just held his gaze steady, letting him draw that conclusion for himself. After a tense moment, he must have. His tense shoulders sagged, and his gaze dropped from mine as he gave a nod.

"Yes, ma'am," he murmured, stepping out of my office.

Zed didn't waste any time pushing the door shut again, slamming it behind Lucas's perfect ass, and turned to me with raised brows. "What—"

"Shut it," I barked, cutting him off before he could start on what he'd just witnessed. "What are you even doing here? I thought you were otherwise occupied." There was way too much emotion in my voice as I said it, and I cringed hearing the words out loud.

Zed heard it too, the perceptive bastard. His eyes widened, and the corners of his lips tugged up. "Are you jealous?"

Oh, hell no. Even if I were—which I wasn't—I sure as fuck wouldn't admit it to his face.

My glare flattened, and I wiped all traces of emotion from my expression. "Tell me something, Zed. When you opened the door a moment ago, did that look like a woman still pining for a guy who turned her down seven years ago?"

I didn't give him a chance to reply—I really didn't want to hear what he had to say—instead crossing over to my desk to grab my phone where I'd left it, along with my empty martini glass.

"Come on," I told him. "We can talk in the mezzanine bar. I need another cocktail."

No, seriously. If I was going to keep up with the whiplash of my own conflicting personas, I needed shots. Zed could join me or not; I didn't much care.

Yet when I heard his footsteps follow and felt the featherlight touch of his fingers on my lower back as he pushed the door open for me at the end of the corridor, I let out a small sigh of relief. I couldn't afford to fuck things up with Zed. Not now, when I needed him to have my back more than ever before.

"So, Vega?" Zed prompted as we sat down on one of the low sofas overlooking the main stage. Whoops, did I subconsciously just want to see Lucas dance again? Possible. Very damn possible.

Zed sat beside me, rather than opposite, but it worked for me pulling up the documents on my phone to show him.

A waitress delivered drinks to us both, not needing to take our orders to know what we usually drank while working, and I opened the files Vega had sent. The first one was a scanned copy of the medical records for the kids in question.

Sure, it wasn't something I—or Vega—should have been able

to access, but normal rules didn't really apply to us. My understanding of medical notes, though, wasn't amazing, so I just gave the document a quick scan and handed the phone to Zed. He would have a much better understanding of what was included in those reports.

"Thoughts?" I asked after a moment.

He gave a small shrug and handed my phone back. "Not much useful info there. Logical conclusion from their tox screening is that they took a dirty batch of PCP, which isn't unusual in other areas of the country."

I grimaced. "Except in my territory where it's strictly prohibited. Fuck's sake." I ruffled my fingers through my hair, staring out over the main club as I thought it through. Below us, "Save a Horse (Ride a Cowboy)" started playing, and a jaw-droppingly gorgeous cowboy strutted his shit out onto the stage.

"If it were an isolated incident, I'd say it was just one of Vega's boys trying to make a name for himself by expanding his portfolio," Zed commented, dragging my attention away from Lucas.

I nodded my agreement. "But it's not an isolated incident. Not with Sonny and that tattoo." With a long, frustrated exhale, I opened the next file Vega had sent over. It was typed up like a police report but without any official logos, probably a copy from whatever local law enforcement was on his payroll.

"Surprise, surprise," I muttered, dread souring the drink in my stomach. "The kids described the plastic bag as being stamped with a geometric design of some sort." I raised my gaze to meet Zed's and gave a tight, bitter smile. "Wanna bet we know what that design looks like?"

Zed's jaw clenched, and I could almost hear his teeth grinding together. "If you hadn't already shot Chase in the head, I'd want to kill that bastard myself," he muttered, reaching out for his drink on the table and bringing it to his lips.

I had nothing to say to that, so I just echoed his movement and sipped my own drink. When our waitress drifted past a moment later, I grabbed her attention and ordered a couple of plates of food for us. No way was I getting sloppy drunk again like I had on the weekend.

Not that it would matter. I'd already thrown myself at Cass. And look how *that* turned out. Evidently, he was only interested when I wasn't Hades.

Insecure fucker. Then again, I shouldn't have been surprised; he wouldn't be the first guy to be intimidated by a powerful woman. Aunt Demi liked to joke that was half the reason she had ended up marrying a woman.

"So, what was the drama over at 22?" I asked Zed, leaning back on the sofa and not even trying to take my attention away from the stage. Lucas had stripped out of his shirt, showing all those chiseled abs off. Damn, I wanted to lick him all over.

Zed finished his drink in a gulp, dropped the glass onto the table, and signaled for another before giving me a narrow-eyed look. "Nothing major, just a fuckup with the beer delivery. The supplier sent light beer instead of the normal stuff and wanted to blame it on Rodney for ordering the wrong one."

"Idiots," I muttered, rolling my eyes. I was glad not to be handling that side of the bars, that was for sure. It seemed like every damn day there was some issue that Zed needed to personally handle, even though I'd told him to hire more management staff.

"So, the stripper kid, huh?" Zed's tone was laced with amusement, and I groaned inwardly. I fucking *knew* he wasn't going to just let that one go.

Still, I couldn't deny it when he'd literally walked in on me mauling Lucas in my office. And now I couldn't tear my eyes off him as he worked the stage like a pro. There was no freaking way anyone would think it was his first night. Or that he was only eighteen. Cringe.

"Just scratching an itch," I bullshitted with a casual shrug. "Even the big bad Hades is entitled to get some decent dick every now and then, Zed. You're certainly not in a position to judge."

With Herculean effort, I turned my face away from the stage and cocked a brow at Zed. He just held his hands up defensively, an odd smile sitting on his lips.

"Hey, I wasn't judging, Boss. Just surprised." His attention shifted past me to the stage, where Lucas was hanging from the pole in some deadly-looking pose that would easily break his neck if he fell. "Although I can't fault your choice. Holy shit, if I was into dudes…" His brows high, he shook his head with a short laugh.

The idea of Zed and Lucas together really shouldn't have intrigued me as much as it did, so I cleared my throat and sipped my drink. Food needed to hurry up and come out, or I'd end up dragging Lucas off the stage by his thong.

A familiar set of leather-jacketed shoulders moved through the crowd below us, heading toward the stairs to the mezzanine bar, and my stomach flipped.

"What's Cass doing here?" I asked with a scowl, tracking Cass as he made his way through the crowd, totally oblivious to the women undressing him with their eyes.

Zed leaned forward to see what I was glaring at, then shrugged. "No idea, but I'm sure we're about to find out."

He was right, too. Cass disappeared up the stairwell, then popped out a moment later at the end of the bar. He headed straight over to where Zed and I sat, pausing only briefly to order himself a drink.

His long legs ate the distance up, and before I could even remember to breathe, he was looming over our table.

"Hades," he greeted me in that gruff voice of his. "Mind if I join you?"

His scarred brow quirked up as he met my gaze like he was challenging me to acknowledge what had gone down between us the day before. It was almost laughable, considering how cold he'd gone when I transformed back into *Hades* after he'd dropped me at my car.

I hadn't heard from him since he'd driven away, not a word. So, no. I wasn't acknowledging *shit*.

Keeping my face blank, I waved to the vacant sofa opposite the one Zed and I occupied.

Cass's eyes narrowed, but after a short pause he sank onto the plush velvet seat. Our waitress arrived then with all the food I'd ordered, piling the small table between us with the most delicious-smelling shared plates, and amusement flashed over the Reaper leader's face.

"Expecting company?" he asked, eyeing all the food—considerably more than one or two people might consume.

I didn't rise to the bait, though, meeting his gaze calmly. "I haven't sampled the new menu here," I informed him, "so I wanted to try one of everything. Quality control is important to me."

Zed, laughing softly under his breath, leaned forward to snag one of the duck spring rolls and dunk it in plum sauce. "What can we do for you tonight, Cass?"

Cass gave my second a long look, his expression totally unreadable. His poker face was almost as crack-free as my own, and it drove me nuts. I liked being able to read people, but I could never read him. Nope. Cass wasn't just a closed book, he was a locked vault.

"Nothing," the tattooed bastard grunted. "I was here discussing terms of surrender with a couple of the remaining Wraiths. Figured it was a waste of talent to just kill them all."

Zed crunched on his spring roll, sitting back again in his seat. For a couple of moments, there was a tense silence between the three of us, and it weighed down on me like a lead cloak. Swallowing my sigh—because showing emotions in a professional capacity simply wasn't done—I shifted my gaze back to the main stage.

Lucas had done a speedy costume change and was now dressed in an imitation SWAT uniform and lap-dancing a girl onstage. Lucky bitch.

"Isn't that three-minute man from the other night?" Cass asked, his question shocking the absolute shit out of me. Not just that it was so personal, but that it was totally out of character for *him*. Also, how the fuck did he just recognize Lucas from the grainy CCTV footage in his supply room?

Zed choked on the sip of liquor he'd just taken, covering his mouth as he coughed and shaking his head at my death glare.

"Three minutes?" Zed gasped out when he stopped spluttering. "More like three hours. Or more. How long was your phone off on Sunday?" His smirk was pure evil, and I was reeling. Should I threaten to shoot him again? I felt like maybe I'd gone too long without making him fear for his life, that things were getting too friendly again.

Then again...I liked it when we were friends.

"Sunday?" Cass rumbled. "I was talking about Saturday." He cocked his head to the side, his eyes hard as he glared at me.

Nope. No way. I wasn't taking that shit, not when he'd kissed me like I was his goddamn soulmate yesterday, then *totally* ghosted me since. Fuck that noise.

"None of your fucking business," I snapped, then shifted my glare back to Zed. "Neither of you. And when did we start acting all friendly in front of rival gang leaders, huh?"

Cass was the one to answer that, giving me a one-sided smirk. "I'm not a rival, remember? Besides, all of Hades's clubs in Shadow Grove are neutral territory."

How the hell could I argue with that? He was quite literally throwing my own words back at me. Motherfucker. So I shook it off like it wasn't making me uncomfortable in the least.

"Eat some food, Cass," I told him, ignoring his pointed reminder of our kiss. "You're wasting away."

He huffed something vaguely similar to a laugh, but helped himself to one of the miniature pulled-pork sliders on the table between us. The tiny burger looked beyond ridiculous in his huge ink-covered hand, and I shifted my gaze back to Lucas.

Lucas. Jesus fuck, what was I going to do about Lucas?

He was watching me again, just like he had been the whole time he'd been onstage, and this time our eyes locked for an extended moment. His hips rolled, simulating… Well, shit. Like he was simulating what he wanted to be doing to me, just like he'd told me he would.

My nipples hardened against my top and my pussy throbbed as I watched him dance, picturing what it would have been like if Zed hadn't interrupted us earlier. But my daydream was broken when Zed casually stretched an arm around me, his fingers stroking down my upper arm.

I frowned, shooting him a confused look. "What the hell are you doing?"

He met my stare, giving me a half smile. "What? You had some dirt or something on your sleeve. Probably from the office wall earlier." He shot me a wink, then withdrew his arm. Slowly.

What the *fuck*?

CHAPTER 17

I was too stubborn to extract myself from the awkward-as-hell situation I'd found myself in with Zed and Cass, not wanting them to think I'd run from a challenge. So instead, I polished up my big old lady-balls of steel and stuck it out.

To my surprise, I didn't hate it as much as I'd expected. Cass even spoke in full sentences—occasionally—and only looked at Zed like he hated him about half the time we sat there. But then I was pretty confident Cass didn't like *anyone* except my little sister, so that wasn't a shocker.

We shared information with him about the kids overdosing on dirty angel dust down in Vega's zone but kept the tattoo on Sonny-boy to ourselves. Cass might have kissed me, but it didn't mean I trusted him.

Sometime later, when we'd eaten everything on the menu—Cass and Zed mostly—I brushed off my skirt and stood up.

"This was…" I let my voice trail off before saying *fun*. Because I wasn't in the habit of having *fun*, the word just sat awkwardly in my mouth. Instead I just walked away without any words at all. I wasn't one for polite goodbyes anyway, so fuck it.

I'd barely made it to the first step of the staircase when I noticed

I was being followed. The stairs from the main bar up to the mezzanine were enclosed as they twisted around a corner and the lights low enough that only red LED strip lights under each step prevented people falling.

"Was there something else, Cass?" I asked, not turning to look and confirm it was in fact him. He just had a quiet presence that was unmistakable.

He grunted a sound of annoyance, then took two long strides, overtaking me on the stairs and turning to face me from a step lower.

"Actually, yeah," he told me, his eyes flashing like black diamonds in the low light, "this." His hand cupped the back of my neck, his fingers threading into my hair as he crushed his lips to mine in a kiss that made my balance falter.

He was ready to catch me, though, sweeping his other arm around my waist and spinning me against the wall. Thankfully, there was no one else on the stairs to see, but the risk was too great. The last thing I needed was rumors of favoritism sparking a gang war with Maurice or Vega.

"Cass," I breathed, pushing him away with a firm hand to his chest. "Not the time or the place."

His chest vibrated with a frustrated sound, but he took a step away nonetheless, swiping his hand over his face. "Right. My apologies, Hades."

My temper flared. "Don't fucking start with me, Cassiel."

His gaze snapped back to mine, anger flaring in those stony depths, then fading again as he gave an irritated shake of his head.

"You didn't text," he commented, his tone neutral and his face guarded.

I scowled. "Neither did you."

For a moment we just glared at one another, then a pair of women in short skirts and high heels came up the stairs, brushing past us with giggles and sly looks, breaking the moment and allowing me to look away.

With my jaw tight and my spine like steel, I started down the stairs again. I needed to get the fuck out of 7th Circle. Away from Cass. Away from Lucas. And away from whatever the fuck had Zed acting so strange.

I could only hope he was still in the bar watching the girls on the other stage, rather than back in my office looking at security feeds.

Cass shadowed me the whole way out of the club, then across to my car in the reserved space beside my bike.

He frowned at my vehicle double-up. "Why's Fat Bob still here?" he asked.

I stifled a sigh, unlocking my Corvette and popping the door open. "Because, Cass, I was too wasted to drive it home the other night. I haven't had a chance to pick it up since, what with my gang being targeted by a ghost."

Cass knew of Chase—he'd probably even met him at some stage—but he didn't know everything that'd gone down between us in the lead-up to the Timberwolf massacre. Reapers had not been my friends back then, with the exceptions of Archer, Kody, and Steele.

But he knew enough of the Lockhart family to know why I said I was being targeted by a ghost. Dead men didn't infiltrate gangs, and they didn't plant drugs. And yet here we were.

"I'll drive it home for you," he grunted, stepping over to my bike.

I frowned. "Hell no. Besides, I don't have the key with me."

He just held my gaze steady then he bent down and swiftly hot-wired my Harley-Davidson Fat Bob motorcycle with nothing more than a utility knife. Bastard.

"I hate you a little bit," I admitted in a whisper, envious as all hell. Hot-wiring vehicles was a skill I'd never had the patience to learn, but it seemed so incredibly useful.

One corner of Cass's lips hiked up in a small smile at my

comment, and he swung a leg over the seat. "It's not good for it to be outside in the weather, Red. You know that."

He was way too big for my bike, but somehow he made it look effortlessly sexy as he caressed the handlebars and waited for me to get into my Corvette. I debated for a couple of moments whether to tell him to fuck off and come back for Fat Bob another day. But he already had it running, and it *was* bad for it to be outside in the weather. So with a small groan, I slid into my driver's seat and pulled the door shut.

He waited while I rolled out of the parking lot first, then followed me back to my apartment building. I opened the underground parking with a clicker on my dash and descended to my parking level. I had a whole level of parking because I owned a whole floor of the building. Some of the other apartments on my floor had been incorporated into my floor space, and some were just empty. I didn't like neighbors.

Plus I needed the parking spaces for my multiple cars. If a gang leader only had one mode of transport, were they even successful? Doubtful.

Cass rolled my Harley to a stop in the vacant space beside me, and I noted that Seph's Camaro was back. Which was a good thing, seeing as she should have been asleep hours ago.

"Thanks for dropping Bob home," I grudgingly told Cass as I climbed out of my Corvette and locked it. "You can't come upstairs, though." I arched a brow at him, implying that was what he'd been angling toward.

Despite the number of times Cass had given Seph a safe lift home or kept an eye on her while Zed and I had been away on business, he'd never been inside my apartment. It seemed a bit contradictory that I trusted him to drive with my sister on the back of his bike but not to see our personal space, but it was what it was.

I, for one, wasn't going to go psychoanalyzing my fucked-up damage. That was a job for a very well-paid doctor that I would eventually get around to finding. One day. Probably never. I'd likely get killed before getting a chance to work on my mental health.

Cass didn't seem offended, though. He just arched a brow at me, a tiny crease in his lips as he walked beside me toward the elevator. The doors slid open a moment later, and we stepped inside. I pressed the button for the ground floor—to let him out—then the level for my apartment as well.

"What are you going to do about this angel dust problem?" Cass asked in a quiet voice as the elevator closed us in.

I gave him a sharp look, suspicious. "Whatever I need to do," I replied. "It isn't the first time someone has challenged my authority, and I'll deal with it the same way I always have."

He made a low, thoughtful sound, his jaw twitching with tension. "You can't always shoot your problems, Red."

I scoffed. "Maybe not, but I can damn well try."

The doors slid open to the ground floor lobby, and I waited for Cass to get out. But…he didn't. Instead, he let the doors close again, then hit the emergency stop button.

"What do you think you're doing?" I demanded.

He turned to face me, and I wondered for a moment if he was going to kiss me again. And did I want him to? Yes, so badly yes.

His gaze trailed over me, no doubt taking in my scarlet lipstick, the hint of cleavage from my half-unbuttoned blouse, my tight pencil skirt and deadly stilettos… Then he sighed and ran a hand over his face.

"What is your fucking problem, Cass?" I demanded, reading disapproval in his body language. "You're only attracted to me when I'm in jeans and sneakers? If that's not the definition of judgmental—"

"What?" He cut me off, his scowl deep. "What the fuck makes you think—" He cut himself off with a frustrated snarl. "Forget it."

He smacked his hand against the door release and stomped out into the lobby of my apartment building. For a man of so few words, he sure seemed to be grumbling a hell of a lot of them about me as he walked away. All I managed to catch, though, was *infuriating woman*, and it weirdly made me smile.

Cass thought of me as a woman. Not a rival or associate or even as a *child*. That had to be a step in the right direction, even if our communication sucked big-time.

My phone buzzed with an incoming call as I reached my floor, and I smiled when I saw the caller ID.

"Hey, Demi," I answered, stifling a yawn with my hand. "Bit late for you, isn't it?"

My aunt just chuckled over the phone. "Don't treat me like I'm a geriatric, Hades. Forty-five is the new twenty-one. Didn't you know?"

I chuckled. "My mistake, party girl. What do you have for me?" The only reason my aunt would call so late at night was if she'd just received the information I'd requested or if she had a mess that needed cleaning up. Hopefully, it was the former.

"I'm sending over the file on this Lucas kid now," she told me. "Most things seem to check out. The only fabrications were his date of birth and surname, otherwise he's squeaky clean."

That genuinely surprised me. "Squeaky clean?" I repeated. "Surely not. He must have some hidden gang affiliation or something. There's no way he's just...*normal*."

Demi huffed. "Don't question my researchers, you know they're the best. When I say he's squeaky clean, I mean it. No gang affiliations *at all*, not even two generations back. His dad was a Marine and died when Lucas was two. His mom used to be a ballet teacher but was diagnosed with multiple sclerosis around six years ago. Lucas was just twelve and working his way toward nationals for men's gymnastics but gave it up to look after his mom. Now that he's back in the school system, he's a year behind from all the time he lost trying to homeschool himself. I promise you, he's just a hard-working kid doing his best to care for his single mom."

159

"Huh." I frowned as I unlocked my apartment. "What about this uncle who paid for his schooling and shit? Anything questionable there?"

"Nope," Demi replied with a short laugh. "Probably one of the few longtime residents of Shadow Grove who never once stepped foot on the dark side. Hon, he's clean. Aside from taking a job in *your* club and lying about his age, the boy is an angel. Seriously. You should probably do the world a favor and fire his ass before you corrupt him."

God*dammit*.

Gritting my teeth, I tossed my keys and bag onto the hall table and made my way to my room.

"Are you sure?" I asked again. I'd really thought Demi would uncover some deep, dark secret about Lucas—something that would make it easy for me to completely cut him out of my life for good. Or…out of life in general, depending how bad it was.

"One hundred percent," my aunt replied. "I'm not even going to offer to dig deeper because there *is* no deeper. He's a choirboy. Quit seeing monsters in every shadow, hon." She and her wife were the only people on the planet that were brave enough to call me *hon* like that, but I quietly loved it.

I kicked off my heels and collapsed onto my bed, staring up at the ceiling. "Okay, well…thanks, I guess."

"Anytime, as always. Stacey asked if you and Seph are coming over for dinner on Friday." We had a monthly family dinner, seeing as Demi, Seph, and I were the last of the Timber bloodline.

I let out a small groan. "Not me, not this week. There's some shit going down…" My voice trailed off. Demi was useful as hell and she'd always be a Timber, but since my hostile takeover, she'd no longer been a Timberwolf—by her own choice.

Demi clicked her tongue. "Heard. I'll see Seph, though?"

"Probably," I replied with another yawn. "Just…keep your eyes open, okay? Maybe it wouldn't be a bad idea to go visit that winery of yours in Tuscany."

There was a short pause. "That bad?"

I breathed out, feeling the panic and uncertainty in my gut. "Yeah."

"Well, shit."

I had nothing else to say to that, so I just wished her a good night and ended the call. Then I spent the rest of the night reading and rereading the file she'd sent over on Lucas Wildeboer, eighteen—almost nineteen—year-old dancer, gymnast, and all-around *normal* guy.

Fuck. Demi was right. I was going to corrupt the hell out of him.

CHAPTER 18

By some stroke of luck, I managed to navigate the next few days without too much drama. I mean, Lucas still texted me when he knew he shouldn't, but I'd managed to stay strong and not reply.

I'd also avoided going back to 7th Circle when I knew he would be dancing—I was only so strong—and thanks to having access to his roster, it was easy enough to maintain that avoidance.

Toward the end of the week, I started to suspect I was being followed, and it pissed me right the fuck off.

"Zed," I barked as I strode into the training room at Anarchy. It was our newest venue, just over a year old, and converted from an abandoned amusement park. Now the big top was the arena for wildly popular cage fights, and the fun house was a nightclub that hosted international DJs and performers.

My second was sparring with one of our upper management, Alexi, and they were both wearing nothing but gloves and shorts. Sweat coated their muscles, and the Timberwolf tattoos displayed prominently on their bare skin.

I pulled up short as I got closer, my breath catching in my throat. When was the last time I'd seen Zed stripped down like this? He was…*wow*.

He tapped gloves with Alexi, ending their session, and padded across the mat to where I stood, a curious look on his face.

"What's up, Boss?" he asked, his gaze cautious. It wasn't like me to show up unannounced while he was working out, but the feeling of being tailed was making me all twitchy and short-tempered. I didn't have the patience to leave him a voicemail, knowing his phone was in his bag and wouldn't be checked for another hour.

Alexi gave me a grin and a small salute from across the training ring, and I gave him a tight nod in response. He was a looker, no doubt, and had made it pretty damn clear he was interested in me as more than just a terrifying boss. But I simply wasn't interested. He struck me as a watered-down version of Cass.

"I have a tail," I told Zed in a low voice, not wanting Alexi to overhear. He was a valuable employee, but that was as far as my trust in him went.

Zed gave me a smirk and craned his neck to look at my ass. "Do you? That's new."

"Fuck you, this isn't funny. Someone has been following me since Tuesday." I folded my arms under my breasts and glared. "And whoever it is, they're good at not being caught."

Zed's brows flicked up. "So how do you know you're being followed?"

My eyes narrowed further, and my jaw clenched. "Seriously?"

He gave a one-shouldered shrug while unstrapping his gloves. "Sorry, forgot who I was talking to for a moment. All right, gimme ten minutes to shower." He headed across the training room toward the showers, and I frowned after him. The Timberwolf tattoo covering his whole back flexed as he moved, and I found myself weirdly fascinated by it. Zed was acting...strange.

But then, so was I. My whole vibe had been off all week...but surely that was understandable given the fact that someone was playing at being the ghost of my ex-fiancé.

"Hey, Boss," Alexi said, strolling over to me and snapping me out of my trance. Zed had just disappeared inside the locker room, but I needed to blink a couple of times before refocusing on Alexi. He fucking knew it, too, glancing over his shoulder in the direction I'd been staring, then shooting me a sly grin.

"You got something to say, Alexi?" I asked in a cool don't-fuck-with-me voice.

He quickly shook his head, his smile slipping. "Uh, no, sir. Nope. Just wanted to ask if you're coming to the fight next month."

There was a fight at Anarchy every weekend, but I knew Alexi was talking about our main event of the season. There was a lineup of several hyped-up pairings, and Alexi was fighting Archer. He didn't stand a chance, but it'd be a good show. They both fought professionally within the UFC, so it'd draw a hell of a crowd. Great for liquor sales, even better for laundering money on bets.

"I expect so," I replied with an arched brow. I didn't carry the conversation, and a moment later he awkwardly shifted his weight and scratched the back of his neck.

"Cool," he murmured after a painfully long pause. "Well, I should..." He jerked a thumb in the direction of the lockers. When I said nothing in response, he gave a tight smile and backed away.

When he was out of sight, I let out a sigh and ruffled my fingers through my hair, then anxiously tied it up in a high ponytail with the black rubber band on my wrist. I paced the length of the room about sixteen times before Zed emerged in a pair of fresh shorts, sneakers, and a tank top. His short-cropped hair was glistening wet from the shower, and he smelled of soap and would be hot as hell—if he wasn't Zed.

"Let's go." I whirled on my heel and stalked out of the training gym ahead of him before he could catch me perving like he were a guy I wanted to fuck. Because I didn't. Not anymore, anyway. We'd established the boundaries of our relationship a long-ass time ago, and they didn't include any kind of sexual activity.

"Where are we going?" Zed asked, hurrying to catch up and

walk beside me. The training building was toward the back of the Anarchy complex, so it was a bit of a walk to get back to the parking lot. We'd left the creepy, huge clown face over the main entrance, just cleaned it up a bit and given it a paint job to make it look demonic. I loved it, but I was also one of those sick fucks who wasn't scared of clowns.

I blew out a long breath, thinking. "Let's go to Zanzibar. I'm starving."

"Sounds good to me," Zed agreed, clicking the key fob to his Ferrari. "Meet you there?"

I nodded. "Hang back, though. See if you can spot anyone."

He gave a small shrug like that wasn't likely—and it wasn't—but still did as I asked. Sure enough, I didn't get the feeling anyone was following me too closely on the way to Zanzibar, an upmarket lunch spot with plenty of outdoor seating, but that wasn't shocking. If I had been followed to Anarchy, they had to know I'd gone to get Zed. So they'd know to hang back from *his* car, too.

So either I was officially paranoid or they knew what they were doing. Both options were equally concerning.

After we dropped our cars off at the valet, I requested an outdoor table, and the maître d' showed us to it. Neither Zed nor I spoke until we were seated, and then he arched a brow at me.

"I didn't see anyone," he commented, his voice low and quiet.

I gave a shrug. "They're there. Somewhere."

Zed stared at me for a long moment, then ran a hand over his damp hair and nodded. "Yeah, I bet. They must be pretty good if you haven't pinpointed them yet." It was an observation, not an expression of doubt. Zed knew not to question my gut. Fuck, I hoped my instincts weren't going as screwy as my mood.

Our waitress came back and took our lunch orders, then left us in silence for a bit. Zed just sat back in his chair, casual as fuck despite wearing gym clothes in a fancy restaurant. His eyes were glued to my face, unnerving me as my own gaze scanned the street beside us. I'd asked to sit outside in the hopes of spotting someone watching.

"Stop it," I muttered after a few minutes.

His lips twitched with a smile. "Stop what?"

I gave him a deadpan glare. "Stop staring at me."

"You never used to mind." His tone was even, not betraying any emotion at all. I frowned deeper, and he shrugged. "Or maybe you just never used to notice."

"You're acting so fucking strange at the moment, Zed," I grumbled. "Did the revolving door to your bedroom get stuck or something?"

Amusement flashed over his face, but he didn't reply. Our waitress arrived with a bottle of sparkling water, and Zed took it from her to open and pour, then handed me a glass.

"I think someone made it out of the massacre alive," I told him after a sip of water. "It's the only thing that makes sense here, isn't it?"

He sipped his water, his blue eyes still fixed on my face. "The only thing that *actually* makes sense to me," he murmured, "is that Chase made it out alive. But even that makes no sense. We both saw him die. You fired the damn gun yourself."

My stomach flipped, and I swallowed heavily, reliving the moment I'd looked my fiancé in the eye, then fired *his* Desert Eagle at his head. Yeah. My favorite gun used to belong to Chase. I'd grabbed it in the bloody fight where we'd beaten each other half to death, and it'd seemed like such poetic justice to kill him with his own weapon.

"I feel like I'm losing my fucking mind, Zed," I whispered, hardly believing I was saying the words out loud. "He's been dead five years, and I'm seeing his ghost in every shadow. What the fuck is wrong with me?"

Zed shifted in his seat, and his leg brushed mine under the table. It was probably an accident, but a small part of my brain remembered how he used to do shit like that when Chase was in a mood and verbally abusing me. Zed would touch his ankle to mine or lean his shoulder in to me, small gestures that reminded me he was on my side, that I wasn't alone.

"You're not losing your mind, Hades," he told me, his tone serious and his gaze direct. "But that's what someone wants you to think. They're playing up your biggest fear. That worries me. Who in the fire-breathing fuck knows the only thing the big bad Hades is scared of?"

It was a rhetorical question, but it didn't make me feel any better. No one. No one knew, aside from those I trusted: Zed and Seph. And I had a really hard time believing either my best friend or my little sister were tormenting me and destabilizing my operation.

"Fuck it. I need a vacation." I gave a bitter laugh, and Zed grinned. It was our running joke, that we both badly needed a vacation. Like that was *ever* going to happen. "All right, tell me how the Timber build is going. I saw an email from Charlotte that they had to rethink the lighting for the poker room?"

Zed nodded, then shifted gears into his role as my group's manager. He ran me through all the progress and changes on our new build, then gave me recaps of how all the other bars were running.

By the time we'd finished our meals, my head was pounding with a stress headache. While Zed had talked, I'd scrutinized what felt like every single man, woman, and child within my line of sight and found no one suspicious—or everyone suspicious. But I was no closer to putting a face on my tail.

"Are you going to Demi's for dinner tonight?" Zed asked as he paid our bill, knowing my schedule better than I did.

I shook my head. "Not tonight. I don't want to go bringing unnecessary attention to them." I chewed the edge of my scarlet thumbnail, and Zed tugged my wrist to stop me. "I'll send Seph over, but I told Demi to book a trip with Stacey and get out of town for a bit."

Zed grimaced but gave an understanding nod. "Maybe they should take Seph with them."

I wrinkled my nose. "You know that's not an option." Because if my sister was halfway around the world, how could I protect her? It was why I'd never *actually* send her to boarding school like I kept threatening to do.

"I know," Zed murmured, not sounding thrilled, but at least he understood. "Well, get some sleep or something. I can throw a guard on your building if you'd like."

We'd just reached the entrance to the restaurant and handed our tickets to the valet, so I turned to him with an arched brow. "I think I've got my own security handled, thanks, Zed."

He rolled his eyes. "I didn't mean… Never mind. Oh look, your boyfriend is here."

I scowled at him in confusion, then turned to see what he was looking at. Part of me thought I'd see Lucas there; then I needed to ask why the fuck I associated Lucas with the word *boyfriend*. That was a train of thought I didn't want to pursue. But nonetheless, I was surprised to see Cass striding down the sidewalk toward us.

"Not my fucking boyfriend," I muttered under my breath to Zed, and he snorted a laugh.

"Hades," Cass rumbled as he approached, his face like stone. "Bad news."

Great. Just what I needed.

CHAPTER 19

Cass wasn't exaggerating when he said he had bad news. As much as I might have hoped he'd tracked me down just because he wanted to see me, that simply wasn't the case. He came bearing more information about whoever was using my name logo for their angel-dust distribution.

I didn't want to discuss business on the side of the road and I didn't want to wait until we got somewhere more private, so when my car rolled up to the valet, I told him to get in. Zed looked less than impressed—there wasn't space for him to join us in my two-seater car—but I called him and put the phone on speaker so I wouldn't need to repeat everything later.

"The Wraith weasel that I've been squeezing for information finally cracked," Cass told me when he slid into the passenger seat of my Corvette.

"I didn't realize you had anyone left to squeeze," I murmured, pulling out of the valet area and merging into traffic. I'd stayed out of it; the Reapers' takeover of the Wraiths, after I'd shot Skate a week earlier, was nothing to involve myself in. But I had kept my ears open, and I knew that Cass and his guys had been *brutal* in cleaning house.

He made a growly sound. "They weren't all two-faced, disloyal bastards. Just most of them."

I quirked a smile at him, then realized what I'd done and turned my attention back to the road. That was one of the major reasons I'd kept my feelings for Cass to myself for so long. The second I let myself explore the possibility of a romance with him, I would no longer hold him to the same standards as all the other gang leaders under my purview.

Then again, if I was being totally honest, I'd been giving Cass preferential treatment for *years*—well before he took over the Reapers from Zane D'Ath.

"So, your snitch started singing?" Zed asked from my phone speaker, and I cleared my throat. I'd forgotten he was listening for a second there.

"He did," Cass replied with a twist of distaste to his mouth. "But too fucking late. Couple of Skate's guys coming back to town from an East Coast weapons deal got jumped about an hour ago. Bastards never even saw it coming. Turned up to the money drop and got shot full of lead."

"Could have been any opportunistic fuck taking advantage of the Wraiths' dissolution," Zed offered, not sounding like he believed that for a second.

Cass huffed. "Coulda. Except there was a message left beside their bodies, drawn in blood on the concrete." He pulled his own phone out to open a picture and held it out for me to see.

I stomped my foot on the brake pedal, then snatched the phone from his hand to zoom in.

"Motherfucker," I hissed.

"Let me guess," Zed drawled on speakerphone. "Darling?"

I was too angry to reply and instead just tossed the phone back to Cass and accelerated once more.

"I don't know what 'Darling' means," Cass said cautiously, his eyes glued to the side of my face as I drove, "but I'm gonna go out on a limb and assume this means something to you both."

A slightly hysterical laugh bubbled up in my throat, and I swallowed it down, coughing lightly as I shook my head. "Yeah, something like that. Anything else?"

Cass scowled, clearly pissed that I wasn't clueing him in. "Nothing. Just that they didn't even take the money, just shot the Wraiths full of holes, left that calling card, and disappeared. No one has any leads."

"Of course not," I said with a sigh.

"Text me the address," Zed ordered. "I'll check it out."

Cass made a noise that I assumed meant "Absolutely, sending it to you now!" Zed ended the call a moment later, leaving me trapped in a small space with Cass.

"Where did you leave your bike?" I asked after a long silence. "I'll drop you off."

He didn't reply for a handful of breaths, just stared at the side of my face until I cracked and glanced over at him in irritation.

"Just pull over here," he told me in a rumble.

I quirked a brow but shrugged and pulled over onto the shoulder. We were in a middle-class suburban neighborhood, but whatever. I wasn't even remotely in the mood to play chauffeur, so the sooner I got him out of my car, the better.

He didn't get out, though. Of course not, that would have been far too cooperative.

I let out a sigh and swung my head around to face him, only to get myself snared in his intense-as-fuck stare. Like he was trying to mentally strip away my *Hades* shell to see what was underneath.

"Was there something else, Cass? Because I have shit to deal with."

"Yeah," he replied, "there is. I wanna know what you're hiding."

I barked a sharp laugh. "You're joking, right? Get the fuck out of my car, Cass."

He just glared. "Nope."

My brows raised, and my glare turned glacial. "Excuse me?"

He folded his huge arms over his chest and got comfy in his seat, visibly settling in for a long argument. That motherfucker knew he was too damn heavy for me to physically kick out of the car, and we'd already established the fact that I didn't want to shoot him. Not for real.

"You heard me, Red," he growled. "I'm not getting out until you tell me what the fuck is going on."

Anger burned through me at his demand. Who the hell did he think he was dealing with?

"Cass—" I started, my voice like death.

"Hades," he replied, cutting me off. "I'm not going to blow smoke and placate you here. I'm asking you to trust me and let me help. Something bad is going down, and you know more than you're telling me."

I scoffed. "No shit. Last I checked, you're not on my list of trusted confidants, Cassiel. Just because I want you to throw me around your bedroom a bit doesn't mean I trust you. Sex and trust don't automatically go hand in hand. You should know that." Yeah, I was taking a jab at his reputation of using women like they were disposable. I'd had more than one of my strippers sob her eyes out after catching his eye for a night, only to be sent home in the early hours of the morning.

His dark gaze heated. Then he gave a small nod and seemed to be thinking. "All right. Let's go. Lexington Six."

I froze. Lexington Six was the name of the building he lived in, along with a handful of other upper-level Reapers and their families.

"You want me to drive you home?" I was confused. Okay, so I wasn't totally confused. I just wanted him to spell it the fuck out so there was no misunderstanding.

He gave me a droll look. "No, I want to give you what you

172

fucking want so maybe you can start thinking with your brain instead of your cunt. Clearly you need it."

Stunned didn't even begin to describe what I felt at that statement. So, after blinking at him like a possum in headlights for a moment, I shook my head, pulled my gun, and pointed it at his head.

"Get the fuck out, Cass."

He cocked one brow. "No."

I flicked the safety off with my thumb, my stare hard and uncompromising. "Get the fuck out. Apparently, kissing you has provided you a false sense of security. I will *not* be spoken to like that. Not from a lover and certainly not from a subordinate. Right now you're only one of those, and you're goddamn close to becoming neither. Get. Out."

He stared at me for a long, tense moment. I didn't blink, though, and I didn't back down. If that was how he treated women he was interested in, it was no fucking wonder he was still single.

Eventually, though, he backed down. His gaze flicked away from mine, and he let out a heavy sigh. Then he scrubbed a tattooed hand over his scruffy stubble and muttered a curse under his breath.

"You're right," he mumbled. "I shouldn't have said that. I apologize, Hades." His tone was all resigned professionalism that cut me deeper than his crass offer to fuck me just now.

I put my gun away, giving a bitter laugh. He hadn't done what I'd asked; he was still sitting in my car. But he'd backed down first, and that was what counted.

"Fuck you, Cass," I said softly. "You blow so hot and cold I can't keep up. What the fuck was all that the other day? Kissing me, then backing the hell off? You're too damn old for stupid games."

He grunted a sound of agreement. "Exactly. I'm too damn old."

I gave him a hard side-eye. "You clearly think I'm stupider than I look if you believe I'm buying that bullshit."

Cass shifted in his seat, turning slightly to face me. "You're right, that is bullshit. You wanna know the truth?"

I narrowed my eyes. "No, Cass, I enjoy being lied to. It's so much more fun this way." Sarcasm dripped from every word, and he just waited patiently. "Yes," I snarled after a moment, "I want to know."

He gave a nod. "Then tell me what that pattern was beside the Wraiths' bodies. Trust me with something."

My heart raced so hard I could have sworn it was bruising my ribs, and my palms sweated. But I didn't let any of that panic show on my face as I considered his request. He wanted me to *trust* him... and deep down I did want to.

I ran a quick risk assessment of sharing that one detail, then ultimately decided there was no real risk. Sooner or later, I would need his help. I could already sense that whoever was attacking us wouldn't stop at being a small-time nuisance.

"It means 'Darling,'" I told him after a painfully long silence between us. "It's my middle name. Zed designed the logo a long time ago."

Cass's brows flicked up a fraction, then dropped into a scowl. "Why leave it beside these bodies?"

I drew a deep breath, then let it out slowly. "It's a message to me. We think all these little attacks are somehow retaliation for Chase's death."

Cass didn't say anything immediately, running his hand over his stubbled chin as he thought this new information over, frowning all the while.

"Chase Lockhart?" he asked. "He died with the rest of your father's men, didn't he?"

I jerked a nod. Cass and I hadn't met until after I'd taken over the Timberwolves. He probably had no idea just how deep the Lockharts had been mixed up with my father. He also didn't know about my history with Chase.

"We were engaged," I admitted, then snapped my mouth shut. So much for just offering up one innocent, hard-to-bite-me-in-the-ass piece of information.

That seemed to shock Cass more than anything. "You were only eighteen," he said, and I shrugged. I wasn't suddenly spilling my guts about my damaged fucking upbringing to him now that we were having a rare moment of open communication.

"So?" I prompted. "Your turn. What's your deal?"

His gaze swung back to mine, and I just *knew* he was going to lie to me.

"I'm not attracted to you," he said, his voice a flat growl. "You're too young for me."

I held his unblinking stare for a moment, my expression frozen in a blank mask to hide the way disappointment crashed through my chest. Truth or not, those words hurt more than I'd have liked them to.

"Go work on your damage with a professional, Cass," I told him in a cool voice. "I've got enough shit to deal with." I looked away from him, turning my attention to the road ahead as I turned the engine back on.

There was no mistaking the dismissal, and a second later Cass popped his door open and climbed out without another word.

I peeled away from the curb before his door had even fully closed, feeling the unfamiliar and unwelcome burn of unshed tears at the backs of my eyeballs.

Fuck that, though. No freaking way was I wasting tears on a lying man when I hadn't cried in over ten years.

So, I did what I always did. I compartmentalized. Took those painful, barbed feelings of hurt and disappointment and rejection, then stuffed them into a little mental box, locked it, and threw away the fucking key.

Cass could kiss my goddamn ass. I wasn't wasting another second on him.

CHAPTER 20

By the time I got home, I was calm. Detached and drained, but calm. Seph's car was in the parking lot, and I let out a small sigh of relief. My little sister was such a bubbly little ray of sunshine that she could make me smile no matter how sour my mood. I called in an order for her favorite Chinese food from the restaurant around the corner, even though it was still early. My lunch with Zed had been late, but the argument with Cass had left me hollow inside, so I could use the MSG in my stomach.

I could only hope she wasn't going to be gushing all over Lucas again, like she had been all damn week. As if it wasn't hard enough deleting his messages and declining his calls. To be safe, though, I'd changed his contact in my phone to something more anonymous.

As the elevator carried me up to our floor, I tugged my hair tie out and fluffed my hair, feeling the relief from tension on my scalp.

When the doors opened to my hallway, I kicked my heels off and picked them up to walk barefoot down to my door. The biometric scanner read my fingerprint and gave a soft bleep as it unlocked for me, and I yawned as I entered the apartment.

"Seph!" I called out as I closed the door and tossed my shoes on the carpet near the hall table. "I'm home! I ordered Chinese. Is it too early for dinner?"

I glanced around, not seeing her, but figured she was probably in her room. So I went to the kitchen to pour a glass of wine.

"Hey!" My sister appeared from around the corner, where our second living area was located. The area had a massive ninety-inch flat screen TV and a huge suede couch that was way too easy to fall asleep on. "Dare, you're not usually home this early on a Friday. Shouldn't you be at the clubs?"

She was acting weird. Her eyes were too wide and her cheeks flushed.

I squinted at her suspiciously. "I wasn't in the mood," I replied. "Why are you…" I gasped. "Do you have a boy here?"

Seph's brows shot up, her lips parting but no sound exiting her mouth.

"Oh my god, Seph!" I shouted, automatically pulling my gun out. "You brought a boy home? Here? What the hell were you thinking?"

Panic flashed over her face, but it was gone in an instant and her chin tilted up in a familiar, stubborn set.

"I was thinking that this is *my home* and I'm allowed to invite my friends over just like any other teenage girl. You always go on about me having a *normal* life? Well, *normal* girls can invite people home and not have their sister pull a fucking gun on them!" Her pretty face was all hard edges, and she balled her fists at her sides, refusing to back down. Fucker. She got that from me.

I ground my teeth together, desperately seeking the patience to actually have a discussion with my sister and not just throw my scary-ass weight around. That—I knew from experience—got me nowhere with her.

"Seph, you don't fucking get it," I growled. "You have no idea how dangerous—"

"Oh my god, Dare." She cut me off, giving a bitter laugh.

"Don't even start on that shit. We're *constantly* in danger. We have been every damn day since you killed Dad. At some point, you have to just let me live my own life and not helicopter parent the fuck outta me."

I reeled back, stunned at the resentment in her voice. But she had no clue what had really sparked the war between me and our father. She had *no idea* how close she'd been to being sold as a thirteen-year-old sex slave to a Saudi billionaire.

So instead of arguing with her, I shoved her aside and went to find whatever brain-dead, suicidal fuckboy had accepted her invitation to come home with her. Because there was no way in hell her cheeks were all flushed like that from an innocent study session with a girlfriend.

"Dare! Stop!" Seph shrieked, grabbing my arm to try to pull me back. "You're acting totally insane! Just leave me the fuck alone and stop trying to ruin my life!"

I had nothing to say to that, so I just rolled my eyes and shook her off. I didn't give two shits if she thought I was ruining her life because I knew better. I knew what the alternative would have been if I hadn't intervened, and I wouldn't wish that fate on my worst enemy, let alone the one person I loved more than anything in the world.

Seph continued yelling at me about how I was the worst sister in the whole world as I marched through to the living room and confronted her "study buddy" on the couch. But I pulled up short when I saw actual schoolbooks and art supplies scattered all over the floor...then laid eyes on the *boy* she'd brought home.

Fucking hell.

"Lucas," I gritted out from behind clenched teeth. "Fancy seeing *you* here."

He met my glare unflinchingly, the corners of his lush lips kicking up. "Oh hey, Dare, right? You have a lovely home here."

That little *shit*. I tucked my gun away because I really wasn't planning on shooting Lucas anytime soon, and there was no way he could be scared off like the other spineless bastards in Seph's school.

"What the fuck are you doing here?" I snapped, not caring how rude I sounded. Seph was the only one who was going to freak out over my apparent lack of manners; Lucas already knew he was in huge trouble.

My sister interceded, though, stepping in front of me and glaring up at me with her face flaming red. "He's my project partner for art class," she snarled. "I told you that the other day. Now seriously, screw off and let us finish this assignment in peace." Her eyes said everything else, like how she was so mad at me she was thinking about cutting my hair off in my sleep or some messed-up prank shit like that.

I looked past her, though, cocking a brow at Lucas like I could silently demand to know what he thought he was going to achieve here. But he didn't look even *slightly* fazed by how angry I was.

Dude had balls for days.

So, I rapidly changed tack. I shrugged, then smiled at my sister. "Sure thing. Wouldn't want to interfere with your grades."

Lucas's eyes narrowed slightly, and I knew I'd thrown him off. About fucking time.

Seph squinted at me with suspicion, but I just started on my way back to the kitchen before snapping my fingers like I'd just remembered something. "Oh, don't forget Demi is expecting you for dinner. So, you know, maybe wrap this up quickly." I indicated to their school supplies, then shot Seph a smile. "Have fun!"

She glared harder, mouthing *fuck you* at me, but I maintained my smile and left the living area in search of wine. I needed it more now than ever, that was for damn sure.

Back in the kitchen, I found myself hovering. I *should* have taken my wine and retreated to my room or something. Or, really, I should have tossed Lucas out on his ass. Yet instead, I found myself lurking in the kitchen and straining my ears to listen in on what they were talking about.

As badly as I wanted to tell myself I was just trying to protect Seph, I couldn't deny the fact that I wanted to know if he was flirting with her. Was he leading my little sister on? If he was, I'd kill him. No one messed around with her heart and lived.

But part of me was really, *really* hoping it actually was the innocent study session Seph was making it out to be. I wanted Lucas not to be a douchebag. I had enough of those in my life already.

For the most part, they kept their voices low enough that I couldn't make out the words. Every time Seph giggled, though, I tensed up with anger and…something *else*.

After about fifteen minutes and a couple of sips of wine, I forced myself to go into my room and change out of my skintight black jeans and formfitting black bodysuit. When I returned to the kitchen in a pair of yoga pants and a loose tank top, I found Lucas getting himself a glass of water at the sink.

Gritting my teeth, I slid back onto the barstool at the counter, where I'd left my wine, and opened my laptop, which I'd grabbed from my room.

Lucas turned the tap off, then leaned his ass against the counter as he took a long sip from his glass. Fucker.

Ignoring him, I raised my own glass to my lips and took a mouthful of the light, fruity Sangiovese I'd chosen. I placed my glass down again, and Lucas leaned over the island to pick it up.

My gaze flicked up, catching on his as he brought my wineglass to his mouth and drank from it. Holy fuck, that was sexy. It shouldn't have been, but somehow my mouth went dry and my panties went…well…*not* dry.

"Mmm," he hummed, licking his lips way too damn sexily. "What's that one?"

I drew a deep breath, rolling his seemingly innocent question around my brain. I knew full well what he was doing, though—reminding me how I'd introduced him to Barolo last time he'd been in my kitchen.

"Sangiovese," I replied, my voice low so Seph didn't come running to save Lucas from her big bad sister.

He took another sip, his eyes still locked on mine. "It's delicious."

I gave him a cool smile. "I'll be sure to send you a bottle when you're of legal drinking age."

He gave a soft laugh, placing my glass back down and running his hand through his hair. The move was *so* calculated, tugging his loose Shadow Prep shirt up and showing off those mouthwatering lower abs.

"What are you doing here, Lucas?" I asked in a near whisper. "The fuck do you think you're going to achieve by leading my sister on?"

His gaze flicked over my shoulder in the direction of the living room, and then he leaned his elbows on the counter opposite me. His shirt was rolled up to the elbows, revealing those strongly muscled forearms, and his eyes were intense.

"I'm not leading her on, Hayden," he whispered back, his tone earnest. "I've made it crystal clear that I'm not interested in being anything more than friends with her. She's just not hearing me."

I huffed. That did sound like Seph, especially with how much she'd gone *on and on* about Lucas all week.

"Trust me," he continued, his low voice full of sincerity. "I would never mess anyone around like that. But when she asked me to come over after school and work on our project..." He gave a shrug as if to say *What's a guy to do?*

I shook my head slowly, astounded at his tenacity after I'd all but ghosted him all week. "Lucas..." I said his name on a tired exhale and let my voice trail off when his fingers wove together with mine on the countertop. His touch was pure electricity, and I swallowed the protests I'd been about to make.

"I needed to see you again," he murmured. "You're all I can

think about. That kiss in your office the other night… I know you want me too."

I couldn't even deny that fact.

"Lucas?" Seph called out, and I jerked my hand free of his a split second before she came into view. "Oh. I wondered what was taking you so long…" She gave me a hard glare, and I just met her gaze with bored eyes as I took a sip of my wine.

Lucas's eyes flicked to my mouth as I rested the glass between my lips. Then he straightened up and gave Seph a bland, friendly smile. "I just got caught up talking to your sister," he told her with a small shrug. "Sorry I kept you waiting."

"Uh…" Seph's suspicious gaze bounced between the two of us, and my stomach twisted with guilt. Then she gave him a bright smile and batted her lashes a couple of times. "No worries. I hope she was being polite." Her hard look told me she didn't for a second believe I'd been remotely polite, but whatever. I'd rather she think I was threatening him than know the truth.

"Of course," Lucas replied with a sly smirk in my direction. "Actually, she was just offering to drive me home so you're not late to that dinner thing. I think my place is on the other side of town."

He was guessing, I could tell, but he was also right. It was an easy enough guess, considering how the wealth of Shadow Grove was split up into distinct neighborhoods.

Seph looked stunned for a moment, giving me a confused frown. "Oh. Uh…that's *nice* of you, Dare."

I gave her a tight smile in return. "Yep." Because I couldn't exactly call Lucas out for lying, could I? Not if I didn't want my sister to find out Lucas and I were more than *friendly* already.

"We should probably finish this project then," she said to him, jerking her thumb toward the living room.

Lucas just picked up his glass of water and followed her. Not before he shot me a mischievous wink, though. God*damn*, he was trouble.

CHAPTER 21

Seph and Lucas probably spent another half an hour on their home-work, and I forced myself to stay in the kitchen and not send Seph to Demi's early on some bullshit excuse.

Zed called me during that time, letting me know that the SGPD had been making a nuisance of themselves in several of our venues tonight, spot-checking IDs of patrons—no one's idea of a good time—and questioning the bar staff about whether they knew about any illegal activity within the premises.

Not a single one of my employees would ever rat out the Timberwolves, but it didn't make the whole thing any less irritating.

"We need to get our hold back on them," I told Zed when he finished his verbal report. "It's becoming inconvenient to have the cops working for someone else."

He grunted a sound of agreement. "No shit. Life was a hell of a lot easier a year ago when they could simply be paid to look the other way."

"It's a challenge to my authority, Zed," I muttered, picking at a hole in the hem of my tank top. "Sooner or later, people will start noticing. Then we're going to be back at square one, defending what's ours against greedy bastards looking to expand."

He let out a sigh on the other end of the phone. "Agreed. So what do we do?"

I chewed the edge of my nail, thinking about his question. "Grab one of them and make him squeal. One of the higher-ups that used to take payouts from Charon, preferably. There's no way those slime buckets suddenly turned into model citizens."

"Yes, sir," Zed replied with an edge of amusement. "I'll get Alexi and his guys on it, and I'll call with an update when we know more."

"Good. Don't hold back." I ended the call with an internal scream of frustration, tossed my phone onto the counter, and pressed my forehead to the marble. Just over the course of my conversation with Zed, a blinding headache had built up behind my eyes, and I wanted nothing more than to hit something. Maybe I needed to drop down to KJ-Fit, my local training gym, and beat the ever-loving crap out of some wannabe MMA fighters to burn off some steam.

The sound of my little sister's voice made me lift my head back up from the counter, though.

"You sure?" she was asking. "It's really not that far out of my way, and my aunt Demi won't mind if I'm late for dinner."

"Yes, she will," I snapped, my irritation temporarily disabling my filter. "Besides, Lucas and I need to have a chat on the way home. Don't we?"

I kept my tone flat and hard. Seph would assume I wanted to threaten him into leaving her alone, and I was going to let her think that. Better she think he was scared off by her violent, borderline-sociopathic sister than suspect the truth behind his disinterest.

Then again, there's no way she would think he was unavailable because of me. Hell, even I barely believed it, and I was involved.

"Absolutely," Lucas agreed with an easy smile. "I'll see you in class on Monday, Seph."

She glared daggers at me, silently demanding I not scare him off, but I just stared back at her unblinking. "Ask Demi how her travel plans are going while you're there," I told her, a not-so-subtle push to leave.

Seph scowled. "You're not coming down to the parking level with me?"

"I need to change," I told her, lying as easily as I breathed. "I have to stop by Club 22 later to check on things."

She hesitated a moment longer, then gave a frustrated little sound and grabbed her keys from the hall table. The door slammed after her, but I didn't move from my stool until I was sure she must be in the elevator.

"So, you need to get changed?" Lucas murmured, stepping up behind me and trailing his fingertips ever so gently down my bare arms. It sent shivers chasing across my skin, and I swallowed the sigh that wanted to escape at his touch. "I can probably lend a hand with that. Or…with the *un*dressing part, anyway." He brushed my hair away from one shoulder and dropped his lips to my neck.

I let out a low chuckle, hiding how turned on he was already getting me. "I'm not fucking you, Lucas. I just didn't want Seph getting her hopes up that you might kiss her in the car. This way you have a convincing reason to decline all her offers in the future. She's used to me chasing away her admirers."

He gripped the seat of my stool and spun me around, then placed his hands on the counter to either side of me.

"I'm not one of her admirers, though," he told me with a small grin. "I'm one of *yours*, Dare."

"Don't call me that," I told him with a frown. "Only Seph calls me that."

Lucas inclined his head in acknowledgment. "Fair enough. I prefer Hayden, anyway."

I rolled my eyes, not pushing the issue on that one. I liked the sound of my name in his mouth.

"I'm still not fucking you, Lucas." My voice lacked the hard

185

edge of *Hades*, though. Hell, not even I believed me, so it was no great shock when he didn't immediately back away.

That was one of the major things that kept drawing me back to Lucas. He didn't let me push him around. He didn't let me push him *away*. He knew what he wanted, and he wasn't afraid to go balls to the wall in pursuing it.

In this case, what he wanted…was *me*.

"Because of my age?" he asked in a low murmur, his tone coaxing and seductive. "I never picked you as one for conforming to societal expectations, Hayden. Besides, I turn nineteen in a month. That'll make you only four years older."

I glared back at him, entranced by the gorgeous emerald depths of his eyes. "You're still in high school, Lucas."

He shrugged. "So? I bet you've dated older guys before. What difference does it make?"

Cass flashed across my mind, and then I remembered how Chase had been three years older than me. We'd been officially engaged before I'd even turned fifteen—entirely due to our fathers' manipulation. Or mine, at the very least.

So yeah, Lucas had a point. He wasn't a child; he'd made that all too clear. If he was old enough to go looking for a job in a whorehouse like Swinging Dick's, then who the fuck was I to split hairs?

"This isn't a game, Lucas. You can't even *begin* to imagine how dangerous it is being close to me. People would hurt you, use you, betray you…just to get to me. You don't need that shit in your life." It was a last-ditch effort because with every passing second I was less convinced that he was a bad idea.

"I'm willing to take that risk," he replied without even a moment's hesitation. He had *no* idea what he was neck-deep in— that much was painfully clear.

"Seph likes you," I told him softly. "I can't hurt my sister. Not for anything."

He gave a slow headshake and a small smile. "But I don't like her. Not like that. No one can even come close to what I feel for you, not since the moment I laid eyes on you last weekend, Hayden."

Internal groan. Where did he learn those smooth moves? He was like a fictional character, for fuck's sake.

"Just give me a chance," he pleaded, echoing what he'd said in my office earlier in the week. "Please, just give me one chance to convince you that this *isn't* a bad idea, that I could be exactly what you need in your life. Someone with no ulterior motive. Someone who sees the real you." He paused, wetting his lips as my heart pounded hard in my chest. "No one ever needs to know. I can be discreet, and I won't tell a soul."

Jesus *Christ*. Why did that turn me on so hard? Maybe it was just the way he leaned in to me as he spoke, like we were being pulled together by a magnetic force.

"You want to be my dirty little secret, Lucas?" I couldn't fight the smile creeping over my lips as I said this.

He raised one brow in a facial shrug. "If that's what it takes? Yes. I want *you*, Hayden. In whatever way you're offering." He paused and grimaced. "Even if it is just to kill time until that big scary tattooed fuck from the other night comes to his senses."

My brows shot up in surprise. I hadn't realized Lucas was paying attention to Cass while he was onstage. Or that he'd accurately guessed who it was that'd had me all tied up in knots this week.

I drew a deep breath, knowing I needed to send him home. Nothing good could come from me caving now. Demi's warning echoed through my mind about corrupting a genuinely nice, normal guy, and I started to shake my head.

Lucas wasn't giving up so easily, though. He leaned in, his lips capturing mine in a smolderingly hot kiss before I could come up with any more weak excuses for why I should *not* give him a chance.

I kissed him back, letting him sweep me up in his arms and carry me halfway to my room before I managed to pry my lips free.

"Lucas, this is—"

"A fucking fantastic idea," he growled, finishing my statement the way he wanted it to end. "I'm not asking for forever, Hayden. Just a chance. You carry so much weight on your shoulders... Let me be an outlet for all that stress, beautiful. I could be your lighthouse if you let me."

My heart pounded so hard in my chest it hurt, and I saw nothing but sincerity in his face. I groaned.

"Fuck it," I muttered, then tightened my legs around his waist and crushed my lips back to his once more.

Then the doorbell rang.

"Ignore it," Lucas suggested, still walking with me wrapped around his waist until he reached the edge of my enormous bed. He lowered me down with staggeringly impressive control and strength, his mouth against my throat the whole time, sucking and biting my skin and probably leaving his mark.

The doorbell rang again, then another time in quick succession, and I groaned.

"Fucking hell," I muttered, "I have to get that. It's my Chinese delivery. I'd forgotten Seph was going out for dinner tonight and ordered for her."

Lucas pulled back far enough to give me a puzzled look, his lips puffy from kissing me already. "Are you hungry?"

I grinned. "Not really, but he won't go away without being paid. Trust me, he's a stubborn old goat."

Lucas stared at me a moment, like he was trying to work out if I was serious or not, then gave a quick nod. "I'll get it," he told me, rising from the bed. "You stay *right* there."

A laugh slipped past my lips as he raced out of my bedroom, but I was stunned enough not to argue until it was too late. He was already opening my front door, paying Linoel, the delivery man, and running—*actually* running—back through to my bedroom.

It was stupid. He should have had better sense than to answer my door. I bet he hadn't even checked the video feed before opening it. Someone could have shot him, just like that. Then again, Lucas easily had the worst sense of danger of anyone I'd ever met, so it shouldn't have been surprising.

"You shouldn't have done that," I told him as he kicked my bedroom door shut behind him. He wasn't carrying the food, so he must have dropped it on the kitchen counter on his way past.

He gave a small shrug. "No big deal. I made almost four grand in tips this week."

I groaned and flopped back onto the mattress, my hands covering my face. "That's not what I meant," I replied, my voice muffled by my hands.

The mattress dipped as he knelt on it. Then his warm hands slipped under my tank top, raising it up so he could kiss my stomach.

"I know," he murmured, sounding serious, "but if your Chinese delivery guy wanted to commit murder, I'd rather he shoot me than you."

Oh dear god. Who even was Lucas Wildeboer?

I moved my hands away from my face so I could look down at him, and he just smirked as he kissed my stomach and teased the waistband of my yoga pants.

"Fucking hell," I whispered, "you're still in your school uniform, Lucas."

His brows hitched. "That's easily fixed."

Oh yeah, Lucas was a stripper in his spare time. It really shouldn't have surprised me how effortlessly he shed his clothes all the way down to a pair of tight black boxer briefs that deliciously outlined his huge erection.

"Better?" he asked with a wicked grin.

"Much," I murmured, trying really fucking hard not to drool.

It was easy to see how I'd accepted him as twenty-one when he was near-naked. Lucas had the body of a man, not a boy.

He took that as the permission it was intended as, returning his mouth to mine as he helped relieve me of my own clothes. After my panties hit the floor, Lucas gripped me by the waist and slid me further up the bed, then grinned as he lay between my spread legs with one of my thighs resting on his broad shoulder.

"This is such a bad idea," I whispered as his long fingers stroked the length of my throbbing pussy.

Lucas's response was to slide two fingers inside me, then stroke along my inner walls as he dragged them back like he was summoning a fucking genie or something.

"Holy Christ," I groaned as he stroked a spot that made my body quake.

He grinned wider at my response, then tentatively lowered his face to my cunt. It took him all of about three seconds to find my clit, and then my whole world exploded into stars and rainbows and shit.

Between his fingers and his mouth, he delivered, hands down, the best oral sex I'd ever experienced. I came twice before literally *begging* him to fuck me properly.

He shifted our positions, rising up to his knees and lifting my ass up off the bed to meet his hard cock, which already glistened with precum as he lined us up. As soaking as I already was, it only took one firm thrust for him to fill me completely, and he let out a low moan. His teeth gripped his lower lip, and his eyes squeezed tight shut for a breath. Then a delirious smile creased his face as his long lashes flicked open once more.

"You feel incredible," he whispered in a husky voice before swiping his tongue over his lower lip and moaning. "And taste incredible. I'm so fucking addicted to you, Hayden."

I had nothing to say back to that because quite truthfully...the feeling was mutual. So instead of replying out loud, I hooked my arms up around his neck and pulled myself up to sitting, straddling him with his dick impaling me in the best possible way.

Our lips met smoothly, like he was already living inside my brain, and he let me push him back onto the mattress. I wanted to return the favor and blow his fucking mind with my mouth, but first…first I needed to get off on his dick. Just once.

Okay, fine. Maybe twice.

His hand found my breast as I rode him, cupping and squeezing it, and then he did one of those panty-melting ab curls to suck my nipple into his mouth.

His teeth scraped over my sensitive flesh, and his other hand gripped my hip hard, urging me to go faster, to fuck him harder. It was maddening and before long I was screaming as I came again. This time, though, I got the satisfaction of seeing his jaw clench and his eyes close while my cunt pulsed and tightened around his dick.

"Hayden, oh my fuck," Lucas groaned, his breath coming in short gasps. "You're gonna make me come any second…"

"Good." Laughing, I climbed off him and ran my hands down his unbelievable body until I gripped his slick cock. "Come in my mouth."

At his sharp inhale, I closed my lips around his tip, tasting my own pleasure as I sucked him. His fingers threaded into my hair, encouraging me to take him deeper, and I obliged. To a point. The rest of him could remain in my hand because even with no gag reflex, I wasn't a damn snake.

Small moans and whispered curses fell from his lips as I sucked him off, and it was only a matter of moments before his body jerked and tensed, and then his hot seed spurted down my throat.

I waited until his grip on my hair relaxed, then wiped my mouth on the back of my hand before collapsing on the mattress beside him, breathing heavily.

We lay there in near silence for a bit, and then he rolled onto his side to face me and cupped my face with one callused hand.

He didn't speak, though, just stared at me while his thumb stroked a gentle path over my cheek, then traced the outline of my lips.

It was such a featherlight caress. I let my eyes close and breathed out all my stress on a long exhale. He'd been more right than he even knew when he'd said I needed someone like him. Someone separate from everything else.

A lighthouse in the wild storm that was my life.

CHAPTER 22

"Dare! You here? I'm home!" Seph's voice jerked me awake, and I sat up with a panicked gasp. I hadn't meant to fall asleep and certainly not all curled up naked in Lucas's embrace.

My eyes flew to my bedroom door as I remembered that we definitely *hadn't* locked it and my sister had no sense of personal space.

Fuck.

"Lucas," I hissed, shaking him awake.

He blinked up at me, all sleepy and gorgeous, and a euphoric smile crossed his face when he saw me. It was the kind of smile that made my pulse race and my chest tighten. The sort of look that said he was already falling way too damn hard for a fuckup like me.

"Sorry, I fell asleep," he murmured, his voice thick with sleep.

"Yeah," I whispered, "me too. But Seph just got home, and you need to hide. Like, right fucking now." I slid out of bed as I spoke, hunting my floor for some underwear. I tossed his boxers at him as he scrambled out the other side, then I pointed at my walk-in closet.

"Dare!" Seph called out again. "Why is there untouched Chinese on the counter?"

The handle on my bedroom door twisted, and I gathered up Lucas's school uniform and threw it into the closet with him at lightning speed, then pulled the door shut and tossed a robe on.

"What..." Seph frowned at me, her eyes suspicious as I belted my robe and tried to slow my breathing. "What are you doing?"

"Me?" I replied, folding my arms under my breasts defensively. "What are *you* doing? You know closed doors generally mean someone wants privacy, don't you? What if I was asleep?"

She wrinkled her nose. "Your light was on. I could see it under the door when I came in. What *were* you doing?" Her gaze traveled over me, then snapped to the bed, and she gasped dramatically.

"Oh my god!" she squealed. "You had a guy over! No fucking wonder you wanted me to go to Aunt Demi's so bad!"

I looked at the bed, cringing inwardly at the way both sides of the blanket had been tossed back. "No, I didn't," I lied. "I just didn't make my bed this morning."

Seph scoffed a laugh. "Bullshit, you always make your bed. Oh wow. And you got all shitty at me for inviting Lucas over to study while you've had *random dudes* here fucking your brains out? Holy shit, look at that sex hair, Dare!" She grinned wide, and I ran a self-conscious hand over my wild curls.

Yep, a quick glance in my dresser mirror told me just how obvious I looked. Not only did I have sex hair, as accused, but I also had a mark on the side of my throat where Lucas had sucked at my skin and my lips were all red and puffy from his stubble.

Fuck's sake. Good planning, Hayden.

"Who was he, huh?" Seph teased, flopping down on the end of my bed—in a section where the blankets weren't disturbed—and smirking at me. "Just some guy? Nah, you wouldn't have brought him here, you're too anal about people being in your space. The only guy I've *ever* seen inside our home is—" She cut herself off with another gasp. "You're totally fucking Zed! I *knew* it! You guys are *so* freaking obvious."

194

I glared. "I'm not fucking Zed, Seph. Jesus, you need to let that go." To distract myself from her intense stare, I grabbed my black jeans from earlier and found my panties on the floor where they'd been tossed, then pulled them on.

"Uh-huh, sure," she replied with a laugh. "If not him, then who? Don't tell me it was Cass. Actually, do. Please tell me it was Cass. You guys are, like, fated mates or some shit. You're *perfect* for each other."

"Seph, what's your sudden interest in my sex life?" I exclaimed, my cheeks heating. Her mention of Cass just resurfaced all the hurt of him saying he wasn't attracted to me...that I was too young for him. It reminded me of how he'd rejected me the first time I made a move and how he'd shut down when I'd transformed back into Hades after he'd kissed me. Cass had pissed me right off.

She just shrugged, oblivious or unconcerned with my attitude. "What? You won't let me have a sex life, so obviously, I need to be unnaturally interested in yours. So? Was it Cass? Pretty sure he's been in love with you for, like, ever."

"It wasn't Cass," I snapped at her. I found my bra on the far side of my bed and shed my robe to put it on. Then I pulled on a black tank top and parked my hands on my hips. "Can you get out of my bedroom now? You're probably lying in a wet patch anyway."

I smirked at how fast she shot off my bed, and she gave me the middle finger.

"If it wasn't Cass, then I'm sticking by my first guess. Oh. Wait. Was it both of them? That'd be hot as hell. I mean, don't get me wrong, those two are practically dead, they're so old, but, like, so are you, so whatever. Get it, girl." She shot me a saucy wink, making her way for my door as I seethed.

"I'm twenty-three, you little shit!" I threw a pillow at her, which she caught with a cackle. "And you've been spending too much damn time with Madison Kate! She's a bad influence on you."

"Maybe you should spend *more* time with her," Seph shot back. "She's living the reverse harem dream, Dare. You could learn a few things."

"Out!" I shouted, but she was already through my doorway and making her way to her own room.

I marched over to push my door shut, and she blew a kiss over her shoulder at me. "Demi and Stace send their love, by the way!" she called out. "Don't forget to put that food in the fridge."

Rolling my eyes, I flipped her off, but she was already closing her bedroom door. I waited a beat, just in case she reemerged for something, but when I heard her TV turn on, I released the breath I was holding.

With my heart racing, I closed my door and flipped the lock before crossing over to my closet to let Lucas out. He immediately clasped my waist, capturing my mouth with his and kissing me until I lost track of whose air I was breathing.

"Cass and Zed are fucking idiots," he told me in a rough voice when we broke apart, both our chests heaving.

I snorted a laugh. "No, my sister is a fucking idiot. A bored idiot who spends too much time fantasizing relationships that don't exist." Or...at the very least she'd overexaggerated the relationships that *did* exist. Cass and I were over before we'd even begun, and Zed was just a friend.

"Come on," I whispered, peeling his hands off my waist before I became tempted to drag him back to bed. "I need to get you out of here before Seph finds out."

Guilt clenched my gut at that prospect, and I shook my head to try to clear those uncomfortable feelings. It didn't work, though. If my sister found out I was fucking the boy she liked, it was going to result in World War III.

Not an option. Not even close to being an option.

With Lucas's hand in mine, I led the way silently through the apartment, holding my breath as we passed close to Seph's bedroom door. I grabbed a pair of flat boots from near the door and ushered Lucas out into the hall while I held the door open.

Just in time, too. Seph's door opened a second later, and she gave me a sly grin.

"Heading out for round two, huh?" She shot me a wink, then grabbed a box of cold Chinese from the counter. "Have fun, you bitch!"

I didn't answer her, just exited the apartment and closed the door firmly behind me. The locks engaged, giving a small bleep and blinking to show they were active, and then I hurried along the hall to where Lucas waited at the elevator.

"That was close," he murmured with a laugh.

I shook my head, my eyes still on my front door as I prayed Seph wouldn't open it. "Too close."

The elevator arrived, and I let out a long sigh of relief when the doors slid closed once more. This was *way* too much tension for having just woken up. My nerves were all kinds of frayed like they hadn't been in a long, long time.

"Hayden," Lucas murmured, turning to me and cupping my face in his hand. He tilted my face up to meet his gaze, then gave a small smile. "You're so short without heels on. It's freaking adorable."

I let out a shocked laugh. "You did not just call me *adorable*. Do you have any idea how many people I've killed, Lucas?"

His smile faded, and he shook his head. "I don't. But you're still adorable to me. I'm sorry I fell asleep. That was too risky."

Goddamn, he knew exactly what to say to wiggle past all my defenses.

"Equally my fault," I admitted with regret. His thumb brushed over my lips again, just like he'd done before I fell asleep, but this time I nipped him with my teeth. "Come on, I'll drive you home."

The elevator had just reached the parking level, and I let him link his fingers through mine as we walked past my modest collection of cars.

"You okay on my bike?" I asked him, stopping beside my Fat Bob. I grabbed a spare helmet from the shelf behind the parking space and held it out to him.

Lucas's brows hitched, but he took the helmet from me. "I've actually never been on a motorcycle before, but yeah, I'm game."

I gave a soft laugh as I pulled my own helmet on and swung my leg over Bob, then kicked the engine over. "I kinda like being your first, then."

He chuckled and slid onto the seat behind me. "Good. That was my first time giving head too. I hope it was okay."

I almost swallowed my damn tongue, then recovered by nodding firmly. "Uh, what? I mean, yep. Yes, you... Yeah, you nailed that." Then I grinned like a damn idiot as I drove out into the night with his hot body draped around me.

The drive to his house was over way too soon, and he reluctantly climbed off the back of my bike when I stopped at the end of his driveway.

"So...uh, I'll text you?" He said it as a question this time, and I got the impression he was actually asking permission, like he was checking if his *one chance* had run its course already.

I took his helmet back and clipped it onto a strap for the trip home, then screwed my face up as I thought. I should tell him no. He'd asked for one chance, and he'd gotten it. Trouble was, he hadn't asked for one night. He'd asked for a *chance* to prove he was what I needed in my life. Trouble was, he'd done that.

No matter how badly I wanted to live in denial, I had to admit that he'd proved his point. Sure, we'd mostly fucked. But those few things he *had* said, they'd all struck a nerve. His persistence had paid off before we'd even gotten naked tonight.

"Sure," I finally conceded. "But no one finds out, understood?"

He jerked a quick nod, a wide grin on his lips. "Understood."

"And we're not *dating*."

His grin deepened. "I promise I won't get jealous next time

Zed marks his territory by putting an arm around you. I'm not asking to be your one and only, Hayden. I just want you…in whatever way you're willing to give."

I shook my head in disbelief. "You're something else, Lucas Wildeboer."

His eyes widened in shock at my use of his real name, and I gave a soft chuckle.

"Good night, Lucas."

He ran a hand over the back of his neck, his smile pure joy. "Sweet dreams, Hayden."

I bit the inside of my cheek as I drove away, trying so damn hard to wipe the echoing smile from my own face. It was no use, though. That goddamn lying teenage stripper was worming his way straight into my life…and my heart. And I wasn't even mad about it.

Until I sensed someone watching me again. Then I just felt sick with anxiety, thinking I'd slapped a target on Lucas's back.

CHAPTER 23

The sun was well up in the sky by the time I dragged my ass out of bed the next day. I'd been awake until dawn, worrying that Lucas might be in the firing line of whoever was attacking my power structure. Ultimately, though, I'd decided they were probably just watching me, like they had been all week.

I hadn't kissed Lucas outside his house, and we'd only exchanged a couple of words. Even then, I hadn't noticed a tail until I was on my way home, so there was every chance they hadn't even seen me drop Lucas off. Hopefully.

As long as we were careful—more careful than we'd already been—he could remain safe.

With a long yawn, I checked my phone for the time and groaned. It was already midafternoon, and I had a bunch of missed calls and texts. There was just one that made me smile like an idiot, though.

Wild Card: Good morning, H. I dreamed about you…

He'd sent it hours ago, and I yawned again before replying with a single heart emoji. It made me feel like a total dork but also gave me belly flutters of excitement, so I went with it.

The rest of my messages were just normal Saturday updates, plus a few from Zed advising me that he and Alexi were having a friendly chat with a certain Detective Sambal. He'd been one of the major beneficiaries of Wraith money in the past, so it was safe to assume he was currently on the take for this new player.

I texted him back, telling him to meet me at Anarchy later with an update, then went to shower.

When I was clean, my hair washed and blow-dried, I wrapped up in a robe and went out to the kitchen to make coffee.

The TV was on in the living room, and after filling my megamug with caffeinated goodness, I wandered through to find my sister moping.

"What's up with you, brat?" I asked her, shoving her legs off the sofa so I could sit down. "You've got that sulky face going on."

She pouted at me, then turned her attention back to the TV.

I didn't push her for information, knowing perfectly well that she'd talk when she wanted to talk and not a moment sooner. This time it only took about five minutes of watching *Julie and the Phantoms* before she let out a melodramatic sigh and sat up.

"I don't think Lucas is interested in me," she admitted, and I stiffened. She misinterpreted my body language, though—as she often did—and threw her hands up in the air. "You totally warned him off, didn't you? Goddammit, Dare, I thought maybe, just *maybe*, this time you'd let me make my own damn decisions. He's not like other boys! Surely, even you could see that?"

Oh, I wholeheartedly agreed with her on that statement, but not for the reasons she was thinking.

Taking a careful sip of my coffee, I schooled my face into that neutral mask I wore so often and met her eyes. "What happened?"

She scowled at me, then shrugged. "I asked if he wanted to see a movie tonight with me and some of the other Shadow Prep girls." Her cheeks pinked, and she looked away, picking at the frayed sleeve of her sweater. "He made some total bullshit excuse about needing to work tonight."

I frowned, confused. "So? Maybe he needs to work." I didn't know why I was trying to placate her; I should be agreeing that he wasn't interested. But I hated seeing my sister upset…

She scoffed a laugh. "He goes to Shadow Prep, Dare. Not on a scholarship, either. Pretty sure he doesn't need to work. Also, he got super evasive when I asked where he worked and wouldn't even say what time he got off. So, yeah, pretty sure he's lying to blow me off."

I sipped my coffee again, silently disagreeing with her. Maybe he worked as a stripper in her sister's club and didn't want his whole class to know about it. Maybe he didn't get off work until three in the morning but couldn't say that without betraying what his job was.

Maybe. Maybe…he was blowing her off because he was already involved with someone else. Maybe.

But instead, I just shrugged. "Guess he is like other boys after all. Besides, didn't you say he had a girlfriend?"

Maybe I should just *tell* Seph that Lucas was stripping in one of my clubs. Surely that would be a good enough reason why she shouldn't be pursuing him?

Seph pouted. "I figured maybe she's still in Colorado or something. He only moved here about three weeks ago. But whatever. We're seeing that remake of the old witchcraft movie from the sixties or something."

I rolled my eyes. The movie she was thinking of came out in '96, but I couldn't be bothered to argue with her.

"Well, enjoy," I said, taking another sip of my coffee and standing up.

She cocked her head to the side as she looked up at me. "Your hair and makeup are on point, Dare. Got a hot date tonight?"

I gave a small laugh. "I wish. Just need to stop by Anarchy to check on things."

Her smile turned knowing, and she nodded. "Oh, I see. Gonna see Zed there too? You should wear that crimson satin lace-up skirt with the black corset top. He's always checking out your ass and tits when you wear that combo."

Ignoring her, I drained the rest of my coffee on the way back to the kitchen, then headed to my room to get dressed. It was nothing more than a coincidence that when I emerged from my room again, I was wearing the outfit Seph had suggested. I mean, sure, she hadn't specified that I add a black leather shoulder holster for my gun, but that went without saying. No way in hell was I wandering around unarmed right now.

She let out a catcall when she saw me, and I flipped her off. Little shit.

My skirt—which laced up in a corset pattern from knee to waist—was way too tight to even consider riding Bob, so I slid into my Corvette instead. I still had several hours before I was due to meet Zed at Anarchy, so I drove across to Rainybanks to catch up on some office work. One of the end-of-night reports had hinted at inventory discrepancies—a polite way of implying someone was stealing—and I wanted to review the last few weeks' figures.

There was a magazine stand near the front entrance to the sky-scraper Copper Wolf HQ was located in, and I grabbed a newspaper before heading inside. It never hurt to run my eyes over what was making headlines, just in case my people were being noticed. But I also had a slightly morbid fascination with reading the obituaries and memorials.

Saturday newspapers always had the most, and they were so varied. In some of them, love for the deceased person rang true with every word, while others were cringeworthy in how little care was put into the composition. I liked to think it spoke to what kind of person had just died. Were their surviving relatives grieving their loss or dancing on their grave? It always made me curious what would be written about me.

The Copper Wolf offices were mostly empty. Just a couple of desks were occupied by the women who ran our reservations and events team, and they gave me friendly smiles as I passed.

I let myself into my office, flicked on the lights, then sat down in my overly masculine leather chair. Crossing my legs, I flipped open the newspaper and scanned over the headlines quickly. I didn't need to read the articles about a giant fish being caught off the coast by a ten-year-old or a head-on collision that killed six. I just needed to make sure nothing was raising red flags about the continued existence of the Tri-State Timberwolves.

Anonymity to the general public was working for us, and I was dreading the day that changed. To be fair, though, I was amazed it hadn't already.

Finding nothing alarming in the news, I flicked over to the obits and memorials.

They were in alphabetical order, and I was pleasantly surprised at the sincerity of the first few I read. Then I reached the Ds.

Darling, I miss you more with every passing day. Five years has gone in the blink of an eye, but we'll meet again soon. I promise. I'll chase you.

I read the simple memorial six times before throwing the newspaper across my office.

"Mother*fucker!*" I shouted. Rage and fear coursed through me in equal measure, making my hands shake as I pulled my phone out of my purse. It took me three attempts to open my camera app, then I needed to go and retrieve the scattered newspaper to take a picture of the message and text it to Zed.

Fuck reviewing inventory; some bastard was trying to make me think Chase himself was still alive. Little did they know I had been the one who'd personally fired a bullet through his face.

Zed called me as I was stalking back to the elevators.

"You're shitting me," he said when I answered.

My fingers tightened on my phone, and I needed to resist the urge to throw it. I was *so angry*, though.

"I'm at Copper Wolf," I snapped, my voice threaded with fury. "I'll be at Anarchy in an hour."

"Understood, Boss," Zed replied, all business. "I'll be waiting."

I ended the call and dropped my phone back into my purse before I could break it. Paranoid didn't even begin to describe how I was feeling as I exited the building and made my way back to my car. It felt as if a million eyes were on me, watching my every step. A million people just waiting for me to slip up.

I wouldn't, though. I wouldn't fall. Because the second I did, someone would be there to slit my throat and toss me to the sharks. After all, it's what I would do.

CHAPTER 24

Anarchy was buzzing with life when I arrived, despite how early in the evening it was. I bypassed the big top—the fight arena—and headed straight for the Fun Zone where I knew I'd find Zed waiting.

We had a VIP lounge area set aside in all our venues, and most nights they were kept for either visiting celebrities or just stinking-rich party girls who could afford to rent them. Tonight, though, it was totally empty except for my second-in-charge.

"Boss," he greeted me, indicating I should take a seat at our favorite table. It was one that overlooked the main club, same as we liked to sit at all our venues. He sat opposite me, hooking his arm along the back of the seat and giving me an intense stare. "It's not him."

Him. Chase *fucking* Lockhart. As if he hadn't tried enough to break me in life, he was still messing with my mind five years after his death.

"Of course it's not *him*," I snarled. "I shot him in the face with a .44-caliber bullet from four feet away. Chase is currently worm food six feet under. But *that message* was personal. Whoever this is, they want me to think Chase is alive."

Zed nodded, his gaze still glued to my face. "There's so much personal information being used. First the Darling design, then knowing you read the obits for fun? Who the fuck else knows you do that?"

I grimaced. "No one. Just you." I let out a bitter laugh. "I don't suppose you're behind this, are you?"

His brows dipped in a deep frown. "You—"

"I'm joking," I assured him with a wave of my hand. "You and Seph are literally the only people on this whole fucking planet above suspicion." I arched a rueful smile at him. "But I wouldn't entirely put it past Seph to think something like this was funny. So you're the *only* person I trust, Zed."

His eyes tightened, and he started to say something before shaking his head. He shifted his gaze out to the club below us, which was about a third full of patrons already, and for several minutes we just sat there in silence.

One of the bartenders from the main bar came by and delivered drinks for us both, and Zed gave him a tight smile of thanks.

I sipped my drink, an Aviation, and watched my friend carefully. He had something on his mind, that much was obvious, but something was making him hesitate to confide in me.

"Whatever is eating away at you," I said after placing my drink back down on the table between us, "you know you can tell me." It wasn't a question; it was a fact. He did know. So why was he hesitating?

His gaze returned to mine, and he leaned forward to rest his elbows on his knees. "You know I'd never do anything to put you in danger, don't you? I'd never hurt you."

I frowned in confusion. Was this about my joking suggestion that he'd submitted the creepy memorial?

"Of course I know that," I murmured, squinting at him.

He gave a small nod, the lines of his face still tight and his fingers clenched in a fist. "I love you, Dare. More than anyone. Ever."

I smiled. He didn't even seem to notice that he'd slipped and used my nickname. "I should fucking hope so. You're my best friend. We've literally killed for each other."

His brow seemed to draw tighter at my response, though, like that wasn't the answer he'd been looking for. Then his gaze flicked away from mine once more to look out over the crowd below us.

"Is it just me, or is Cass lurking around a whole lot more than he used to?" Zed punctuated his change of subject by sitting back in his seat and unclenching his fist. It was a very obvious, forced shift in his mood, and that worried me. Had he really thought I suspected him of being behind the fake-Chase messages?

Still, I followed his line of sight and groaned when I spotted the big tattooed Reaper staring up at us from his position at the bar.

"Miserable bastard," I muttered under my breath when his eyes locked on me. He raised his drink in a small salute, like he'd heard me and agreed.

Zed coughed a laugh, then smirked. "Come over here for a second? There's something I want to see." He beckoned for me to join him on his seat, and I did so without hesitation.

"What's up?" I asked, perching on the velvet lounge beside him. A brief memory of Seph telling me that Zed liked this outfit flashed across my mind, but I shoved it aside. Zed was my friend, nothing more.

He leaned closer, a teasing smile on his face as he brushed my hair back from my shoulder. "Dare...is this a bite mark?" His fingertip stroked a line down the side of my throat, pressing against the tender spot Lucas had left behind, and for some reason I let him. I didn't smack his hand away or lean out of his touch. Hell, I *liked* it.

Seph was officially messing with my head. All her teasing about me and Zed fucking had made me start reading too much into every interaction with him. Now I was getting turned on by an innocent touch? Yeah, I was going to kill her.

208

"Maybe," I murmured, letting a smirk cross my lips. "None of your business, Zayden."

His brows rose in surprise, then he laughed.

"Well, if it's not my favorite niece and her gorgeous partner in crime," a woman said, and I jerked my head around to meet my aunt Demi's amused gaze. "I thought I might find you two here."

"Because I texted you and said to meet us here?" Zed offered, his tone dry as he leaned back in his seat again.

Demi just shrugged and sat down opposite us—in the seat I'd just vacated, so I stayed where I was.

"That too," she agreed with a smile at Zed, then shifted her attention to me. "Darling, you look flushed."

I winced. "Please don't call me that."

Demi cocked her head to the side in confusion, and I pulled up the picture of the memorial on my phone, then handed it to her.

"Oh, shit," she breathed. With a frown, she read it over, grimaced, and handed it back. "I see."

Zed leaned forward to sip his drink, then settled back once more, propping his arm on the back of the sofa behind me. "Boss, I hope you don't mind. I thought Demi might help us in the research department."

I nodded. As badly as I wanted to keep my aunt clear of Timberwolf business, I wouldn't trust information from anyone else.

"Will you look into the Lockharts for me, Demi?"

My aunt nodded, folding her hands in her lap. "What am I looking for?"

I shrugged and sat back in the seat. My back rested against Zed's arm, but I was okay with that. "Anything. Anyone even slightly connected that might have motive to attack us now."

She pursed her lips, thinking. "Someone has to know a whole lot about you to leave a message so personal and to know you'd look there and find it. I don't suppose your ex-fiancé liked to keep a journal?"

209

I snorted a laugh. "As amusing as that mental image is, no. Chase wasn't a journaler."

Zed grunted a sound that seemed close enough to disagreement that I shifted to look at him.

He grimaced when he met my stare. "Look... No, he didn't have a journal. But he did...sort of have something similar. I don't know. Maybe that's where this personal information is coming from."

"Explain," I demanded, shocked beyond belief that he'd kept something a secret about Chase.

Zed ran a hand over his face, then sighed. "He had a hidden camera in his room."

"What?" I spluttered the word, rising halfway out of my seat. Zed reached out, his fingers circling my forearm like he wanted to stop me from fleeing...but that wasn't even remotely in my nature. I was much more likely to shoot first, ask questions later, and *flee* fucking never. He knew that. So why the fuck was he touching me?

"You know what?" Demi interjected. "I'm going to leave you to this. It's starting to look like a conversation above my pay grade." She picked up her handbag and blew me a kiss before making a quick exit.

"Dare—" Zed started, and I shook my head.

"Do *not* try to manipulate me right now, Zayden de Rosa." My voice was pure fury, and he must have known he'd pushed too far. He cleared his throat and released my arm carefully, then drew a deep breath.

"My apologies, Boss," he said in a clipped voice, like *he* was angry at *me*. "I guess I forgot my place for a moment there."

That statement almost cut me deeper than the revelation of Chase having a hidden camera in his bedroom.

"Fuck you, Zed. Don't fucking do that. Just tell me what the hell you mean about Chase's goddamn *camera*. I can't..." I let my voice trail off, shaking my head in frustration and disbelief. My

210

emotions were all over the damn place, my shoulders tighter than a bowstring and my hands shaking.

If I were with anyone else, I'd never *ever* let them see me so damn weak. But it was just Zed. So I tucked my hands under my thighs and tried to calm myself.

"Zed...his *bedroom?*" my voice was no longer murderous, just stricken.

He nodded, his lips tight. He knew. I knew that he knew. Whether he'd seen the footage himself or Chase had told him... *bragged*, it didn't matter. Fact was, he knew something I'd hoped had gone to the damn grave.

"I destroyed it when I found it," he told me in a soft voice. His gaze wasn't pitying, and that was the only saving grace. It was just regretful. What the hell *he* had regrets about, though, I had no idea. "I burned all the tapes too. But...I don't know if anyone had already seen them. It seems like a long shot, but I can't think of anything else."

I swallowed hard, letting my gaze drift over the club below us in an attempt to detach from the memories clawing at their cage in my mind.

"You're sure you burned them all?" I asked in a hoarse, far-too-vulnerable voice.

Zed leaned forward, blocking my line of sight to the club. He raised a hand to my face, stroking my hair away from my cheek with the backs of his fingers in a gesture that made my chest tight.

"Every last one," he assured me. "It's why I never told you. They're gone, destroyed. You didn't need to know."

I drew a deep breath, letting it ground me and wash away some panic. "Why? I never needed you to protect me, Zed."

His lips twisted in a sorrowful grimace. "Yes, you did. I was just too late."

That statement struck me right in the heart, stealing my breath away. But I didn't get a chance to unpack all the baggage piled into those few words as screams rose from the club below.

CHAPTER 25

Zed and I both jerked at that first scream, leaping to our feet and peering over the railing to get a read on what exactly was causing such a commotion.

"You must be fucking *kidding* me," I uttered, hardly believing what I was seeing with my own eyes. "Has everyone lost their goddamn minds?"

Zed huffed, pulling his gun, and led the way out of the VIP lounge. "Not everyone, Boss. Just Vega and Cass, apparently."

"And their men," I snarled. "They seriously chose the wrong night to break my rules." I drew my own gun as I followed my second down the stairs to the main club. I usually let him handle fights within the venues, but I was already in a rare mood. This might be just what I needed.

By the time we got down there, a lot of the patrons had scattered into the parking lot or were staying well out of the way while the Anarchy security team tried to break up fights between the Reapers and the Death Squad.

In the middle of it all were the leaders themselves. Vega had Cass by the front of his shirt and was punching the shit out of the bigger man...yet Cass wasn't fighting back.

Zed glanced over at me, his brows raised, and I aimed my gun at Vega's head.

"What," I said in a voice like glacial ice, "do you think you're doing, Vega?"

I didn't need to yell. He heard me loud and fucking clear. His spine stiffened, and he released Cass like he'd just realized he was holding a poisonous creature.

"Hades," he croaked, spinning around to face me with a stricken look on his face. "I didn't realize you were here tonight."

I raised one brow. "And that would make it okay? You know the rules, Vega. You *all* know the rules." At this, I shifted my cool stare to Cass, who sat on the floor, dabbing at his split lip with the corner of his T-shirt.

"Respectfully, Hades," Cass spoke up, "I broke no rules. Vega attacked *me*."

Silently, I was impressed. That sly son of a bitch had known I would crack down on this breach of my law with an iron fist and had made a *point* of not striking Vega back.

"Confirmed," Zed told me, his phone to his ear. He would have one of the security guards on the other end reviewing the CCTV footage already.

Vega looked gobsmacked, like he'd been set up. Then he shook his head in disbelief.

"Hades, please, give me a chance to explain myself." His face was sheet-white, despite his Hispanic complexion, and he spread his hands wide in open surrender. "He set me up. My whole shipment was stolen last night, and Tito was killed. It had Reapers written all over it." He swallowed heavily, his throat bobbing and sweat beading on his brow.

I stared at him for a long moment, letting him sweat in his panic. But I could already sense there was so much more to this than it appeared. Tito was Vega's cousin, but he treated him like a

213

brother. I could understand how something like that might drive him into a drastic, *stupid* move like this.

Without a word, I lowered my gun, and Vega let out a huge sigh of relief. Far too soon, though, in my opinion.

"Take Vega and his men down to one of the old storerooms," I ordered my security team. "Hold them there until further notice."

"Hades, please…" Vega begged again, but my guards were already escorting him out of the club as I shifted my attention to Cass.

He hauled himself up off the floor, wincing at some damage Vega had managed to inflict, and blood was still smeared across his lower lip.

"Cass, take your boys over to the training building and wait for me there. I'll review the security footage and deal with you shortly." There was no polite request in my tone; it was a clear order. Do it or die.

His brows dipped in a scowl and arguments flashed through his dark gaze, but I gave him a granite stare back.

"You may not have broken the rules, Cassiel, but can you make that same claim for all of your guys?" I arched a brow, and his furious glare lit on the handful of Reapers who'd jumped in to—presumably—defend their boss.

He jerked a nod of understanding, then barked an order for his guys to follow as he left the club.

"Need us to keep an eye on them too?" one of my remaining security guards asked. Security was all run by Timberwolves because everyone needed a day job and what better use for highly trained fighters and killers than nightclub security?

I shook my head, tucking my gun back in its holster. "No, Cass will do as he's told." Because he damn well knew he'd already pushed me too damn far. One more misstep and I really would shoot him. "Let's review the footage and leave them all to sweat it out a bit."

A couple of my guys were already helping the bar staff sweep up broken glasses and mop spilled drinks, so Zed and I made our way through to the security office where the footage was up on the screens.

"Evening, Boss." The bouncer stationed at the desk nodded, hopping up from his seat and offering it to me. "All cued up, ready to play."

Sitting down in his seat, I clicked the mouse to start the video, and the three of us watched it in silence. A couple of times I rewound, freeze-framed, then replayed, but it didn't take a lot of time to get a grasp on what had happened.

"What do you want done, Boss?" Zed asked in a low murmur as I stood up from my seat once more.

I pursed my lips, thinking. "Let's deal with the Reapers first. Vega can stew in regret and panic a bit longer."

We needed to cross back through the main club on our way out of the security office, and it was satisfying to see everything back to normal, if a little less crowded than before. Still, it would take more than a bar fight to dampen the mood in a Copper Wolf club.

"What are you thinking?" Zed murmured as we stepped out into the darkness behind the Fun Zone. It was just the two of us, no one else around to hear us speak, so I shrugged.

"No fucking clue," I admitted. "I can't deal with replacing two gang leaders tonight. I know how Vega and Cass work. I know they're loyal...to a degree. I don't know or trust their seconds, so..." My voice trailed off, but he knew what I meant. Better the devil you know than the devil you don't.

"They broke your rules, Hades. Publicly." As if I needed the reminder.

I shot him a glare as we strode across the shadowed park grounds toward the training building. "I'm well aware, Zed. They need to be punished for fighting in a neutral zone, but I just don't think I can afford to kill them."

Zed grunted. "Agreed. Fucking bastards couldn't have picked a better time to start this shit."

My thoughts exactly. With an internal sigh, I pushed open the door to the training room and pulled on my hardened face of death.

Cass and the four Reapers who'd been involved in the fight were waiting for me in the middle of the padded floor and I had to commend them for not flinching away from my cool gaze as I approached.

I stopped at the edge of the mats, not wanting to risk walking on the padding in my heels and possibly breaking an ankle. Cass met my stare and tilted his chin up in invitation like he was telling me to get on with it and make it quick.

Fucker thought I was going to shoot him and wasn't even scared.

I let the silence sit between us for a long, tense moment, and one of the Reapers shifted his weight uncomfortably.

"You're being taxed forty percent for the next four months. Ten percent and one month per infraction," I announced, my voice bouncing ominously off the walls of the vast room. "You can go."

The four bruised-up Reapers hesitated, giving Cass uncertain looks, but I was in no mood to be questioned.

"I said go," I snapped, my eyes narrowing at the gangsters in fury.

This time, they did as they were told, mumbling apologies and promising it would never happen again. But Cass? Nope, he didn't move a muscle. He just stood there, stubborn as a damn mule, staring at me like he had something to say.

The door slammed after the fleeing Reapers, and I raised a brow at the infuriating shithead staring me down.

"Did I stutter, Cass? Or has your hearing gone in your old age?"

He grunted a sound of amusement, the corner of his mouth twitching, and he shifted his gaze to Zed at my side.

"Mind giving us a moment?" he rumbled the question to my second, but it really wasn't a question.

Zed scoffed. "Yeah. I mind."

A sly look crossed Cass's face. "You worried Hades can't handle herself against me? Sounds a whole lot like you're doubting her ability, Zed."

Zed jerked in alarm, shooting a lightning-fast look at me, then back at Cass. Talk about a catch-22—either concede to Cass's request and allow a momentary power shift between the two men...or undermine my authority by doubting my strength.

"Zed," I said, sparing him the decision, "go and check on Vega. I'll meet you down there."

The storeroom that my security would have the Death Squad secured in was one of many underground cellars that had been used to store props, machinery, stock...all sorts of crap when the property had been a functioning amusement park. We planned to seal up a lot of them, but occasionally they came in handy, like when I needed a holding cell for disobedient gangsters.

"Hades—" Zed started to say, then cut himself off with a sharp nod. "Understood, sir."

He hesitated a moment longer, like he had more to say, then stalked out of the training room with his spine rigid and left Cass and me totally alone.

"Well?" I prompted when the silence stretched. "In case you failed to notice, I'm a busy woman."

Cass's eyes narrowed, and he swiped a hand over his long stubble. "You don't want to ask if I had anything to do with Vega's shipment being stolen?"

"If I did, I wouldn't be letting you off with a tax." And he damn well knew it. But there was no way in hell the Reapers were starting a gang war right now, not while they were in the middle of a hostile takeover of the Wraiths, so I wasn't going to waste my breath questioning him over it.

I'd get all the information I needed from Vega directly.

Cass nodded, then reached into the pocket of his jacket and pulled out a key. "Here," he said. "I picked this up for you."

I raised a brow at his extended hand but made no move to step closer and take it. My days of meeting Cass halfway—or more—were done. If he was trying to make some kind of weak peace attempt, he needed to try a hell of a lot harder.

With a frustrated sigh, he strode across the training mats until he was right in front of me, then took my hand, turned it over, and placed the key in my palm.

"Fat Bob needs some work, and you need something faster." He muttered the words like they were physically hurting him, and I looked down at the key with curiosity.

"You're giving me a new motorcycle?" I let out a sharp laugh, recognizing the Ducati badge on the key. "Seriously?"

His brow dipped deeper as he scowled down at me. He stood close enough that I needed to tip my head back to meet his gaze, and I caught the lightning-fast glance at the mark on my neck.

"Yes, seriously," he rumbled. "Call it an apology."

Now both my brows rose, and I shook my head slowly. "I can't think of anything that requires a new motorcycle as an apology, Cass. Unless you've broken any more of my rules that I'm not aware of?"

He scowled, not buying my bullshit. Not that I expected him to; my voice had been loaded with sarcasm as I'd said that.

"You're gonna make me spell it out?" he growled, frustration tightening his features. "Fine. I'm sorry. The way I spoke to you yesterday was unacceptable, and I…" His voice trailed off for a second, like he was searching for the right words. "I regret that choice."

Bitterness carried my tongue before I could hold it. "You seem to be regretting a lot of things lately, Cass. Maybe stop being a colossal cunt-plug in the first place, and you won't need to live with so many regrets." I held the key out to him, indicating that I didn't want it. "Take your guilt gift and shove it up your tight ass, Cassiel Saint. I have no interest in being bought."

He just scowled harder and folded his arms over his chest.

Fucking hell. "What are you, twelve?" I rolled my eyes and stuffed the key back in his pocket myself when he refused to take it. "I've got places to be. Turn the lights off when you leave."

I spun on the toe of my shoe, my hair fanning out as I turned, then started stomping my irritated ass toward the door. Just when I thought Cass couldn't be *more* insulting, he tried to erase his poor behavior by buying me a bike? What the fuck even went on inside his head?

"Hades, wait," he called out after me, but I didn't take orders from him. So I barely even slowed my stride as I flipped him off and continued across the room. He caught up to me as I reached for the industrial bar handle, his own huge hand covering mine and holding it still. "Just…wait. Can we pretend for a minute like I didn't throw a live goddamn hand grenade at this thing between us yesterday?"

Well shit, now he had my attention.

"Sure, Cass," I replied with a wry, sarcastic laugh. "Let's pretend." My back was still to him, his hand over mine against the door, so I tugged my fingers free and turned around. "But let's get something perfectly clear. A couple of lukewarm kisses is not a *thing* between us."

His hand still braced against the door, he was right up in my personal space. I didn't even attempt to push him away. I was fucked up enough that his push-pull bullshit was *actually* keeping me interested, and I quietly loved having him looming over me close enough to kiss.

He huffed a short laugh. "Your definition of lukewarm must differ from mine, Red, because I remember them being hotter than hell."

"Get to the point, Cass. I have blood to shed tonight, and unless you want it to be yours…"

He stared down at me for a long moment, then nodded and stepped back. I thought he was backing down, but he just pulled a matte-black butterfly blade from his pocket and held it out to me, handle first.

"Fine," he said. "If that's what it takes to prove my loyalty."

I took the blade from him, simply because I preferred to be the one holding the weapons, and squinted up at him in confusion. "How fucking hard did Vega hit you in the head?" I muttered. "You're not making any fucking sense, and I don't have time for word games. Say what you mean, or stop wasting my goddamn time."

His jaw clenched tight, and a growling sound came from his chest. "I want you to trust me, Hades. You need my help with this Lockhart mess, but I can't help if you keep me in the dark. So, what will it take? Do I need to bleed for you like Zed did? If so, have at it." His words were clipped with anger and frustration, and he spread his hands wide, inviting me to…what? Stab him? Carve my initials in his flesh and decorate it with a love heart?

"Zed had earned my trust long before he almost bled to death, Cass," I told him, shuddering slightly as I remembered the state my best friend had been in at the end of the massacre. He'd been stabbed six times by Chase before I'd gotten to them, then had to lie there dying as I finished the fight.

Cass dropped his arms with a sigh. "Then what will it take?"

"Why do you care?" I shot back. "Just keep your own house clean, and this doesn't need to affect you in the least."

His expression turned murderous. "It will affect me plenty if you get killed, Red. I don't want you dead."

Surprise rippled through me, and I felt the need to push him harder. "No? Why not? Without me in charge, you could have free run of Shadow Grove. You wouldn't have me skimming from every aspect of your business and pushing you around like a big bully. Some might think you'd be a hell of a lot better off if I were dead."

He glared. "You know why."

I tilted my head to the side, spinning his knife around my finger. "Do I? Spell it out for me. Maybe I'm too *young* to get it."

His jaw tightened again and his hands balled to fists at his sides, but no words exited his mouth. Stubborn fucking donkey.

"Forget it, Cass," I said with a disappointed shake of my head. "You want me to trust you, but you can't even admit how you feel. And no, Grumpy Cat, I didn't buy your bullshit for a damn second yesterday."

When he still said nothing, I twirled his knife again, then flicked it closed. "Keep the bike," I told him. "I'll accept your knife as an olive branch instead—between platonic, professional acquaintances." I shot him a wink, then slid the folded blade into my cleavage for safekeeping. Sounded stupid—sticking a knife between my tits—but my outfit was severely lacking in pockets.

This time I made it halfway through the door before he cracked.

"You're right," he snarled. "I lied. I've wanted to kiss you for goddamn years."

I scoffed a laugh, turning back to face him but remaining in the doorway. "Just kiss? Come on, Cass. Don't go all innocent now."

"What do you want from me, a fucking love letter?"

A sly smile creased my lips. "Well, now that you've suggested it…"

His glare flattened in a way that almost made me laugh, but he didn't immediately tell me to get fucked.

"What about the rest?" he rumbled. "This attack on you and the Lockhart shit? I want to help."

I shrugged. "Write me that letter, and I'll think about it."

Cass blinked at me in disbelief, so I winked again, blew him a kiss, and left.

If he thought it was going to be an easy comeback from that

moody, hot-and-cold crap in my car yesterday, he was delusional. The path back into my good graces was going to be paved with broken glass and jagged rocks.

CHAPTER 26

It took a couple of guesses to work out *which* storeroom Vega and his guys had been taken to, and I made a mental note to be more specific next time. Or speed up the timeline in sealing the rooms that were structurally unstable and unusable.

When I entered the right room, I found Zed crouched down on the floor having a conversation with the leader of the Death Squad, who sat against the wall.

No one else was in the room, though, and I arched a brow at Zed in question.

"One of Vega's boys thought he could mouth off," my second told me. "Serge and Malik are a couple doors down showing him the error of his ways while his buddies watch."

"Just kill them." Vega's voice was dull and hopeless. "We fucked up. We know the consequences for breaking the rules of neutral ground."

I propped my ass against a stack of boxes and looked down at him with disgust. "Pull yourself together, Vega. You're better than this. Someone set you up, and I want to work out who. Start from the beginning and don't leave out anything."

Vega drew a deep breath, his shoulders losing a bit of their slump as he started his story. There wasn't much to tell. Someone had hijacked his drug shipment at the handover point. The entire truck was taken, and the three Death Squad assigned to taking possession—including Vega's cousin, Tito—were gunned down.

"What led you to think it was the Reapers?" I asked when he paused for breath.

Vega winced. "One of my guys got an anonymous tip."

My brows shot up. "Are you fucking kidding me? You came here to *my* club and started a fight with a rival gang leader on the information of an *anonymous tip*?" Incredulous didn't even begin to describe where I was at.

He hung his head in disgrace. "I know. My only excuse is that I was blinded by rage and grief over Tito…"

I shot Zed a look, but he just shook his head and shrugged.

"Jesus Christ," I muttered, running a hand through my hair. "Who got the tip?"

Vega grimaced. "Adrien."

"Your second?" I didn't know the man well; Vega was a lot like Cass in that he preferred to run things hands-on and not rely too heavily on his second. I'd met Adrien in passing but didn't have a good grasp of what sort of guy he was.

"He's the smart-ass currently taking an ass-kicking from Serge," Zed added, and I straightened up with a nod.

I let myself out of the room and easily found the storeroom where one of my head security guards was beating the crap out of Vega's second.

"Boss," Malik acknowledged as I entered the room. His gun was drawn and pointed at one of the other guys, who looked like he was about three seconds away from doing something stupid.

"Serge," I said, interrupting the other guard before he delivered another blow to Adrien. "I have a question for your friend here."

"Yes, sir," he grunted, hauling Adrien up by the front of his shirt, and nodded for me to proceed.

I gave the bloody, semiconscious guy a tight, cold smile. "Adrien. I understand you had a tip-off. Care to tell me who that call came from?" There was no need to elaborate more than that; he knew perfectly well what I was asking to know.

He knew, and he laughed.

The sound of my gun firing a bullet through his skull reverberated through the room, making a couple of guys cringe and cover their ears. I'd grown used to the noise, though, and the way the ringing in my ears faded in its own time.

"Shit, Boss," Serge muttered, dropping the dead man to wipe his bloody hand on his pants. "Didn't feel like questioning him first?" It wasn't judgment, more amusement.

I scowled. "He didn't know anything more than I already know. The prick who orchestrated this is too fucking smart to give away anything useful to cannon fodder like him." I scanned the remaining Death Squad guys, then put my gun away. "Give these three a warning about breaking the rules of neutral ground, then send them on their way."

Without waiting for a response, I made my way back to the room where Zed was keeping Vega company.

"I'm going to give you the benefit of the doubt here, Vega, and accept that your grief made you temporarily *stupid as fuck*." I paused, tapping my toe against the concrete floor as he peered up at me with sheer relief on his face. "But this can't go unpunished."

He nodded frantically. "Yes, of course. Absolutely. I deserve it. Hades, you have to understand I would never—"

"I do. That's why you're still alive, Vega. But you'll be taking one of my guys on as your new second. He's going to audit your whole crew and weed out any other turncoats. Clear?" He babbled understanding, and I kept talking over him. "You're also being taxed fifty percent for five months. Do you have anything else to tell me?"

He shook his head. "No, sir. No. I swear I'll make this up to you."

I stared down at him another moment, then gave a tight nod. "I know you will. Zed?" I tilted my head to my second, and he cracked his knuckles.

"Yes, sir," he replied with a slightly feral grin. He was just as bloodthirsty as me most days, and today I could tell he had some tension to work through.

I flicked another glance at Vega, then nodded to Zed. "Make it look good. We don't want Maurice getting ideas that I've gone soft."

Zed's lips kicked up, and Vega paled further. But he couldn't complain when he knew he would come out of it alive, and he *knew* he was going to have to take some damage for breaking my rules. Not just monetary, either. If he was leaving my property with his heart still beating, then he would damn well be wearing the visible consequences of his actions.

I wasn't sticking around for the show, though, and started back toward the stairs that would carry me aboveground once more. A couple more Anarchy security guards passed me in the tight corridor, and I made it all of four steps past them before I paused, frowning.

"Hold up," I barked, spinning around to face the guards.

They stopped and turned around at my command, and I squinted at the guy on the left. He was in his late twenties or early thirties with a short, sandy-blond beard hiding his lower face, but his eyes flicked to the side nervously as I scrutinized him.

"What's your name?" I asked him, stepping closer. I tried to recognize all my employees by sight, but with almost two hundred just within the Timberwolves, it wasn't always possible. Add Copper Wolf staff to that number and the faces started to blur together a bit.

The other guy stammered out his own name, but I waved him off.

"Not you, Rixby, I know you. What's *your* name?" I addressed Blondie again. "I haven't seen you around Anarchy before."

"Uh, Puck, ma'am. Adam Puck. I just started a couple days ago," he stammered, and his tongue nervously wet his lips.

Rixby cringed when Puck called me *ma'am* and took a deliberate step away from the other man like he wanted to physically show me that they were *not* friends.

I flashed him a knowing smile, then flicked my gaze back to the nervous blond guard.

"Hmm, I see. Who hired you?" Because someone owed me some answers.

He licked his lips again. "Ah, Alexi himself. Ma'am."

I held his gaze, drawing a deep breath through my nose. "Rixby," I said, not taking my eyes off Puck for a second, "I'm going to need you to call Alexi in."

"Yes, sir," the other guard responded, pulling his phone out of his pocket.

Puck shot a nervous look at Rixby, then back to me. "Is there… is there a problem?"

I gave him a tight smile. "Yes, you could say that. But I'd really like to hear from my head of security directly as to why there's an undercover FBI agent in my employment. Do you happen to have the answer to that, *Adam Puck?*"

The blond liar blanched, then bolted. He shoved straight past me, sprinting toward the end of the corridor where the stairs would take him out to ground level. It was the only way out—that we'd found so far—so his only hope for escape.

Also a pointless effort because I had more than enough time to pull my gun and shoot him through the knee before he even came close to the stairs and freedom.

"Holy shit," Rixby breathed, his face a picture of shock. "I didn't expect that. How'd you know?"

I flicked a quick look at him as the imposter howled in pain further down the hallway. "That he was FBI? I've seen him before. The beard was new, but I recognized him from the team who investigated last year when Archer's wedding got shot up. I didn't expect him to bolt, though. The FBI needs to train their operatives to grow a pair and stand their ground."

Rixby gaped at me in awe. "You're scary impressive sometimes, Boss."

I scoffed a laugh. "Sometimes? I'm insulted." The screaming was dying down along the corridor, so I made my way closer. "Go grab Zed for me, Rixby. And tell Alexi to hurry the fuck up."

"Yes, sir," the young guard replied. "You need help here first?"

I shook my head as I reached Adam Puck's bleeding form. He was too quiet all of a sudden, and there was something about the way he was lying… He seemed to be trembling. Or convulsing.

"Shit," I breathed, using the toe of my stiletto to roll him over. Foam coated his mouth, bubbling over and dripping down his face as his eyes rolled back in his head. Motherfucker had just taken a poison pill.

Fury washed through me at the lost opportunity, and I let out a short scream of frustration and kicked the son of a bitch in the side. It didn't matter—he was already dead—but it helped me get a rein on my temper.

"Fucking *fuck*," I hissed, putting my gun away, then running my hand through my hair in agitation. Not only had an undercover agent made his way into my organization, but he'd been equipped with a cyanide capsule? I wasn't high-profile enough of a target to warrant that level of planning…not from the FBI anyway.

But if *Adam Puck*—whoever the fuck he really was—had infiltrated my team as a double agent, who was to say he wasn't doublecrossing the FBI too?

Ugh. What a goddamn mess.

CHAPTER 27

Alexi was less than useful in working out how the fuck the FBI had wormed their way into our house. He showed us all the vetting paperwork done on "Adam Puck," and it'd been verified by Zed himself.

Trouble was, it was a forgery of Zed's signature. Luckily for me, one of my new Timberwolves, who I'd acquired as a favor to Archer a year ago, had come with a whole host of useful skills. Spotting a forged signature was one of those skills.

"It's damn close," Dallas murmured, increasing the image on his screen so much that it became a blur of pixels to my eye. "But no forgery is foolproof. This wasn't signed by Zed."

"Obviously," Zed growled from across the room. We were in my office at Copper Wolf headquarters, and Dallas was using my computer to review the signatures.

Dallas shrugged and closed the images down, then sat back in my chair. "I can't really give you much more than that. They used a standard blue-ink ballpoint, and they're right-handed. That's about it."

"That's plenty," I told him with a small smile. "I trust you'll keep this to yourself."

He jerked a nod. "Of course, sir. As always."

I pointed to the splotch of what I guessed might be baby snot on his black T-shirt. "I'll let you get home. I hope baby Maddox is behaving for you."

Dallas grimaced, but it was immediately followed by a fond smile. I got the impression he was the most doting father out there, even with his less-than-legal day job.

"He's going through a sleep regression now and only sleeps on Bree, so she's having a hard time. We'll get through it, though." He arched a lopsided smile at me, then nodded to Zed, who was trying to bandage his own split knuckles and doing a crappy job of it. "Need me to help with that?"

Zed just glared death at our resident hacker, and Dallas raised his hands defensively.

"Never mind then. I'll go." He hurried out of my office, and I crossed over to where Zed sat with an open box of medical supplies. He'd made a hell of a mess of his knuckles on Vega's face, but it wasn't anything Zed wasn't used to.

"I can handle it," he snapped when I reached for the bandage he was fumbling.

I firmly took his hand in mine, pressing down on his split knuckles as I placed it in my lap. "I never said you couldn't," I replied, grabbing the bandage roll from the couch beside him and tearing open a fresh dressing.

Silently, I dressed his injuries, winding the bandage around the dressing patch to hold it in place on each hand, then securing the ends.

"You always do it too loose," I told him with a teasing smirk.

He just glared at me, then gathered up all the wrappers and disposed of them in the trash basket under my desk.

"I do not," he muttered, returning to the sofa, then dropping onto it once more with a heavy sigh. "FBI, huh? Are you certain?"

I jerked a nod, sitting sideways to face him and leaning my

head on the back of the sofa. We'd been up all night dealing with the drama at Anarchy, then spent all damn day in my office working through *how* this slipup had occurred in the first place. It was almost dusk again, and we both had heavy dark circles under our eyes.

"After that mess at Archer's wedding, remember the FBI sent in a couple of investigators to tick their fucking boxes because of public exposure?" I yawned, covering my mouth with my hand, then blinked sleepily at Zed. "I stopped by the church briefly to check on things while they were there. He wasn't one of the lead investigators, but I spotted him smoking beside their van. You know I never forget a face that might try to bite my ass later."

Zed huffed a short laugh, sliding down the sofa until his head rested on the back too. "True that. Wanna hear the information we got out of our good friend Detective Sambal?"

Fucking hell, I'd totally forgotten telling him to squeeze the local law enforcement. "I'm assuming if it was anything useful, you'd have told me already."

He grimaced. "You guessed it. He had no fucking clue who was pulling the strings now, only that they were paying in a currency we aren't willing to provide."

I sat up with a jerk. "No."

He nodded, yawning as he ran a hand over his face. "Unfortunately, yes. So, whoever is behind this isn't just flouting your rules about angel dust. They're also paying off the scum of SGPD with child pornography."

My stomach churned, and a shudder rippled through me. "We need to find this fucker, Zed. We need to end this. Soon."

"We will," he agreed. "He had the element of surprise, but we're on his trail now. No one gets the better of Hades, remember? You're a force to be fucking reckoned with."

I groaned, dropping my face into my hands. There was nothing to say back to that. Zed didn't want to hear my feelings of self-doubt or exhaustion. He wouldn't want to know how tired I was of being *me*.

He sat forward too, shifting on the sofa beside me, and swept my hair over one shoulder.

"Remind me again where we're going on vacation?" he joked, his bandaged hand cupping the back of my neck. His fingertips rubbed small, firm circles in my tense muscles there, and I exhaled heavily as I turned my face to look at him.

"Maybe when we're dead? I'll leave instructions in my will to be buried somewhere exotic." It was funny because it was probably closer to the truth than a joke.

Zed just rolled his eyes and continued rubbing my neck.

"That's probably not doing wonders for your split knuckles, idiot," I muttered, but leaned further into his touch, nonetheless.

He huffed a laugh. "Oh, sorry, want me to stop?" So damn sarcastic.

"Hell no," I groaned. In fact, I shifted around until I was lying down with my head in his lap, then yawned again. "Just get that knot at the base of my skull, then you're free to go."

"Yes, sir." He chuckled, digging his thumb into the tight spot in my neck.

Next thing I knew, I was waking up to sunlight filling my office. My cheek was resting on Zed's chest, his heartbeat slow and steady and his arm banded around my back.

I didn't immediately get up—I couldn't explain why—instead just lay there for some time, listening to his deep breaths and soaking in the way my whole body had totally relaxed, as if that small massage he'd given my neck had alleviated years of tension from my limbs.

He stirred a few minutes later, his fingers flexing against my back as he woke slowly. Then he must have realized where we were—how we were sleeping all snuggled together—and his whole body stiffened up.

Wanting to spare us the awkwardness of the situation, I yawned dramatically and sat up. Zed's hand seemed reluctant to release my waist as I did so, but maybe that was just him still waking up.

"Yeah, uh, I think we both needed that," I told him with a small laugh. My hair must be all over the damn place because when he sat up, he reached out and combed his fingers through it with a slight smile.

"We did," he murmured, his voice thick from sleep.

Something about the way he looked at me, though, gave me the impression he was talking about more than our over-twelve-hour nap on my office couch.

Weird.

Wrinkling my nose, I stood and smoothed my skirt down as well as possible. My shoes had been kicked off at some point, so I slipped my feet into them and headed for the mirror beside my bookshelf.

"Fucking hell, that's a good look." I wiped a finger under my eyes to try to clear some of the black smudges of mascara, then gave up. Stupid waterproof makeup.

Zed just grinned, standing up and stretching his arms above his head with a yawn. Dammit. Seph had definitely gotten into my head because I found my gaze automatically drawn to that strip of skin above his jeans when his shirt rode up.

"Boss, did you just check me out?" Zed asked, and I jerked like I'd been electrocuted.

"What? No." I cringed inwardly but kept my face smooth. "I should get home and let Seph know I'm still alive." I grabbed my gun and holster from where I'd left them on my desk the night before and shrugged them on.

Zed did the same with his weapons, which he'd left on the lamp table beside the couch, then grimaced as he flexed his fingers. "Fucking Vega has a hard face, I'll give him that. Come on, I'll buy you breakfast. Seph will already be at school."

I started to decline, but my stomach rumbled loud enough to raise the dead and I grimaced. "Yeah, good call. I'm not eating that health-food bullshit though. Take me somewhere that serves bacon and coffee."

He just laughed at me, shaking his head, then packed up the first aid kit that we'd left out on the coffee table and put it back on the shelf where it lived.

"Yes, sir." He chuckled, holding the door open for me to leave ahead of him. "Bacon and coffee. Your wish is my command."

I glared at his teasing, then almost stumbled when he shot me a wink.

What the fuck?

As we made our way through the Copper Wolf headquarters, already busy with people well into their workday, I couldn't help but notice a difference between us. Somehow the forced reminder of our past, of how we'd both been fooled by Chase's charms and what we'd eventually done to fight back, had also reminded us of who *we* used to be. How close we'd once been.

In a way, being my second meant Zed was closer to me than any person alive. But I could see now how we'd lost the closeness of friendship, and damn, I missed it.

Now definitely wasn't the time to start rekindling my eight-year-old crush on him.

CHAPTER 28

It was afternoon by the time I made it home, and after a long soak in the bathtub, I fell back into my bed for an afternoon nap. I needed it.

When I woke up again, my internal clock was all screwed up, and it took me several minutes of blinking at my clock to work out if it was seven in the evening or morning. Eventually, the darkness clued me in to the fact that it was, indeed, evening.

I could smell pizza, so it was a safe bet that Seph had sorted out dinner for herself with takeout, seeing as she was a lousy cook. Yes, I was failing at parenting her, but on the upside, she was still alive. So, fuck it. She had plenty of time to learn how to cook.

Driven by hunger, I dragged my ass out of bed and made my way out to the kitchen to check if she'd ordered enough for me too.

"Seph!" I yelled when I found the kitchen empty. "Where's the pizza?"

"Get your own!" she shouted back from the living room. "I didn't even know you were home, so I didn't get you one!"

Grumbling insults at my little sister under my breath, I stomped through to the living room to steal a slice. Then froze midstride and let out a string of silent curses.

"Dare, what the fuck?" Seph shrieked when she saw me standing there like an idiot. "Put some clothes on!"

I glowered at her. "Maybe you need to tell me in advance if this is going to be a regular thing. How was I supposed to know you had company?" With a shrug, I sat my ass down on the sofa and grabbed a slice of pizza from the open box on the table. "Hey, Lucas. Nice to see you again. Still working on that art project?"

He shook his head, a wide grin splitting his face, and quickly flicked his gaze over my outfit. Or lack thereof. I had come straight from bed and was only wearing a pair of red bikini briefs and a loose tank top that did *nothing* to hide my nipples or generous side boob. In my defense, he'd already seen me naked plenty of times, so this wasn't so scandalous... But Seph didn't know that.

"Actually, we finished that last week," he replied, subtly shifting in his seat and pulling a pillow into his lap. "Seph generously offered to tutor me in economics so I could catch up. My homeschooling over the last few years has been a bit lacking, so I'm behind."

Seph was still glaring brutal death at me, so she hadn't seen the way Lucas's line of sight kept dipping to my hard nipples. But I was probably pushing my luck, so I scooped up another slice of pizza and stood up once more.

"I should leave you to it, then," I told her with a teasing smile. "Good luck on your homework, Lucas. Seph sucks at economics."

"I do not!" she hissed, throwing a pillow at me as I left the room laughing.

I didn't go far, lurking in the kitchen to eat my stolen pizza and eavesdrop on my sister's study session. Yes, I was at that level of pathetic, but fucking whatever. The distraction of my naughty little liaison with Lucas was the perfect mental relief after the stress of Saturday night at Anarchy. Like he'd said...I needed him in my life right now. He was keeping me sane, reminding me that I was still human. That I was more than the image I'd built for myself.

For the most part, their voices were low enough that I couldn't hear anything that was being said, so I just ate my food, then went to the fridge to find a drink. Just as I was opening a bottle of orange juice, Lucas's words met my ears clearly.

"Really sorry," he was saying, and I froze to listen. "I thought I was really clear. I don't want to lead you on, Seph. You're crazy beautiful, obviously, and an awesome girl. But I have a girlfriend. I've already told you that."

Oh *shit*. That had to sting. I bit my lip, torn between wanting to comfort my sister—because she was a goddamn catch—and cursing her for not respecting his boundaries when he'd made it clear he wasn't available.

"Yeah, sorry," Seph replied, giving a forced laugh. "Yeah, I know. Sorry, I wasn't trying to... Look, can we just forget it and move on? I didn't—"

"It's cool," he cut her off before she could ramble anymore. "I don't want to make you uncomfortable either. I just want to be transparent. Your sister would probably cut me into a million tiny pieces or something if I led you on." He said it with a small laugh, but he damn well knew he was right. I would.

Seph groaned. "Fuck, she totally would. Christ, can we just keep this between us? She can be a bit of a psycho..."

Ouch. That hurt.

"She just loves you," he told her, his tone serious. "You're lucky to have her."

Seph made a sound like she disagreed but didn't argue. Instead, she changed the subject back to their homework, and I drummed my fingertips on the counter. I should go back to my room and leave them to study in privacy. I didn't mistrust *either* of them; I was just fucking curious. I'd lost so much of my own teen years that it was fascinating for me to observe from the outside.

Just as I was about to retreat into my room, Lucas said he was going to the bathroom. A second later, he appeared around the corner to the kitchen with a look of determination on his face.

My lips parted to ask what he was doing, but he pressed a finger to his lips. Two long strides had him crossing over to me, then he grabbed my wrist and dragged me around the corner into the guest bathroom with him.

His lips slammed into mine a split second before the door closed behind us, his hard body shoved me against the tiled wall, and his hands cupped my face.

Fuck it. I kissed him back, digging my fingers into his back and pulling myself closer. He gave a quiet moan against my mouth, his hands sliding down my body to cup my ass, then he lifted me until my legs wrapped around his waist and his hard cock ground against my panties.

"Fuck," he breathed after a moment, his chest heaving just as much as mine was. "Fuck. I shouldn't have done that. Now all I can think about is burying my dick in your incredible pussy..."

I rolled my hips, groaning at how hard he was against my clit. "You called me your girlfriend," I whispered, and his hands tightened on my butt.

"You heard that?"

I gave him a long look. "Lucas..."

"I know. Trust me." His gaze was serious as he stared back at me, searching my eyes for...something. Then he gave a rueful smile. "You're gonna have to put some clothes on or I'm never getting rid of this boner."

I grinned, then leaned in to kiss him again. This time it was less of an intense, desperate thing, and my stomach flipped over and over.

"Okay, seriously," he groaned, several moments later. "I need to splash some cold water on my dick or something before Seph comes looking for me."

I snickered quietly, then dropped my feet back to the floor to leave him to it.

"Hey," he whispered, halting me with a hand on my waist as I reached for the door. "Will I see you tonight? I'm on from ten."

I turned my face to look at him over my shoulder. Bad move. I couldn't say no to him, not when he looked at me with such open adoration.

"I'll be there," I promised, then quickly slipped out of the bathroom and raced to my room before Seph could see my puffy lips and lust-filled eyes.

Holy hell, Lucas was turning into the worst kind of addiction. Soon I needed to think about what the fuck I was doing with him because nothing stayed a secret forever. Not between sisters.

Back in my room, I decided I was in need of another shower. A cold one this time.

By the time I had showered, dressed, and done my hair and makeup, Lucas had already left and Seph was sulking on the couch in front of the TV. Okay, sure, she could have just been watching TV, but the fact that she was eating ice cream directly from the tub suggested she was feeling a bit sorry for herself.

"Hey, you," I said, sitting down beside her and trying to take the tub out of her hands. She tightened her grip on it and glared, so I backed off. "Good study session, then?"

"Fuck you," she muttered, scooping more ice cream into her mouth. "Did you have to go shaking your ass in his face like that? You know he has a girlfriend, right? That's just rude, flirting with a guy who's not available."

My jaw dropped as I stared at her, initially thinking she was joking, but then I realized she was serious. Apparently, she had no idea I'd heard her doing *exactly* that.

"Are you kidding?" I laughed. "I had no idea you'd brought your friend home, so it wasn't exactly a deliberate clothing choice. Furthermore, I wasn't *flirting* with anyone." I rolled my eyes, then pushed up off the sofa. "I've got to go to 7th. See you in the morning."

Seph just grunted something that might have been "Okay, see ya!" or might have been "Screw you, asshole."

239

Deciding not to engage when she was being a bitch, I just left her to it and grabbed my keys to head out. Lucas's shift wouldn't start for a while yet, but I still had an empire to run and a saboteur to root out.

No rest for the wicked, apparently.

CHAPTER 29

It took a couple of days longer than I'd anticipated, but eventually I got the call I'd been expecting from the moment FBI-Adam had died at my feet.

"Ms. Wolff," the woman on the other end of the call said, "this is Special Agent Dorothy Hanson. I wondered if you might be available to meet? I have a few questions."

I was walking back to my car from grabbing a coffee and shifted my phone to the other ear so I could fish out my keys from my bag. "Special Agent Hanson, how lovely to hear from you," I replied with a small smile. "Yes, of course. I'm surprised you called first."

"Uh...I wasn't aware we'd met before, Ms. Wolff." The woman was already off-kilter by my friendly response.

I gave a soft laugh. "Not in person. So, what can I do for you?"

There was a short pause, then she replied, "This morning would be preferable. I have just come from your office in Rainybanks but was told your schedule is fully booked."

I smiled. My staff were the best. "Well, it is. But I'm always happy to make time for the FBI, Agent Hanson. I was heading into one of my clubs today to check inventory. Would you care to meet me there? It's called 7th Circle."

"I know it," she said in a clipped tone. "I can be there in a little over an hour."

"Great." I clicked my key fob to unlock my car. "See you then."

I ended the call before she could, a little power play to mess with her confidence a bit, and dropped my phone into my handbag. Just as I reached for the door handle on my Corvette, I caught a swift movement from the corner of my eye.

Acting on instinct, I dodged. A metal baseball bat smashed straight into the window of my car where I'd been standing. It didn't shatter, thanks to the toughened glass I used in most of my vehicles, but goddamn, that would have hurt if it'd hit me.

My attacker was bigger than me, male, wearing a black hoodie and a mask covering his lower face with a skull grin painted on it. He swung again, his form *terrible*, and I easily maneuvered out of the way before his bat slammed into the hood of my car, leaving a nasty dent.

I scowled, more irritated than anything. "What the fuck is this, idiot hour?" I demanded, dropping my bag and coffee, then pulling a knife from the hidden pocket of my dress.

"Screw you, bitch," the guy snarled back, swinging his bat at me again.

If he he'd been sent to attack some random woman on the street wearing a dress and heels, he'd have probably already killed her. So someone either gave this poor fuck bad info, or...

"Motherfucker," I hissed, changing tactics before I slit his throat like I'd just been planning. Instead, I tossed my knife aside and used my bare hands to disarm and disable my attacker. I was *very* careful to only use self-defensive techniques, which resulted in me catching a lucky elbow to the face while I twisted him up and tossed him to the pavement.

Once I had him locked up in an arm bar, I glanced up at a good Samaritan passerby who'd just run over from the shop across the street to help. Plenty of other people were staring, but only one had tried to come to my rescue.

"Are you okay?" the guy asked, staring down at me in shock where I knelt on my attacker's back. "My wife is calling the cops. Let me hold him for you."

Ugh. Great. Like I needed to deal with dirty cops who *weren't* on my payroll anymore.

"Thank you so much," I told the man with a tight smile. Blood had just started dripping from my nose, so his timing was impeccable. "That would be great." I let him take over holding my attacker, then retrieved my knife from where I'd tossed it. The dickhead on the ground was just spouting insults and profanities, and I got the distinct impression he was new in town. He had *no* clue who he'd been sent to attack. Or how close he'd just come to being killed.

I scanned the area as I picked up my handbag. Luckily I had some tissues in there which I held to my bleeding nose, then grabbed the few things that had rolled out when I'd dropped my bag. I tossed them back inside before straightening up. Sure enough, the CCTV camera across the street that *should* have been pointed at the entrance to the jewelry store was pointing directly at my car.

Some motherfucker had just tried to catch me on camera killing someone.

To what fucking end?

Crouching low, I put my face level with my attacker and peered into his angry eyes. "I hope you know someone sent you here to die," I told him in a quiet voice, dabbing more blood from my nose. "Who hired you?"

"Fuck you," the guy snarled, and I gave a shrug.

"You're kind of lucky cops are already on their way, otherwise I'd be hauling you into my office for questioning myself. Don't worry, though. One of my associates will pop past your cell for a chat later. Be sure to tell him everything you know." I gave him a cold smile, letting him see the violence in my eyes before I patted him on the cheek and straightened up.

My helper frowned at me. "You'll want to get some ice on that," he said, nodding to my face.

I touched my fingers to the bridge of my nose and right eye, where the dickhead's elbow had connected, and sighed. Great. Now I was going to have to explain a black eye to Zed when I saw him. Not to mention the blood that kept dripping from my nose. I had a weak blood vessel on the right side where my nose had been broken years ago and it didn't take much to set it off.

"I'll do that," I said with a tight smile. "Thanks for your help here."

Without hanging around to deal with the cops, I slid into my somewhat dented car, ignoring my helper's protests that I needed to wait. I just gave him a little wave and drove away, passing a police cruiser on my way. When my nose continued bleeding, I got annoyed and twisted up a piece of tissue to pack it. Such a good look.

The further I drove from the scene, the angrier I became. That had been a deliberate setup. But to what end? Sure, killing someone in the street in broad daylight wasn't great PR, but it was the sort of thing that *could* be cleaned up. Especially when there was no physical evidence left by the time law enforcement got on the scene.

"Fucking *fuck*," I exclaimed when I stopped at a red light, slamming my fist against my steering wheel. It was a damn good thing I'd gone for my knife and not my gun, or I wouldn't have had that time to contemplate my options. Then what? I'd have been arrested?

A sick feeling churned my stomach. Whoever had it in for me definitely had a good majority of the SGPD on their books. So what in the hell did they plan to do with me once I was incarcerated?

My imagination was a dark and scary place, so the number of things that flashed across my mind were enough to make me shiver. Thank fuck I'd thought it through…this time. I needed to be more careful in general, though.

By the time I pulled into 7th Circle, I was a tight bundle of anxious energy. There were still forty-five minutes until the special agent would be coming to meet me, though, so I headed into the bar to grab some ice for my eye.

Staff wouldn't start arriving for several hours yet, so the ice wells were all empty and I needed to go through to the storeroom to grab some from the ice maker.

After wrapping a handful of cubes in a cloth, I pressed it to my face with a grimace and made my way up to my office, flicking on lights as I went. The cleaning crew must have only recently left because the whole place smelled sharply of disinfectant, and I sneezed twice on my way up the stairs, setting off the bleeding again.

Once in the office, I sat down with a heavy sigh and placed my ice down on the desk so I could repack my nose with tissue, then hunted through my bag for my phone. I needed to call Zed and inform him what was going on. Maybe he had some ideas...or at the very least, he could sort out a visit to my wannabe attacker in his holding cell.

"God shitting dammit," I muttered when I realized my phone wasn't in there. It had likely fallen out when I'd dropped my bag, and I hadn't seen it when I picked it up. Security wasn't such a concern—my phone was password protected. But it was an inconvenience I didn't have the patience for.

Grumbling to myself, I turned on the desktop computer, activated a remote wipe of my phone, then sent Zed an email asking him to grab me a new one on his way into the club later. Then I moved on to the nightly reports and started my analysis of the stock variances that had been mentioned several times by my managers.

I hadn't been working on it for long when my eyelids started drooping. The third time my lids started to flutter closed, I straightened up in alarm. Spreadsheets and numbers did *not* bore me enough to put me to sleep, and I'd had plenty of sleep. Was I concussed?

Pressing my fingers to my bruised eye, I frowned. Nope, it wasn't that much of an injury; it'd probably barely even darken. The bridge of my nose was a bit puffy, but nothing drastic. A concussion bad enough to make me drowsy had to be from a harder hit than that.

Alarm tripped through me, and my instincts screamed that something else was going on. Something else was wrong.

I tugged the tissue out of my nose now that the bleeding had stopped and stood up from my desk. A wave of dizziness washed through me and I staggered. The only things that stopped me from falling flat on my face were my hold on the edge of my desk and sheer determination.

Something was *very* wrong.

Gritting my teeth, I kicked off my heels and carefully made my way to the door. I needed to call someone for help and get the hell out of the office.

The farther I went, the worse my dizziness seemed to get, until I found myself clinging to the stair railing as I halfway fell down the narrow staircase. The smell of disinfectant was still strong in the main club—distorted by the swelling and blood in my nose—but I doubted a bit of bleach would make me this messed up.

So I gritted my teeth and pushed forward. The club was still totally empty downstairs, and I used furniture to keep my balance as I staggered. After what felt like three years, I finally hit the front door and shoved it.

It didn't move.

"What the fuck?" I moaned, trying the handle again and finding it locked. I hadn't locked it when I came in, knowing the bar staff would be arriving soon.

Most of my staff—the management mostly—had keys to the clubs for access, but I hated needing to remember keys for everything. It was bad enough that my cars still needed them, but I'd decided ages ago I didn't want to carry around a huge bunch of keys for the clubs too.

That was a diva moment I was eternally grateful for now because it meant I could slide open a keypad panel beside the door and unlock it with a biometric lock, same as I'd had installed on my apartment.

The lock bleeped, blinking green and clicking open a moment later, and I grabbed the handle to wrench it open. But I was too slow.

I stumbled out, only making it two steps before the explosion detonated, blowing up 7th Circle and throwing me into the air with all the force of a freight train.

A lightning-fast moment of realization passed through my mind before everything went black. It had been a gas leak. The dizziness, the nausea, the sleepiness… There had been a gas leak. Just like at the Lockhart house the night I killed Chase.

CHAPTER 30

High-pitched ringing wailed on and on as I woke up, and I groaned in pain. I wanted to cover my ears and shut out the noise, but I couldn't move. Why the fuck couldn't I move?

Pain radiated all the way through me, every *single* inch of my body in agony, and I winced as I blinked my eyes open. What the hell had just happened? Where was I?

It took several moments to figure out what the fuck was going on, but once my brain connected the pieces, there was no denying the sight in front of me.

7th Circle, or what was left of it, was engulfed in flames. The information quickly snapped back to the front of my mind as I watched my venue burn down. The gas leak. The explosion. It was a goddamn miracle I was still alive.

The ringing in my ears was still there but not as bad as when I'd woken up, so I ignored it and craned my neck to see why I couldn't move. As best I could tell, a section of the front wall—complete with steel supports—had landed partly on top of me.

My injuries weren't as bad as I'd initially thought, and it only took a bit of pain-filled wiggling to drag myself clear of the weight. When I was free, I was able to push myself into a sitting position, so I didn't think I'd broken anything major.

With my hearing slowly returning, I could make out sirens in the distance. Probably the fire department. Not that there would be anything left to save by the time they arrived. The gas explosion had done a thorough job. If I'd still been inside, I would be little more than bloody, chargrilled chunks now.

Everything hurt. My whole body, my head, but mostly my heart.

I just sat there in the middle of the parking lot, surrounded by smoldering debris under the bright morning sun while my club burned down. Except I wasn't watching my club burn. In my mind, I was right back on the front lawn of the Lockhart mansion, watching it burn to the ground, fully aware of how many innocents had been trapped inside. Knowing it was *my fault*.

My gaze remained locked on the burning building for a long time as the memories haunted my mind. I didn't move as the fire trucks came skidding into the parking lot or when an EMT crouched down beside me and started asking questions.

Logically, I knew I was in shock. I'd had plenty of near-death encounters in my life, but this hit me in a different way. It wasn't just an attempt to kill me… It was an attempt to *terrify* me, and to me, that was a hundred times worse.

The EMT was getting annoying, and I blinked slowly to break my trance and shift my glare to the well-meaning medic. He was spared the scathing words sitting on my tongue, though, when a familiar black Ferrari came screaming into the parking lot.

Zed was out of his car in a shot, not even turning off the engine. He sprinted across the gravel, dodging debris from the building, and fell to his knees in a dramatic skid in front of me.

"Dare, holy shit. Thank god." He knocked the EMT out of the way and hauled me into his arms, hugging me like an anaconda. My body screamed with pain, though, and I let out a groan of protest.

Zed released me as quickly as he'd grabbed me, his face a

picture of alarm. "Fuck, I'm so sorry. Shit, you're hurt. Where are you hurt?"

"That's what I'm trying to work out," the annoyed EMT snapped.

Zed glared absolute *death* at the man, then gave me an accusing scowl. "Cooperate with the medic, Dare."

"I'm fine," I muttered, despite how my limbs had just started trembling uncontrollably. "I was almost out when the explosion happened."

"*Almost* out," Zed snapped back. "You're fucking bleeding and look like death warmed up. Can you stand? We need to get you into the ambulance."

"Agreed," the EMT added, giving me a frown.

I was too fucking wrecked to even argue. I just let Zed wrap his arm around me and support my weight as I gritted my teeth and found my feet.

"No, you shouldn't be walking," the EMT said with a shake of his head. "I'll get the gurney. Just wait a second."

I grunted with the effort but took a little of my weight back from Zed. "Hell no," I growled. "I'm not getting strapped into a fucking gurney right now. Some motherfucker just exploded my club. They declared *war* on the Timberwolves. No fucking way will I do anything but walk out of here on my own damn feet."

Zed hesitated, his expression torn. "Dare..."

"No," I snapped. "No. I *guarantee* whoever did this is watching right now. They set this up to test me, Zed. But now I'm just *mad* as hell."

The EMT looked conflicted, but when I took a couple more pain-filled steps forward, he threw his hands up in defeat. I didn't mind getting checked over in his ambulance—I needed it—but I would walk my ass over there and let it be a show of strength.

Zed kept his arm around my waist, though, and I let him.

"You're so fucking stubborn," he whispered as we stepped over broken, scorched bricks and twisted metal.

I snorted a laugh. "You love it. Did you get my email about my phone?"

He nodded. "Yeah. I saw you'd emailed from the 7th Circle server, then the alarm company called to say there was a fire… I panicked. When I saw the flames as I drove up, I thought—"

"Stop it," I told him firmly. "I'm not so easy to kill."

Zed just shook his head. "You're still human, Dare. Even though you act like you're not. This was close. Really fucking close."

We'd reached the ambulance, and he helped me climb inside and sit on the narrow bed so the EMT could do his thing. Neither Zed nor I spoke any more while my medic—Gareth—checked me over and treated my myriad minor lacerations and burns.

Around the time he was finishing up, telling me that I needed to get checked out for internal bleeding, the fire chief came striding over to us with his helmet in his hand. He'd worked on the Shadow Grove Fire Department for years, and we'd dealt with him plenty of times over fire safety regulations for the clubs.

"Hades, sir." He greeted me with a nod. "Zed. It's not looking good for the structure. Any ideas what caused this?"

I grimaced. "Yeah. Gas leak."

Zed's head snapped around, his expression startled.

The fire chief didn't notice, though, just nodded and rubbed his hand over his beard. "Yeah, that fits the pattern of destruction. Accidental or…"

My gaze flattened and my jaw tightened. "Or."

He winced, then gave a nod. "Understood. We'll keep working to put out the fire, but I reckon you'll need to do a total rebuild. There's just not much left of the framework."

"Thanks, Mitch," Zed said in a rough voice. "Appreciate your work."

The fire chief gave us another nod, then hesitated a moment, his gaze taking in the many patches of dressing dotted all over me.

"If you don't mind me saying, sir, you're goddamn immortal. That blast should have killed you, and you've only got a couple of scrapes to show for it." He let out a low whistle, shaking his head. "Damn blessed, you are."

I snorted a laugh, seeing real humor in that statement. Blessed? Not even close. More like cursed and making the best of it.

Mitch headed back over to where his crew worked to try to extinguish the blaze, and I closed my eyes for a second, searching for more strength deep inside. He was wrong, though... I didn't believe I was meant to die in that blast. It was just a test. A game. Someone trying to get inside my head and make me *scared*.

"A gas leak?" Zed repeated after a couple of moments, and I flicked my lids open once more. "Are you sure?"

I gave a small nod. "Positive. I bet when they do their investigation, they'll find the gas line behind the oven severed."

Zed swallowed heavily, looking sick. "Fuck."

I refused to be taken to the hospital by ambulance but wasn't dumb enough to refuse treatment altogether. Instead, Zed drove me over in his Ferrari. The whole way there, he kept one hand on my grazed knee like he was scared I would disappear if he wasn't holding on to me at all times.

It was an intimate thing, but I didn't stop him and he didn't mention it.

The hospital staff ushered us through quickly when we entered the emergency room, and I was escorted to a private room where a doctor gave me a more thorough examination.

The whole thing took some time, with the doctor ordering a full CT scan to check for internal damage before he reluctantly cleared me to leave. He badly wanted me to stay overnight for further observation, especially when the bruising all down my back started darkening, but I overruled him.

No way in hell would I chill in a hospital room while someone waged war on my gang.

I wasn't even fully listening to the doctor's warnings about what I could and couldn't do while healing, my attention glued to Zed outside my little window. He paced the corridor, his phone to his ear and his expression rigid.

When the doctor left, Zed stepped back into my room, his arms folded over his chest.

"What?" I snapped, tugging my hospital gown tighter around me. My clothes had been pretty much destroyed, and I was naked under the thin material.

"You should stay for observation," he told me, "at least one night."

"Hell no." I shook my head, wincing when it tugged the tape on my neck over a small burn. Fucking shit, burns hurt to high hell. Even with the painkillers the doctor had provided, I could feel a dull ache in every single one of them.

Zed glared at me, exhaling heavily. "Fine. Then just rest for a few minutes until I can get you some clothes."

I gave a small shrug. "Just give me your jacket, then drive me home."

He glowered. "We're not walking you out of here barefoot in a hospital gown with your bare ass on display for the whole damn world. Just fucking chill. Cass will be here in five."

My jaw dropped. "Cass? Why the fuck is Cass coming here?"

Zed gave me a droll look. "Because I wasn't fucking leaving you here alone, and I didn't think you wanted Seph finding out about all of this just yet."

I grunted. "True."

"Right. So, Cass is bringing you some clean clothes, and you can walk out of here as the badass you are and whoever tried to

253

have you killed can go eat a dick." He dragged over a chair and sat down heavily beside my bed, scrubbing his hands over his face. "I think you're prematurely aging me, Boss."

With a grin, I reached out and traced my fingertip down the faint line between his brows. "Well, it suits you. I'll be sure to keep stressing you out."

He grabbed my hand, pulling it away from his forehead with a small growl of irritation. "Please don't."

His pale-blue eyes met mine, and there was a layer of vulnerability and fear in his gaze that I'd never seen before. Or never taken notice of, at any rate. My hand was still captive in his, and he stroked his thumb up the inside of my wrist, making me shiver.

The door to my room opened with a crash, and Zed released his grip on my hand, sitting back smoothly. I tensed, eyeing the broad-shouldered, bad-tempered man standing in the doorway.

"What the *fuck* happened?" Cass snarled.

Zed scoffed a laugh, hooking his ankle over his knee all casual as shit. "I told you. There was an attack on 7th Circle. Did I leave anything out?"

Cass's glower intensified as he stepped into the room and kicked the door shut behind him. "You said an *attack*, but I just drove past and it's completely destroyed. And Hades is in the fucking hospital? Yeah, you left a couple of things out, De Rosa."

Zed parted his lips to reply, probably with something highly sarcastic, and I held up a hand to silence him.

"Quit it, both of you. You're giving me a headache."

Zed shot me a sly look. "I'd say that getting thrown halfway across the parking lot contributed to that headache, but hey, I'm no doctor."

Cass damn near vibrated with tension. "What?"

I stifled a groan. The testosterone was already way too thick for my liking. Madison Kate must be a fucking saint to willingly commit her life to three meathead men; I'd probably rather become a celibate nun than inflict self-torture like that.

"Zed, fuck off for a minute. Get me a coffee or something." I gave him a hard glare, and he just smirked back at me as if he *liked* pushing Cass's buttons.

"Nah, hospital coffee is awful," he replied with a shrug, making no move to get up. "You'd hate it."

I rolled my eyes. "Fine, then just fuck off in general. I need to get dressed, and I doubt you really wanna see my tits."

His brows shot straight up, but I pointed firmly at the door, not giving him any options to argue with me further.

Zed scowled, getting up reluctantly and eyeballing Cass. "What about—"

"Cass can stay if he wants." I slid off the hospital bed and reached for the clothing store bags in the big Reaper's hand. "He's already made it crystal clear he wants to see my tits, so I doubt it'll make him uncomfortable."

Both men stared at me in speechless shock at that comment, and I snorted a sharp laugh. "Jesus Christ, that was a joke. Both of you fuck off."

Cass released the bags into my care, and I waited for them both to leave my hospital room before making any move to open them. They didn't go far, though. As I closed the blind over the little window, I caught Cass's low rumble.

"When the fuck did she start joking?"

CHAPTER 31

The clothes Cass had bought for me fit perfectly, which was impressive, considering he'd chosen skinny jeans. Even the bra he'd selected was the right size, which made me wonder if it was him or Zed who knew all my sizes.

The black leather boots in the shoebox were flat-soled, but I was actually relieved he hadn't grabbed heels. Even if they were my usual look, my aching body couldn't have handled stiletto heels.

Once dressed, I checked my face in the little mirror stuck to the wall and tugged my hair free of the loose ponytail I'd tied it up into. At least with it down, it hid some of the bandages on my neck. Otherwise, my wounds were pretty well disguised. The top Cass had bought was black and long-sleeved, covering the worst of my bruises and scrapes, but tight enough to look sexy with the fashionably distressed jeans.

When I was satisfied that I looked nothing like a *victim*, I gathered up all the clothing tags and disposed of them and the boutique bags in the trash beside the bed.

Tugging my door open, I found Cass and Zed leaning against the wall opposite my room with their heads close as they spoke in low voices. Whatever they'd bonded over, apparently I wasn't to know because they immediately fell silent.

"Acceptable?" I asked when neither one of them said a word.

Cass scowled. "Maybe if you didn't have a black eye."

I wrinkled my nose, feeling the dull ache in my cheek. "That actually wasn't from the explosion." It reminded me that I hadn't told Zed about the staged attack on me in the street this morning. Or the fact that Special Agent Hanson was the only one who'd known I would be at 7th Circle at that time.

"What the fuck was it from then?" Cass demanded, folding those thick, inked arms over his chest and standing his ground like he was going to force the answers from me.

I quirked a brow at him, tempted to laugh. Then I shook my head and looked to Zed. "I think we're done here. Let's go."

"Whoa, what? No." Cass physically stepped in front of me, blocking my path. Instinctively I reached for my gun but silently cursed when my hand touched air. I'd taken my weapons off in Zed's car so the hospital staff wouldn't lose their minds when I was admitted.

"Here, Boss," Zed said, holding out a silver 9mm Beretta to me. "Grabbed an extra for you." He shot me a wink as I took it from him, and Cass just glowered harder. Damn, he had to be part storm cloud for how thunderous he managed to get his expression.

"Hades," he growled.

"Cass," I replied, giving him an unimpressed brow raise. "I appreciate the clothing, but now I need to go deal with some things."

His jaw tightened, a muscle twitching in his cheek under thick black stubble. "Don't shut me out, Red. I wanna help."

Not even getting nearly blown up would make me magically forget how he'd intentionally tried to hurt me rather than tell the truth last week. So I just gave a shrug and tucked Zed's gun into the back of my jeans.

"Well…you know what to do, Grumpy Cat." I gave him a condescending pat on the chest, then simply slipped straight past him. With no heels on, I was a full foot shorter than him—not great when I was having metaphorical dick-measuring competitions, but useful when I needed to be agile.

I didn't hang around, knowing Zed would catch up before I got to the elevators at the end of the hall. He did, too, his shoulder brushing mine as we stepped into the car. As the doors slid closed, I caught a glimpse of Cass punching a wall.

"So…something going on there?" Zed asked after a moment of silence.

I gave him a sharp look, confused for a second, then remembered he had no idea Cass and I had kissed…several times. All Zed knew was that I'd made a pass at Cass and been rejected.

"Uh…" I considered the question. "There was, briefly."

Zed scoffed a laugh. "I'm guessing, based on that interaction, he fucked it up somehow?"

I drew a deep breath, then exhaled heavily. Fuck me, I hurt all over. "Yep."

He shook his head. "What a fucking idiot."

I was inclined to agree. "Well, we have bigger fish to fry right now, Zayden De Rosa." I met his gaze, letting my apathetic mask fall for a moment and giving him a glimpse of the fear coursing through me. Fear that got worse with every additional attack and every paranoid thought. "I think Chase is behind this."

Zed jerked in alarm. "That's impossible."

I shrugged. The elevator doors opened once more, and we stepped out onto the busy ground floor of the hospital. We navigated our way through the people and out into the midafternoon sunlight. It seemed weird for it to be daylight still, given all that had happened in my day. But no matter how badly I might pray for the world to stop, it just kept on turning.

Zed's car was parked in the open-air parking a short walk away with a fine under his windshield wiper. He just plucked it off and wadded it up, then opened the passenger door for me.

"I know it's impossible," I told him when we were safe within the confines of his car. He didn't immediately turn the engine on, instead just shifting to face me in his seat with a deep frown on his face. "I *know* what I did. But…are we totally sure he died?"

Zed's look was incredulous. "You think he could have survived a bullet to the face at point-blank range *and* a gas explosion?"

Frustrated, I chewed the edge of my thumbnail until Zed tugged on my wrist, and I groaned. "I don't know what *else* to think, Zed. Nothing else even remotely makes sense. This is all so…fucking personal. 7th Circle was the last straw. It can't be anyone *but* Chase. Can it?"

He just stared at me, horrified by the suggestion but also not offering me any other explanations. Fucking hell.

"Look, I don't know. I *saw* you shoot him, that's something I know for sure. Whether he survived…with the fire after? It seems too far-fetched." He shook his head, running his hand over his buzzed hair. "But…his body was pretty badly burned up when they pulled him out…"

Dread churned through me. I'd wanted him to tell me I was being hysterical, that there was *no way* Chase could be back, tormenting me.

"We need to know for sure," I murmured, my skin prickling with apprehension. "We need to close this question once and for all, or the paranoia will drive us crazy. That's probably what he fucking wants. You know how he got off on my fear. You saw." Those words tasted like poison on my tongue as I acknowledged the tapes that Zed had seen—my absolute darkest moments that had made me want to die.

Zed swallowed hard. "Yeah," he said, his voice thick with emotion. "I know."

I nodded several times, confirming to myself that this was the right course of action. The *only* course of action.

"So, that's what we need to do, then. We need to dig up his grave and DNA test the remains." That sentence out loud almost sounded like a joke, and I needed to swallow the hysterical laugh that threatened to bubble out of me.

Zed blew out a long breath, whispering a curse. But he didn't disagree. Instead, he just stared out into the distance for a moment, drumming his fingertips on the steering wheel, then nodded.

"All right. But tomorrow. You nearly died today, Dare, and you're black and blue as a result. Promise me one night of rest, and tomorrow I'll help you exhume the body of legitimately the most twisted son of a bitch I've ever known. Deal?"

I wanted to argue and demand we go right now. But he had a point. I was in no state to dig up a grave alone, not tonight, anyway. And I could already tell he wouldn't be persuaded otherwise. So I gave a jerking nod.

"Deal," I agreed. "Tomorrow. Hell, he's been dead for five fucking years. What harm will one more day do?"

Zed winced. "Don't say that. Now I'm going to be all keyed up and jumping at shadows for the next twenty-four hours." He turned his car on, and I buckled my seat belt.

We drove in silence for a while, until I noticed Zed taking a detour from the quickest route to my home and gave him a quizzical look.

"Dallas sorted you out a new phone this afternoon," he answered my silent question. "Figured you'd want it sooner rather than later."

I gave him an appreciative smile. "You know me so well."

He shot me a look from the corner of his eye. "Better than anyone, Boss."

We pulled up outside Dallas's adorable suburban house and

only waited a minute before he came out to the car with a baby carrier strapped to his front and a sleeping infant tucked inside.

He brought his finger to his lips before he reached us and silently handed a phone through the open window to me.

I mouthed my thanks to him, and he gave a little salute before heading back inside with a bouncing gait, clearly paranoid about waking the baby up.

Zed pulled away from the curb, and I pulled a sticky note off the front of the phone to read it. It was just brief instructions for how to unlock it and reactivate all my wiped data from the old phone.

Within a few minutes, I was back up and running. Then I groaned when the unread messages started rolling in.

"Shit," I muttered, "Seph drove past 7th on her way home. She's freaking the fuck out."

Zed wrinkled his nose. "Can't have been long ago. She usually has some after-school shit on a Thursday, doesn't she?"

I checked the time on her messages, then nodded. "Yeah, only ten minutes ago." Biting my lip, I texted my sister back and assured her I was fine and that I had lost my phone earlier in the day.

Her response made me snort a laugh.

Seph: Oh. Cool. Fuck, I was worried and shit. Can you make that garlic and pepper steak thing for dinner? I'm so hungry.

I showed it to Zed, and he just rolled his eyes.

"I love that kid, but goddamn, she doesn't know how good you are to her." He gave me a pointed look, and I shrugged. It was an old disagreement between us that I had never told Seph about our father trying to sell her off as a thirteen-year-old sex slave.

Ignoring his look, I checked my other messages and inwardly groaned.

Wild Card: Hayden, wtf? Jo messaged and said not to come to

work tonight. Then Seph said 7th burned down?! What's going on? Are you okay?

There were several more messages after that, getting increasingly worried as he'd gotten no replies from me, so I quickly tapped out a response.

Hades: I'm fine. Sorry, lost my phone this morning and just replaced it.

I wasn't good at the soothing thing, so after sending that and rereading it, I awkwardly sent some heart emojis too. That would surely soften up my blunt reply, right?

Wild Card: Can I see you?

Flipping down the mirror in the sun visor, I cringed at my reflection.

Hades: Not tonight, I've got a lot going on…

Ugh, it sounded like a brush-off even to me, and I knew that wasn't what I'd meant. Biting my lip, I quickly tried to fix it. I liked Lucas, and the last thing I wanted to do was turn him off because my social skills were lacking. But he simply couldn't see me all messed up like I was.

Hades: Saturday?

He wouldn't be working, so it was just a question of finding somewhere to go where we wouldn't be seen…that was, if I was still alive in two days' time. Who fucking knew what tomorrow would bring.

Wild Card: Done.

Then the little bubble showed he was still typing, so I waited to see what else he would say.

Wild Card: I know you're probably dealing with police and insurance and everything, but…call me when you get home tonight? I just have this bad feeling.

He ended it with a worried emoji face, and my chest tightened. He was right to be worried, but I didn't want to admit that. Not to him. Not when he was my escape from my life as Hades.

Hades: I'll try.

I had no idea whether I would or not, but it seemed like a simple enough request. Maybe. Depended how long I managed to stay awake once I got into my sleep shirt.

"Everything okay with Seph?" Zed asked when I put my phone down, and I blinked at him a couple of times.

"Yeah, she's… You saw. I was just replying to…uh…" I let my voice trail off, suddenly feeling awkward as hell admitting I was on casual texting terms with an eighteen-year-old stripper in my employment. But then how many times had Zed fucked the girls at Club 22?

So, screw it. A little taste of his own medicine for once. "Lucas," I finally finished. "He heard that 7th burned down and was worried."

Zed did a noticeable double take. "The new stripper? That's… You're still fucking him?"

Amusement rippled through me at his response. "Yeah, why not? I figured I'd take a page out of your book, Zed."

Instead of finding my comment funny, though, he just scowled and tightened his grip on the steering wheel. Not the response I'd expected, but whatever. Maybe my humor needed some work.

CHAPTER 32

Rather than just dropping me off at the door, Zed insisted on coming upstairs with me. He claimed he wanted to be sure I didn't pass out in the elevator, but once he was inside, I realized he *probably* just wanted to witness Seph's dramatics when she saw the state I was in.

Bastard.

By the time my sister stopped freaking out, she'd made me strip out of my new clothes and show her every single injury. She then scolded me profusely for being "dumb enough" not to notice a gas leak until it was almost too late.

I loved her. I really did. I'd killed for her many times over and would continue to do so forever…but fuck me, sometimes I wanted to smother her with a pillow.

By the time I'd changed into a pair of shorts and my sleep shirt, Zed had finished cooking dinner for us all, and Seph reluctantly quit lecturing me in favor of batting her lashes at him.

I rolled my eyes at her antics, knowing full well she was being a brat and not actually interested in my second.

"Thank you for cooking," I told him, sweeping my hair up into a high ponytail as I joined them both at the dining table.

Zed turned to look over at me, then froze with a weird look on his face.

I frowned. "What?"

"Nothing," he replied with a smirk, turning his attention back to the food he was serving up for each of us.

I sat down beside him and eyed the perfectly cooked steak with my mouth watering. He was still giving me a weird look, though, so I glared at him.

"What?" I asked again. "I thought I was the one with head trauma, not you."

He snickered softly, reaching for a bottle of wine he'd pulled from my Vintec, and poured himself a glass. Just one, for him.

"Rude." I scowled. "Where's mine?"

He arched a brow, then took a long sip before replying. "*You* have head trauma. No alcohol."

I made a disgusted sound and snagged the glass out of his fingers. "Asshole."

He waited until I had a full mouthful before muttering, "Nice T-shirt, by the way."

I choked on the damn wine. Coughing, I peered down at my favorite sleep shirt and instantly remembered where it'd come from. Yep. It was Zed's signed Blink-182 T-shirt that he'd "lost" about eight years ago and I'd *sworn* I had no idea where it was.

Oops.

"Oh my god, you guys," Seph groaned, "get a room or something. All the eye-fucking is putting me off my food." She made a dramatic fake gagging noise, then smirked as she chewed a mouthful of steak.

Had I mentioned recently how I'd like to smother her?

She must have sensed the murderous vibes rolling off me, too, because she quickly changed the subject and asked Zed what would happen next with 7th Circle and how long it'd take us to rebuild.

I was quietly glad for the shift of focus and just concentrated on eating my food without really participating in the conversation. By the time I finished my meal—which was delicious—I was damn near asleep on the table.

"Okay, bedtime," Zed told me in a firm voice, nudging me with his knee. I was too drained to argue, just nodded and let him support half my weight on the way to my bedroom.

Seph snickered behind us. "Don't fuck too loudly, you guys. I have school in the morning and need my beauty rest."

Zed just chuckled and helped me into my epic-sized bed. "Hey, Dare?" he asked in a whisper after pulling my blanket up. I quietly loved that he was using my nickname more and more these days…even though I'd never admit it to him.

"Mmm, what?" I mumbled, my eyes already closed.

"Why does Seph think we're sleeping together?"

My lids pinged open. "Because she's a sexually frustrated eighteen-year-old virgin and reads too many romance novels."

He grinned down at me, smug as all fuck. "Uh-huh."

I glowered. "She has an overactive imagination. Don't get a big fucking ego about it."

"If you say so. I'll let you sleep." He bent down and placed a kiss against my hair, just like he used to…but hadn't done in over five years.

We both froze, then he started to retreat.

I grabbed his wrist. "Stay with me for a bit?" I asked, cringing inwardly at how weak I sounded.

I held my breath, half expecting him to refuse. But he just kicked his shoes off and lay down beside me with his arm draped over my waist and his face against my hair.

"Sweet dreams, Darling," he whispered.

We slept like the dead, not waking up until well after Seph was gone for school. Then we decided it'd be better to wait until after the cemetery closed before digging up a grave.

Admittedly, we could have paid someone to do it for us. We could have just paid the groundskeepers to look the other way while we did it during daylight. But neither of us wanted to risk breathing a word of our plan to anyone else.

If—*if*—Chase had somehow survived, then we were in bigger shit than either of us were comfortable discussing. So we kept our mouths shut and waited it out. The second the gates to the cemetery closed at dusk, Zed and I got out of our car and popped the trunk to grab our supplies.

"Uh, where's the other one?" I asked when Zed plucked the one and only shovel out and handed me two flashlights.

He shrugged. "Oops. Must have forgotten it." The sarcasm was so thick I could have gotten stuck in it. Bastard.

I glared at him. "Seriously?"

He just closed the trunk and gave me an unapologetic look. "Sorry, Boss. Guess only I can dig. You're cool to hold the light, though?"

"Zed…" I growled, but he was already scaling the decorative wrought-iron fence of the cemetery. Before leaving my place, he and I had argued whether I was physically capable of digging up a grave, considering how bad my bruising was over almost my whole body. But I thought I'd overruled him.

Apparently not.

Grumbling, I followed him over the fence and gritted my teeth against how much it hurt to move my body like that. Sure, maybe he had a point. But I despised being treated as fragile.

"You sure about doing this?" he asked in a quiet voice as we made our way through the picturesquely creepy grounds in search of Chase Lockhart's burial plot.

"Fuck no," I muttered back. "But what other options are there? At least this way, if he's in there—or his remains are—then we can look further afield."

Zed just nodded, leading the way through the narrow pathways until we reached the extensive Lockhart plot. The whole family had all died the same night, so they'd all been buried together with a huge monument marking the family name. Thankfully, each space was individually marked and we didn't have to dig up the entire family to find Chase.

"There he is," Zed grunted, stomping a boot on a patch of grass. The little plaque at the head simply stated Chase's name, year of birth, and year of death, nothing more. No "loving son" or "beloved fiancé of Hayden" because he was neither of those things. Not when he'd died, anyway.

I let out a long breath, placed the flashlight down, and folded my arms to hide the way my hands were shaking. "I thought he was in our past, Zed. I thought this was over."

Zed stabbed his shovel into the dirt and left it standing upright as he moved closer and wrapped his arms around me in a tight hug. "He is *dead*, Dare. I'm sure of it. But if this is what it takes to make you sure, then this is what we do." His big hand rubbed my back in soothing circles, and my anxious shaking eased. "I mean, just think of this as a management bonding experience. I bet Archer's crew never dug up a grave together."

I snorted a laugh and pushed him away. "You're ridiculous. Come on, let's get this over with. I'm nervous about leaving Seph alone at the moment."

She'd still been at school when Zed and I'd left to drive over to where Chase was buried, but I hoped to be back before she went to bed. It was Friday night, so hopefully she'd be up late.

"You've got Cass watching the apartment, though?" Zed asked, quirking a brow at me as he started to dig. I nodded, having called in yet another favor from the big sexy bastard earlier in the day. "He's fast becoming the best babysitter in Shadow Grove," Zed joked. "She'll be fine until we get back."

I blew out a long breath and sat down on Chase's plaque. "Yeah, I know. I just...worry."

Chuckling, he tossed dirt aside into a pile on top of the next grave over. I didn't look to see whose it was because I didn't want to know. Chase hadn't been the only evil, twisted son of a bitch in the Lockhart family, not by a *long* shot, and I had no interest in reliving any painful memories of his other relatives.

"Pretty sure that comes part and parcel with loving someone, Boss." Zed gave a lopsided smile, continuing with his digging.

For a while, neither of us spoke and the only sound was from the thump and scrape of his shovel moving earth from Chase's grave. When he paused for a break an hour into the task, I tried to take over digging. He clung to the shovel with a snarl like it was his favorite chew toy though, and I rolled my eyes.

I didn't push the issue that hard because I *was* hurting. I'd taken a couple of nonprescription painkillers on the drive over but hadn't wanted to impair my reaction time with my prescribed ones in case we ran into trouble. The result was that the drugs had barely taken the edge off my pain.

"This isn't working," I announced after another thirty minutes or so. "We need machinery, or we'll be here all damn night." I scanned the cemetery, thinking. Surely there would be some kind of backhoe to dig new graves.

"What are you thinking?" Zed asked, swiping sweat and dirt off his face with the hem of his T-shirt.

"Let's find some help," I told him, pushing to my feet with a groan. "Can you hot-wire heavy machinery, by any chance?"

He grimaced. "No. But I'm sure we can work something out."

It took us another ten minutes to find the storage shed for the cemetery caretaker's equipment. Sure enough, there was a little mechanical digger parked inside, and I gave Zed a wide grin.

He used his shovel to break the padlock on the big double doors and quickly swept the interior with his gun in hand before nodding to me that it was clear.

Before we started messing around with amateur hot-wiring of

heavy machinery, I figured there was merit in searching for keys first. A caretaker shed in a cemetery didn't seem like the kind of place that went overkill on security or, really, even tried at all. The keys to the digger were hanging on a hook beside an assortment of garden equipment and were even labeled with a tag that read "digger" in case it wasn't easy enough to identify.

"We're in luck," I told Zed as I held the key up.

He gave a small whoop of excitement and held his hand up for me to toss it over. He caught it easily, then slid into the driver's seat of the backhoe and fired it up. The heavy, semi-ancient machine chugged and groaned, but fuck it, it worked.

"Hop up," he said, holding a hand out to me. "Let's get this shit done."

I took his offer, but as there was only one seat in the machine, I ended up perched on his lap as he drove the old digger back along the path to the Lockhart plot.

Once there, I jumped off to grab one of the flashlights I'd left on the grass and let Zed get to work. With the help of the backhoe, it was only another half an hour until the bucket scraped something hard.

I waved my arms at Zed, and he lifted the scoop back out of the hole before shutting the engine off.

"Jesus," he muttered, standing beside me as I peered down at the dirt-covered coffin six feet below us. "I'll do the rest by hand." He climbed into the hole. "Hand me the shovel?"

I did as he asked, then crouched on the edge, watching as he cleared dirt away from the top half of the casket, just enough that we might be able to open it, seeing as it was conveniently a split lid.

"You ready?" he asked, peering up at me with his hand on the edge of the lid.

I nodded, wordless. I needed to know.

Zed heaved, but the lid didn't budge.

"What the shit?" he muttered, annoyed. "Pass me a light? There must be a catch or something."

I snorted a dark laugh. "To keep the corpse inside if it came back to life? Creepy as hell. Here." I handed a flashlight down to him, and he inspected the side of the coffin.

He fumbled around and muttered curses for a moment, then all of a sudden, the lid came free in his grip. It was so sudden that Zed lost his balance and fell backward onto his ass, giving me a clear and unobstructed view of the interior.

My vision swam and my whole damn body went weak with terror. Our plan to collect a DNA sample was pointless. There was no skeleton or decaying corpse inside at all. There was...nothing.

"Oh *shit*," Zed breathed, and I couldn't have agreed more.

CHAPTER 33

The trip home was somber to say the least. We didn't bother filling
the grave in again because what was the fucking point? Even if we
had, it would have been pretty damn obvious the five-year-old
grave had recently been dug up. But more to the point, Chase
wasn't in there. He wasn't in there...which meant he was, what?
Still alive? Or just that he was buried elsewhere?

My head hurt from more than just the mild concussion.

Pulling my phone out, I brought up my contacts list and found
the number for someone who had firsthand experience surviving
a supposedly fatal gunshot.

"Hades," he answered after a couple of moments. "This is a
surprise. What can I do for you?"

I drew a long breath before replying, meeting Zed's worried
gaze as he glanced at me. He was driving, and I had the phone on
speaker.

"Steele. You got shot in the chest last year and lived to tell
the tale," I said, chewing my thumbnail as I considered my words.
"What do you think the odds are of someone surviving a bullet to
the head?"

Max Steele—one of the few people I considered more friend

than acquaintance—made a sound like he was thinking. "Like a graze?" he eventually asked. "I know for sure that's possible."

"No," I replied with a grimace. "I mean a .44 bullet right in the middle of his fucking face, point-blank."

He huffed a laugh. "Pretty fucking bad, I'd say. His brain would likely resemble scrambled eggs. I got shot in the chest, but it just missed the good shit enough that I could get patched up in surgery. There's not much chance of missing important shit with a bullet to the brain, you know?"

I let out a long sigh. "Yeah, that's what I thought too." I didn't even know if that's what I wanted to hear or not.

"What's this about, anyway?" Steele asked. "Or do I not want to know?"

I exchanged a look with Zed. *Should* he know? He had been involved in the Timberwolf massacre, after all.

"You don't *want* to know," Zed answered for me, sounding grim. "But you might wanna dust off your weapons, just in case."

Steele scoffed. "As if I let them get dusty." Then he paused, and there was the sound of tapping on a keyboard in the background. "Look, I don't know if this helps, but there has been a recorded case of a woman being shot with a .44 in a drive-by shooting. Somehow, the bullet shattered against her skull, and she barely even needed stitches. So…yeah, I guess it's possible. Likely? Hell no. Impossible? Also no. Nothing is *impossible*, you guys know that."

I groaned, rubbing a dirt-covered hand across my forehead. That *definitely* wasn't what I wanted to hear.

"Amazing," I muttered, dread rolling through me in waves. "Now would probably be a great time to take a vacation." It was the same advice I'd given Demi, and while I didn't care *that* much about Steele and his family, I also didn't want to see them dead. They were too useful.

He just laughed, though. "That's funny. I never knew you were funny, Hades."

Zed smirked. "It's a new thing, apparently."

"Screw you, Zayden," I snapped, scowling at him. I was quietly pleased at Steele's response, though, given how much assistance I'd provided when his girl was in trouble last year.

"I've been looking for an excuse to buy new guns," Steele commented, like he was already online, shopping. "Just say the word, and we've got your back."

I let out a small, silent sigh of relief. We'd teamed up once before to slaughter my whole family and Chase's, and we were one hell of a team.

"Appreciate it," Zed replied. "Stay alert around SGPD right now too. They're no longer ours."

"Damn," Steele muttered, "that was convenient while it lasted."

"Tell me about it," I said with a sigh. I ended the call and gave Zed a long look. "What are the actual odds that Chase was a one in ten million who could survive a bullet to the face, then manage to crawl out of the Lockhart mansion *before* it went up in a ball of flame? Then also somehow fake his death."

Zed grimaced. "Like Steele said, nothing is impossible, right? Someone has to be that point zero one percent case, why not him?"

I groaned and ran my hands over my face. "Fuck it all to hell and back. I'm so screwed."

Zed dug his fingers into my knee. "Nope, *you're* not. *We* are. What is it that Seph says? Ride or die?"

I snorted an inappropriate laugh at his attempt to use slang. He wasn't fucking wrong, though; he *was* my ride or die. Except I had the horrible feeling our ride was just about finished.

"I'll feel a hell of a lot better when I've got my own eyes on Seph," I admitted, chewing my thumbnail again as I stared out the window. We weren't far from Shadow Grove now, but my anxiety kept building. "This whole thing started when Chase put her in danger."

Zed gave me a worried look from the corner of his eye, then

shook his head. "It started a long time before that, Dare, and you know it. But yeah, I'm worried he'll go for Seph too. Maybe text Cass and check in, but we'll be back in twenty minutes anyway."

Not wanting to acknowledge his comment, I did as he suggested and shot Cass a message to make sure all was still okay at my apartment building.

He replied almost immediately with a thumbs-up. Yep, man of few words right there.

Zed and I drove the rest of the way back in silence, both lost in our own thoughts and haunted by the memories of our past that had been so uncomfortably reawakened.

I couldn't spot Cass's bike as we pulled into the street outside my building, but that was no great shock. He often stayed out of sight so Seph wouldn't know she was being watched. It saved him the drama of her throwing a temper tantrum that no one trusted her.

Zed went straight down to my parking level and left his Ferrari in the space I always kept vacant for him. I climbed out of the passenger side with a groan as my stiff, bruised muscles screamed at me.

"I need a shower," I observed, brushing my dirty hands down the front of my dirtier jeans. Then I quirked a brow at Zed as he came around the car from his side. "Correction, *you* need a shower. You look like you just…" I let my voice trail off, giving a sharp laugh. "You look like you just dug up a grave."

Zed chuckled. "How morbid." I started toward the elevators, but he caught my hand in his, pausing me midstep. "Actually, before we go upstairs there's something I need to say. Something I've been *meaning* to tell you for a really long time, but I just kept losing my nerve."

I gave him a confused frown. "Can it wait until we're not covered in grave dirt? Even though there was no corpse in that coffin, I still feel like I smell of death."

He gave a small headshake. "No, I just… I keep making excuses to myself why I haven't told you, and it's killing me to keep this secret."

That had me worried. I took a step closer, peering up at him. Conflicted emotions filled his familiar gaze. "Zed, whatever it is, you can tell me. We don't keep secrets from each other, remember? Even if it hurts."

Honesty, at least between the two of us, was the whole foundation of our friendship. So for him to say he'd been keeping something from me…?

"Yeah, I remember. That's what makes this worse," he muttered, running a hand over his hair. His gaze left mine, dropping to the floor as he visibly argued with himself over what to say.

It pained me to see him so twisted up, so I stepped closer still and wrapped my arm around his waist. "I know I've changed a lot since we made those promises, but I'm still me. I'm still Dare, deep down."

Zed's hand came up to my cheek, gently tilting my face up as he stared down at me. For a tense moment, it almost seemed like he was about to kiss me. For a moment, I wanted him to.

But then I remembered how Seph had been getting inside my brain lately about me and Zed and how I never, ever wanted to risk our friendship again with misplaced romantic feelings. So I stepped away.

"What did you want to tell me?" I asked him in a rough voice. Fucking hell, I'd just come so close to screwing up the best relationship I'd ever had.

Zed gave me a long look, then sighed. "Nothing, it's nothing. Just…I scratched your McLaren when I drove it last month."

I gaped at him. "What? You drove my McLaren?"

He winced. "Yeah. Sorry. When you were out of town for that meeting with Ezekiel. My car was getting serviced, and Seph told me to grab one of yours for the day. I couldn't resist."

"What the shit, Zed?" I exclaimed, stomping over to the car in question, my one stupidly expensive car that I hardly ever drove because I was paranoid about damaging it. Sure enough, there was a white scrape in the front bumper. "You asshole." I swung a punch at his upper arm, and he grunted when it landed.

"I'm sorry," he said again, "but holy shit, what a dream to drive." His grin was all mischief, and I couldn't even muster the appropriate anger for what he'd done.

Instead, I just shook my head and stalked past him to the elevators. "You're so fucking dead, Zayden De Rosa," I growled as he followed me inside. "Next time I need to transport a body, I'm doing it in your car."

He just barked a sharp laugh. "As if you clean up your own bodies. That's cute."

He continued teasing me about being a princess for not disposing of my kills personally, and I just rolled my eyes and flipped him off when the elevator reached my floor. I only made it a couple of steps more before I froze in panic, though.

My apartment door—the one secured with biometric locks that could only be opened by Seph or me—stood partially open. Seph would *never* leave it open. Not even on her most careless of days.

Zed saw it too, and we both drew our guns as we rushed forward. The inside of the apartment was totally trashed, and I needed to swallow heavily to smother the scream of panic welling up inside me.

"Seph!" I called out, my eyes sharp on every possible hiding place. "Seph, are you here?"

Zed motioned to me, and I moved over to where he stood near the kitchen. Smashed glass was all over the place and my furniture was a mess like there had been a huge fight. The blood he was pointing to suggested the same damn thing.

"Shit," I breathed, terror taking hold. "Seph? *Seph, answer me!*"

I raced through to her room, searching for any sign of her, but found it totally empty.

"No, no, no," I chanted, tossing my gun down on the bed and pulling out my phone. I called her number first, but the sound of her phone peeled out of the living room.

With my panic reaching epic proportions, I dialed Cass.

"Red," he answered, his voice a low drawl. "What's up?"

"Where are you?" I demanded, not even trying to hide the fear in my voice. "Where's Seph? You were supposed to be watching her, Cass! I trusted you to keep her safe!"

"Whoa, what?" His gravelly voice kicked up a notch at my accusation. "She's right here. I'm staring right at her. What the hell is going on?"

My heart stopped a second, then beat twice as fast as those words sank in and confused the fuck out of me.

"Here where? Where are you?"

He made a sound like he was walking while he spoke to me. "The frozen yogurt shop down the street. Apparently, she needed sugar for her period or some shit."

I swallowed heavily, my free hand balled into a fist as my eyes surveyed the mess in my home. "Put her on, Cass. Put her on the phone."

"Two seconds," he replied, and the sound of his boots on the pavement traveled down the phone, followed by the chime of a shop door opening.

Then came the best sound I'd ever heard in my entire damn life. "Dare? What's up? Cass looks like he's ready to murder something."

I needed to take a few breaths as I processed the fact that she was okay. She was safe. Cass had her right there with him.

"N-nothing," I lied, relief washing over me so hard I almost fell. "Nothing. Sorry, brat. I just... I was worried. It's pretty late for a yogurt run." Obviously Seph would see the break-in when she got back, but there was no sense in panicking her now that I knew she was safe.

I made my way back down the hall to tell Zed that she was safe as she replied, "Yeah, well, my period cramps were making me all bitchy and crap. I figured I'd be back before you and you wouldn't know... Are you super pissed?" She sounded guilty as hell, like she expected me to go batshit on her ass. But she was eighteen; if she wanted to go for a late-night frozen yogurt run, she could.

"Pissed? No, why?"

"Boss!" Zed shouted. "Come and see this!" He was in my bedroom, staring down at something on my bed.

Please don't be body parts.

I moved closer, desperate to see what it was, and was instantly relieved not to find my sister's severed head on my quilt, even if I was on the phone with her. Instead, it was a note, and on top of that note was a diamond engagement ring.

"Uh, I dunno," Seph was saying in my ear with a nervous laugh. "Maybe because I left Lucas there while I went out? I know how you feel about security and shit, but, like, I've only been gone ten minutes, max. And you seemed cool with him coming over the other day, so..."

No. *No, no, no!* The blood in the living room... It was *Lucas's* blood.

Whatever else my sister said faded into obscurity as my eyes scanned the note under the engagement ring. The hauntingly familiar engagement ring.

What's yours is mine, Darling girl. 'Til death.

AUTHOR'S NOTE

Hey, reader! I'm so happy to see you here! I'll keep this note brief, because I need to dive straight back into Hades's world and inflict some pain on—er, I mean, *save*—my hard-ass heroine's sanity!

If you came here from Madison Kate, I really hope you've enjoyed immersing yourself back into Shadow Grove for more fuckery. If you're brand new to this world, why don't you head on over and pick up MK's series while you wait for *Anarchy*? I'll keep the crossovers super brief, so as not to spoil that series for anyone reading Hades first.

This book and these characters have been a real challenge for me to write, but I've fallen totally in love with all of them. I hope you have, too! Or…maybe not yet for some of the more stubborn ones, but I have confidence you'll get there eventually. Remember how badly you wanted to shoot You-know-who in my last series? But he redeemed himself, right? So, if you're currently hating on any of Hayden's boys, have faith. I gotchu, boo.

For anyone (hopefully no one, but just in case) still trying to place Hayden in MK's series, I'll clear this up. You, as the reader, never met her. MK and Seph only formed their friendship at the very end, during which time there were two significant time skips.

It was during that time that MK met Hayden—but knew her only as Seph's sister, Dare. It simply didn't make sense for them to have *not* met in that time skip, seeing as the girls had grown so close "off-screen" but...yeeeeah, Hades wasn't ever shown on the page.

Extra-special thanks to my Hades Alpha Team for supporting me through this book! Heather, Jax, Jane, Shaley, Savannah, and my resident medical expert Rebecca. You guys rock my socks.

Right. Back to the writing cave I go! Wish me luck... I have a feeling things are gonna get bloody...

Wanna chat spoilers for Hades? Join us in my dedicated SPOILER group on Facebook:

facebook.com/groups/wtftate

ABOUT THE AUTHOR

Tate James is a *USA Today* bestselling author of contemporary romance and romantic suspense, with occasional forays into fantasy, paranormal romance, and urban fantasy. She was born and raised in Aotearoa (New Zealand) but now lives in Australia with her husband and their adorable crotchfruit.

She is a lover of books, booze, cats, and coffee, and is most definitely not a morning person. Tate is a bit too sarcastic, swears far too much for polite society, and definitely tells too many dirty jokes.

Website: tatejamesauthor.com
Facebook: tatejamesauthor
Instagram: @tatejamesauthor
TikTok: @tatejamesauthor
Pinterest: @tatejamesauthor
Mailing list: eepurl.com/dfFR5v